Pumps
and
Circumstances

Mary Lou Irace

ALSO BY MARY LOU IRACE

Out Of My Dreams

The Magic Of Us

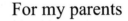

For my parents

CHAPTER ONE

It was a rainy Monday morning after a blissful holiday weekend. My assistant Teresa Jenks was slinking around my office, lurking near the drapes like a viper, waiting to ambush me on this miserable day.

"That reporter is waiting for you in the conference room," she said.

Convinced she was put on this earth to torture me, I decided to challenge her venomous statement. "Excuse me, Teresa. Can't you see I can barely function?"

I slumped against the wall, sunglasses perched on the bridge of my nose, squinting at the unforgiving fluorescent lights overhead. I dragged myself through the door while she scurried about, organizing my desk for the endless day that loomed ahead. I examined the daily itinerary she had printed out. Nudging the specs to my hairline, I flashed my bloodshot eyes at her, delivering the dirtiest of scowls. "If you were a good person and if you respected me more, you would have left me alone this morning so I could ease back into my schedule. Look at this calendar! Is this a joke? I should fire you."

With hands planted on her hips, Teresa was unfazed. "Finished now? Done throwing that hissy fit? It's time for work. You are the boss here—or did you forget? All of us depend on you—Melinda Drake, the magnificent leader of MD Shoes—to be our shining example. Please go fix your makeup and brush that messy, red hair. It looks like you got caught in a wind tunnel. You need to look good for this meeting. He said his photographer would be arriving soon."

I blew a strand of hair out of my eyes. "For your clarification—this," pointing at my head, "is auburn and styled, not red and messy. And don't change the subject. I'm trying to yell at you."

"No time to yell at me. He's waiting for you. Been in there for ten minutes."

"But did you have to schedule this interview for today? Couldn't you have pushed it off until the end of the week? I don't have time, nor do I feel like talking about myself."

"The reporter has a deadline and told me he needs to file it by Wednesday, so you have no choice. Besides, it's an honor to be recognized by *Wealth and Success* magazine. You should be over the moon that you were selected out of all the nominees. Think of the added exposure you'll get not only in the shoe industry but in the fashion world as well. Maybe some famous celebrity will start buying our shoes."

"Celebrities can afford to wear high-end designer heels."

"We can dream, right? Look how far we've come since you started this business. You need a gratitude check today."

I moaned a sigh of surrender. Teresa spoke the truth. She wasn't being a nuisance. As my executive administrative assistant, she was invaluable to me, and she knew it. That's why she could get away with so much. Teresa was my most loyal employee, but she had also earned the title of trusted friend. She was by my side from the beginning and we worked together like a well-oiled machine.

"Please stop complaining, get yourself together, and go talk to the nice man in there, will you? For the love of sweet Jesus in heaven, Melinda—everything is fine. Did something bad happen this weekend? Never mind, you can tell me later. I'll bring in coffee. Run along." Teresa shooed, slipping into her Reverend Jenks persona, which was a complete farce because the woman rarely—if ever—set foot in a church.

Teresa often spoke to me like she was my mother. In reality, she was a few years older, but she radiated maternal love to everyone in our office's inner circle. A pint-sized, bolt of lightning, Teresa has boundless energy and keeps me on task.

Attempting to pull myself together for the interview, I was distracted by the odor of burnt garlic wafting from the break room down the hall. I'd bet a doughnut it was our intern Wyatt heating his nasty leftovers in the microwave again. My stomach growled with hunger pangs, my mind once again consumed by the memory of my mother's holiday feast.

Easter fell the second Sunday in April this year, and due to a blast of balmy weather that blew in from Canada, most of the spring annuals bloomed and tree buds popped a few weeks ahead of schedule. The day was wonderful: purple and pink tulips adorning my mother's dining room table, chocolate bunnies and marshmallow chicks voraciously decapitated by my three nephews, a honey-glazed, spiral-sliced ham the centerpiece of the meal, the entire Drake brood healthy, happy, and together. After surviving a God-awful winter with too many snowstorms, the Northeast was experiencing a welcome thaw. I strolled along the street in my hometown liberated from a heavy coat and cumbersome boots. I relaxed on my parent's front porch alongside the family sharing stories, basking my pale face in the warm sun.

I attended church that Easter morning. I dropped to my knees and prayed for family and friends and world peace. I thanked God for his many blessings. My envelope contained a generous check. I helped an elderly man walk down the steep staircase so he wouldn't fall and injure himself. I relinquished my seat in the packed church—secretly cursing the A&P (ashes and palm) Catholics who only attended twice a year—to a frazzled young mother with three small children, already at the end of her rope at ten in the morning.

Later that evening, I achieved a different state of grace with my current significant other, Steven. I must confess: I fully realized such lustful actions would throw my sacrifices and piety down the drain. I succumbed, nonetheless.

I further exhibited a life of wanton decadence by eating way too much and drinking my weight in wine, which attributed to my self-inflicted state of misery this morning. My brother-in-law, Pete—aka Party Pete—kept goading me to do shots of honey whiskey until my father threatened to throw him out of the house for getting trashed in front of the kids. I experienced a great weekend, but it was time to get back to work.

Bloated and hung over, I was not in the mood for much of anything but coffee, a salty bagel smeared generously with strawberry cream cheese, and great sales figures from my finance department.

I decided to embrace Teresa's advice, taking a moment to appreciate my surroundings. This was mine. I forged a shoe empire out of nothing, and I was damn proud of it. From the innovative, kinetic offices to the imaginative design rooms to my bustling, state-of-the-art factory—I created all of it. The walls were flanked with the numerous Shoestring News Achievement Awards MD Shoes had won over the years plus three PlattForm nods for designer of the year in 2016, women's fashion footwear brand of the year award in 2017, and the marketing campaign award in 2019.

Standing to stretch my fatigued muscles, I smoothed my skirt that thankfully didn't wrinkle, remembering to grab my bifocals. Rounding the corner from behind the desk, I did a lipstick check and glanced at my backside in the mirror over the credenza. Sucking in my gut, I frowned at the thought of all the extra time I would need to put in at the gym to atone for the vast amount of calories consumed over the weekend, now cursing my mother's culinary talents and Pete's shots of alcohol.

"You do realize I could fire you for insubordination, right? I'm watching you, Mrs. Jenks," I threatened, shaking a finger at her as I headed down the hallway to the conference room.

Waiting patiently was an older gentleman, rather handsome, reading the screen on his phone. Sporting a grayish, perfectly manicured beard and a full head of matching hair, his custom navy suit and high-shined shoes screamed quality breeding and boarding school pedigree. When I entered the room, he stood and greeted me with a smug smile, exercising the diction of someone who had a total handle on the proper use of the English language.

"Ah, Ms. Drake, so nice to finally meet you. Phillip Gunderson, *Wealth and Success* magazine."

Thank God I glimpsed at my phone this morning to check my schedule and dressed accordingly in a smart and stylish black skirt and silk blouse. I understood how to play in Mr. Gunderson's hipster, country club sandbox. I shook his hand and motioned for him to have a seat. "The pleasure is all mine, Mr. Gunderson. I hope you haven't been waiting too long?"

His hand was strong and calloused, uncharacteristic for a man who makes his living typing words on a keyboard. I hypothesized he probably pursued a macho hobby like splitting firewood or ripping out drywall. Scrutinizing the package and presentation of Phillip Gunderson, I admired how well he was put together. I appreciated neatness, manners, and maturity, preferring my men on the older side in their late forties or fifties. Having recently turned thirty-nine, I wasn't sure how I felt about the alarming prospect of becoming forty, my milestone mark for middle age.

"Not at all. Congratulations on being named our Woman of the Year in Business. I appreciate you taking time out of your busy day for this interview. The entire article spotlighting you, along with nine other women designated as industry leaders, will be featured in our July issue."

"Well, thank you for this prestigious recognition. I'm truly honored to be this year's recipient. I'm cognizant of the reputation of *Wealth and Success* as the premier standard for business news. If you're ready, we can get started. My assistant will be bringing us coffee and tea, so please make yourself comfortable."

I assumed this interview would be routine, even though I was not in the mood to tout my accomplishments today. After I enjoyed a few minutes of idle chitchat about the weather with the charming Mr. Gunderson, Teresa entered with a tray. He took his coffee black, of course, no sugar. A real reporter, I concluded. He oozed class and elegance, more investigative journalist for *The New York Times* than ink slinger for a glossy magazine. He informed me our discussion would not take too much of my valuable time.

He retrieved a small notepad from his jacket pocket along with a sharp pencil. I expected he would have carried a fancy pen, or whipped out a tablet and stylus to record my answers to his questions. I assumed he would be taking copious notes or, at the least, recording our conversation.

"Going old school there, Mr. Gunderson?"

A confident smirk spread across his weathered face. "I have a photographic memory when it comes to words, Ms. Drake. I use this to write down thoughts that come to me while you are answering my questions. I've been doing this job for a while so don't worry. I won't misquote you."

That was a little creepy, like he read my mind. About three years ago, a reporter had printed incorrect facts about me that he had to retract, so I remained leery regarding interviews.

Easing back in my chair behind the long conference table, I crossed my legs and slipped on my glasses. Although I was annoyed before, I was now eager to brag about the company I had built from nothing. Hell, I would blow Phillip Gunderson away with the tale of my rags-to-riches success. I would give him a great story for his magazine, and he would be astounded they had waited so long to feature me in their publication. Fortified by a healthy dose of caffeine that resuscitated me from my sorry condition, I was back in the zone, delighted Teresa had not cancelled this meeting.

"I have no doubt that you are excellent at your job, Mr. Gunderson."

"Phillip, please." He flashed a flirty grin.

This should be semi-enjoyable after all. The exposure would be fantastic, and MD Shoes would be acknowledged by a preeminent business journal. If the world hadn't yet been aware of my outstanding corporation, the effect of this magazine spread certainly would command attention.

Phillip straightened in his seat, poised to begin.

I smiled with the utmost confidence. "Very well, then. Let's have at it—shall we?"

He nodded, cleared his throat, and embarked on the interview.

Q: Congratulations on your selection as Wealth and Success' Woman of the Year in Business. How does it feel to be singled out from all the possible contenders?

A: It feels wonderful, and I'm thrilled to be recognized along with my staff and the entire organization. As always, I share my accomplishments with them, as we are, and have always been, a team and a family.

Always best to admit that although I am at the helm here, I couldn't have gotten this far on my own. Many things take a village. I always made it a point to give my staff due credit.

Q: For those who don't know about your company, could you provide our readers with a brief overview?
A: I would be happy to. The name of my company is **MD Shoes,** and our tagline is **PUMPS TO HEEL THE SOLE**. We are a mid-size manufacturer of comfortable, yet sexy, stylish pumps, boots, and stilettos for the modern woman. Our complete line of footwear is affordable at a price of $49.95 per pair, manufactured using quality materials, proudly produced in the United States of America.

Perfect introduction—my standard go-to-pitch.

Q: When you first started out, what was your vision for this company?
A: My dream was to create a line of beautiful, designer high-heel shoes for women on a budget—shoes that could be worn at work all day or to a formal or semi-formal function without having to pay the price of aching feet the following morning. The "MD" in MD Shoes stands for my initials and the fact that my pumps treat the needs of the feet, like a doctor. There was nothing filling this need in the stores or on the market. I saw a niche, and after consulting with several respected podiatrists and fitness trainers, I created a concept, and I let my imagination and some skilled artisans get to work. I also wanted to create a sense of family with my employees, a business where hard work and loyalty to the customer and commitment to the product would be tantamount to profit margins and sales figures. In establishing an environment where we could produce a quality product while treating workers with respect and appreciation, we have achieved great success and gratefully boast low turnover rate among our employees. I want them to be happy to come to work every day, because I believe in the customer value chain where a happy employee equates to a satisfied customer.

Keeping it short, concise, positive.

Q: Your sales figures for the past five years have reflected this success. Tell our readers how you got started in this business. Do you design as well as manufacture your line?
A: My grandfather made shoes for a well-known sports manufacturer. In our family, there is no business like shoe business! Sorry, that joke is standard fare at MD Shoes. But, yes, I learned basic shoe design and footwear construction from my grandfather, and his grandfather was a cobbler in Belgium before the war, which is where it all started. Always sketching designs of shoes in elementary and high school, I attended college to learn the business and marketing aspects of running my own company.

Background is critical to any great success story.

Q: Let's start back at the beginning and talk about your education and training in the field. From which college did you receive your bachelor's degree and in what discipline: design, business, or both?
A: Actually, I never finished my degree.

Let's be clear. I hadn't verbalized this fact in ages. Now that I did, it immediately felt like vinegar on my tongue, leaving a bad aftertaste.

Q: What circumstances made you leave college?
A: I was forced to withdraw two months into my senior year. A medical leave of absence due to a car accident forced a change of plans.

Okay, I'm beginning to feel a bit of perspiration in the armpits of my blouse. Why did I agree to this damn interview anyway?

Q: That must have been a difficult time for you, having been so close to the attainment of your degree. What did you do?
A: Well, I didn't wallow in self-pity. I have always been a "make lemonade" sort of person, so I had to strategize for a Plan B. My injuries forced about eight months of physical rehabilitation, and at the end of it, my wonderful, supportive parents sent me on a trip to Paris. It was there I got my life back together and began an apprenticeship with one of the top shoe designers in France, Pierre Roussel. I absorbed everything I

7

could about making a great pump from him and his team, and I had several terrific mentors who taught me the ins and outs of the business, including marketing, management, distribution, and sales. It was the greatest type of on-the-job, real life training. I felt I learned more in Paris in two years than I had in three years, cooped up in a classroom.

Hopefully this will satisfy the now annoying, prying Mr. Phillip Gunderson enough so we can move on and discuss my many awards and accomplishments and philanthropic efforts and...

Q: Ah, but is there a small part of you that wishes to this day that you had gone back to college to earn your degree? You had one year left to complete it. Do you consider that unfinished business in the curriculum vitae of Melinda Drake?

I clutched the arm of my chair as my past reared its veiled head. Gunderson was getting too close to the flame, and I needed to shut this down before a raging inferno ensued. Take a deep breath, Melinda.
A: To be completely honest, Mr. Gunderson, I've been so busy managing a thriving corporation I simply placed it on the back burner of priorities. Besides, a college degree isn't a guarantee of success. Hard work and sales numbers are, and I have accomplished so many of my personal and professional goals with MD Shoes. Now, if I may, as part of your introduction to our fabulous organization, I have arranged to have our director of manufacturing, Maria Carlucci, escort you on a tour of our factory and facilities. She and her associate manager are waiting for you and will be happy to answer any further questions you may have about our operation.

At first, I feared he would be suspicious—or worse—complain I was concluding the interview too soon. But Phillip Gunderson seemed totally fine with it. In fact, he made an odd gesture after my abrupt answer to his outrageous question. Folding his arms across his chest, he stared at the floor with an odd grin on his face, like he had scored the winning point in a tennis match or knew a secret I wasn't privy to. But these writer types were quirky in my experience, so I guessed I was successful in taking control and pushing him off on my production manager.

After a final exchange of pleasantries, I informed him I had to scoot to an important meeting, hoping he had enough copy for his story. I assured him I would pose for any pictures he required after his photographer arrived. Shaking his hand, I thanked him for the distinguished honor. I summoned Teresa to deliver him downstairs to meet Maria. After they left, I hurried into my office and closed the door. I sprawled across the long sofa, rubbing the tension from my temples.

My skin was on fire, and I could feel the blood coursing through my veins. I wasn't sure if it was a heightened sense of panic or excitement. I rambled aloud, in the privacy of my office. If Teresa witnessed my behavior, she would've had me institutionalized.

"Thank you, Mr. Nosy Reporter. Thanks for hitting my Achilles heel. Typical man who obviously harbors his own insecurities in the presence of a high functioning, powerful female."

I jumped off the sofa, pacing the floor in my $49.95 pair of faux, leopard-skin, MD Shoes sling backs. Suddenly I froze, smack in the middle of my opulent office.

There it hovered, glaring at me like an open, festering wound. The sobering realization that Philip Gunderson opened the Pandora's box of my life, the sticking point in a superb story of success, determination, and downright true grit.

"Thanks for nothing, Philip Gunderson."

Because a prying, magazine reporter highlighted one of my shortcomings, my brain had suddenly flipped a switch and gone into overdrive.

He hit a nerve.

He hit *the* nerve.

What the holy hell was that in there—a challenge?

"Damn him." I surrendered, slumping back into the safety of my sofa.

The gauntlet had been thrown at my feet. Could I finally face the demons of my past that haunted me?

Phillip Gunderson shook the hornet's nest. He planted the preposterous notion in my imagination that I—Melinda Drake, Chief Executive Officer and creator of MD Shoes, would (or should) seriously consider resuming my undergraduate career—after an outstanding career.

At my age, was I completely out of my mind?

CHAPTER TWO

After the dashing, albeit annoying Philip Gunderson left my office, I couldn't stop pondering his harmless yet ominous question. I must admit—it had sometimes bothered me I never finished the damn degree, but I always compensated for it by rationalizing how successful I had become and what I built with MD Shoes. A baccalaureate degree wasn't a guarantee of anything. I had amassed extreme wealth and could buy anything I wanted. But I started to think: after all these years, wouldn't it be the ultimate challenge to acquire that elusive piece of paper?

Frustrated, I didn't know where to start and had so many questions swimming around in my head. I wandered around my office, contemplating an issue that for years had not even been on my radar until a random reporter shoved it in my face. Was it because he was so damn good looking with that smirk and those dimples? Was I secretly self-conscious I had an academic deficit in my long list of accomplishments? For the first time, I grappled with feelings of inferiority and, frankly, it irritated the hell out of me. Anyone who knew or met me saw I had a ton of confidence and self-assurance. Hell, I was the epitome of the self-made woman. Hell, I was *Wealth and Success* Woman of the Year in business! Why did I feel so intimidated by a simple interview?

I sat at my desk to ponder this dilemma as if it was a business issue, making a list in my mind:

1. Could I actually go to school part-time and still run a corporation?
2. What are the necessary steps to enrolling back in a college?
3. Was there a statute of limitations on my previous transcript?
4. Where could I take my remaining classes to earn my degree?
5. Who do I contact?

My feet perspired, a strange malady I suffered since childhood, peculiar for a woman who made her claim to fame selling footwear. I kicked off my sling-backs, digging my toes into the plush carpet. Overwhelmed, I paced a wide circle, excited at the prospect of this becoming a realistic goal. Don't get me wrong, I loved my job and adored my life. But maybe I needed a new challenge outside of the shoe business. All my career aspirations had been accomplished. Perhaps now, I could go back and indulge in my long dormant intellectual pursuits. The idea was totally intriguing. Maybe I should be thanking the dazzling Phillip Gunderson instead of cursing him.

I decided to abandon this brainstorm and allow it to unravel and germinate in my brain. Making a rash decision never worked well for me in the past. I needed to research this properly, make a plan, and consult with some trusted advisors. Luckily, Teresa buzzed me.

"Your next appointment is here—the marketing team. Can I send them in?"

"Sure. Thank you. And would you mind bringing me a bagel? I'm starving."

"Be right in. I'll bring you a latte, also."

I love that woman.

I have a great life. I also have a terrific family. My mother and father are the best, and I have an older brother, Kyle, and a younger sister, Serena. My brother is three years older and my sister and I are two years apart. We are a tight group, and I'm happy to report we never had any dysfunction in our home. My mother is the magnificent Marion Drake, and my dad is the fabulous Fred Drake. They, along with two girlfriends from high school, are my main support system. My besties and I get together as much as our schedules allow, and I see my family on a regular basis.

I also like having a man in my life. Not a husband, mind you, just a nice, preferably good looking, caring, non-possessive guy that I can spend time with who takes care of my basic needs. I am not married, never wanted to be. Kids will never be a part of my personal profile, except for three adorable nephews. My little sister is pregnant with her first baby and she's having a girl. She's asked me to be the godmother, so I'm all set in the kid department. People describe me as larger than life. I try to take this as a compliment.

I am the queen of clichés, puns, and all things alliteration. I consider myself witty, and yet, I've been accused of being corny and cheesy. Some of our greatest writers and philosophers have employed a puntastic sense of humor, so I know I walk in good company ☺ Successful marketing of a product requires wordplay and your target audience's ability to relate to the familiar. Running some of the best ad campaigns in the business, I have dazzled the industry with some doozies:

Get over the Wednesday hump in your MD Shoe Pumps

Match those suits with MD Shoes boots

You can't lose in a pair of our shoes

Kick the winter blues with MD Shoes

Our customers want to put their best foot forward

Okay—you get the point.

Physically, I am what you would call a full-figured girl, not fat, but far from thin. I am taller (five-nine without a pair of my heels on) and never desired to be anyone other than who I am. I love good food and wine. I exercise but don't obsess over my body. I am loud, proud, and in your face, a fact that has always been a large part of my success.

I love hosting parties as well as attending them. Once I had a New Year's Eve party where a famous actor (I won't mention any names because I am the soul of discretion when it comes to a person's private life) made a complete fool of himself after too many dirty martinis and ended up in my guest bedroom under a huge pile of coats with a much younger aspiring male actor. His super model spouse discovered them after going in search of her cigarettes, and well, he got burned. After that, I made a point of carefully selecting my guest list to avoid any potential landmines with those who couldn't handle their liquor or negative press. Known around town as a good-time girl with impeccable taste and class, I have an active social life. I am no shrinking violet.

As I entered my apartment that evening, I threw my stuff on a chair and called Steven. We've been a couple for almost three years, and it's comfortable and easy. We don't live together because I treasure my privacy, but we spend equal time shuttling between our respective residences. He is fourteen years my senior, divorced with two grown daughters. We have fun together, and neither one of us pressures the other for anything more than what we have. It's sex and a great kinship—the best kind of friends with benefits.

"Hey, Steven."

"Hey, gorgeous. What's happening?"

"Nothing. You busy tonight?"

"Never too busy for you. What's your pleasure?"

"I think some dinner and then you. Up for that?"

"Always up for you."

Steven never lets me down.

"Give me thirty minutes for a quick shower."

"You got it. I'll text you when I'm leaving. Do you want me to come in, or can you meet me outside?"

"You don't have to fetch me. Wait for me in the car. I'll come down, that way we can go. I'm hungry."

"See you in a few," he said.

Steven's roomy white SUV pulled in front of my building, and Oscar, my doorman, opened the passenger side for me.

"Thank you, Oscar," I said, tucking a twenty-dollar bill in the breast pocket of his uniform jacket. "How are Lena and the girls?" I always inquired about his family and took care of him as he did of me.

"Fine, Miss Drake. Thanks for asking," he smiled. "Evenin' Mr. Hill."

"Good evening, Oscar."

Oscar shut the car door and Steven leaned over and gave me a quick kiss before pulling away from the curb.

"You look beautiful."

Steven and I made a formidable pair. Friends laughingly described us as the ultimate power couple. Steven is built like a linebacker, not overweight, just solid. He's a corporate attorney, and we met at a friend's dinner party. With dark hair, dark eyes, and black eyeglasses, he is striking. He walked up to me the first night we met and flat out told me I was the most intriguing (drawing the word out in several sexy, delicious syllables) woman he had ever seen, and that he was tired of meeting women who looked and felt like skeletons. Steven flirted shamelessly that night—I couldn't help but be attracted to him. He is intelligent, cultured, and funny. We have a good arrangement.

We arrived at one of our favorite casual places to eat. Steven put his arm around my waist and guided me inside the restaurant, where the hostess seated us at a table.

"I am dying for a cheesesteak and fries," Steven said as he perused the extensive menu.

"Oh, God, that sounds like heaven. Would you also split a salad with me?"

"Of course." Steven pulled off his expensive glasses, placing them carefully on the table.

"And how was your day today? Productive, I hope, after our nice, long weekend." He flashed a cocky, confident smirk, referencing our amorous liason on Easter Sunday evening.

"Busy. Meeting after meeting. I swear, I think Teresa is trying to kill me."

"Are you kidding? That woman worships the ground you walk on. If anything ever happened to you, God forbid, she'd need to be sedated for months."

We joked, but it was a statement of fact. Steven had been to my office several times since we started dating, and he considered her loyalty admirable.

"Oh, I also had that interview with the reporter from *Wealth and Success.*" I bragged about the award months before when I received the email.

"Was it long and drawn out or short and sweet? God, I hate being interviewed. Some of those reporters love to twist what you say. Controversy and conflict sell newspapers and magazines."

"No, it was fine, it went fine. Just a litany about how wonderful my company is and how talented I am." I winked.

"What month will it run? I will have to make sure I buy all the copies in New York City. I can plaster your picture on every wall in my apartment."

"I believe you have already plastered me against every wall in your apartment, haven't you?"

Steven glanced up from his menu. "Why, yes, I have. With great pleasure, I might add."

I smiled at the recollection of Steven's walls yet frowned at the memory of the interview. "This reporter seemed to fixate on my educational background, you know, where did I graduate from, what was my degree in, that sort of stuff." Steven was my friend above being my lover and knew me well enough to see that it bothered me.

The waitress appeared and took our order. Steven ordered a nice bottle of pinot noir in addition to our dinner choices.

"And? Did you tell him that you earned your knowledge of the shoe business in the trenches, where it matters most?"

"Sure, I gave him the whole spiel of how I'm a self-made success and that I had to leave college my senior year. Blah, blah, blah..." I rolled my eyes.

"Was he one of those holier-than-thou elitist educational types that looks down on anyone without a college degree?"

"Yup. I looked him up after he left. He graduated Ivy League, of course. Typical, intellectual snob."

Steven had worked several jobs while putting himself through college, earning a degree with honors in political science and history as an undergrad. He continued on to receive his Juris Doctor, and is a successful lawyer who is respected among his peers.

Steven leaned back, glaring at me. "Does this degree nonsense actually bother you? Frankly, I'm surprised. No one intimidates Melinda Drake. This reporter is well aware of the fact that you are worth millions while he makes a measly magazine writers salary. Think about how intimidated he is knowing how much you are worth."

"No, he didn't bother me in that way. It made me think. I've always believed that most things happen for a reason. Maybe this lack of formal education thing is resurfacing at the right time in my life. I mean really, Steven. How many people would let three years of college simply hang there without finishing? It doesn't make sense that I never completed that goal. I was so close—I am so close. Perhaps the time is right for something new. It might actually be fun to take a class here and there and

15

finish the damn thing. Plus, I would look so good in that black cap and gown. I could design a pair of great pumps to go with it and call them Senior Stilettos or, better yet, an entire line called Class of Kicks or Shoes for the Prudent Student. What do you think?"

"Always the queen of shoe puns, thinking about your next marketing scheme. That is what makes you a success, not this high-priced piece of parchment you now seem to be obsessing over," he said, shaking his head.

The wine arrived, and Steven poured two glasses, tapping my glass in an informal toast.

"Thank you for the nice compliment, big guy. My problem is that I'm out of my element here. I have no idea where to start and how to set the wheels in motion to do this."

"Then I would suggest you put Teresa on the case. She'll have it all figured out and organized by the time you finish your first cup of coffee tomorrow morning. Besides, she would love having a hand in your finally doing this," he said.

Steven was right. I would ask Teresa for help tomorrow. I had no doubt she would think my plan was a brilliant idea.

CHAPTER THREE

"That's the dumbest idea I've ever heard, Melinda!" Teresa's voice shrieked. "Why the hell would you want to do something so stupid? You don't need some useless degree. Kids go to college so they can go out and find a decent job. You already own your own company, for God's sake. People come to you for jobs!"

My heart sunk. I was shocked by her negative reaction. Teresa had always been my biggest cheerleader and supporter at MD Shoes, and I could always depend on her to be in my corner. I was certain she would agree with me once I spelled out my plan.

"Calm down. Everything is in the investigative stage. It's something I never accomplished, and maybe I might want to complete it while I'm young enough and still have some active brain cells left in my head. If I wait too many more years, I may not have the energy or opportunity to do this," I tried to explain.

"But why? Why now, all of a sudden?"

Crossing my arms across my chest, I let out an exasperated sigh. "When that snooty Phillip Gunderson asked me about my education in the interview, I felt like I was in steerage and he was in first class. No one ever made me question my choices before. I didn't—I don't—like the fact there is this major dangling participle in the paragraph of my life, and I want to explore the idea of finishing my college degree. Since I've become aware of this, I realized I do in fact, have a bucket list of things I would like to accomplish in my time here on this planet. Surely, you can understand, can't you?"

Teresa eyes glared at me with the look. The one that said she would go to the ends of the earth for me, even if she didn't agree. "But how do you propose to do this? You barely have enough time for lunch every day, let alone sneaking out and going to classes. You don't have any time in your day as it is. I know; I manage your schedule—remember?"

"I realize this would be a challenge, but a good one—for me. An intellectual challenge."

"But you make more money than God. I don't see why you would need to do this. You already have everything you could possibly want. Look at your life!"

I was looking at my life, and maybe now I needed something new.

"Listen to me. I am not planning on making any drastic changes in my world or yours as of this moment so relax. But I do want to explore the possibility. I hope you'll help me."

Teresa's shoulders sagged. "Like I would ever say no to you."

"That's my girl."

Teresa crossed her arms over her chest. "What do you need me to do?"

"Well, for starters—where do I start?" I laughed.

Teresa looked away to think. "I'll call the school you used to attend. Which one was it again?"

"Pennwood University, in Philly. First, can you find out if my old credits are still valid and where I could attend here in New York and I guess transfer the classes back to them? I don't know the right questions to ask. That's why I need you. I need Teresa Jenks the miracle worker to figure it all out for me." I nudged her arm.

"Oh, please. Save the sucking up. You pay me to do a job, and you know I'd never refuse you anything even if it means chasing some way-out-there scheme of yours. Let me make a few phone calls to see what I can find out. I'll get back to you later."

"You're the best, Teresa."

"Yeah, I guess. Meanwhile, can we do some legitimate work around here now?"

I shook my head. Who exactly was the boss?

"Sure, Mrs. Jenks. What's first on the agenda today?"

I threw myself into work that day with the renewed enthusiasm of someone who had a singular goal in mind. Now that the idea was embedded in my brain, I couldn't stop thinking about it. Approaching this like I had everything else in my life, with determination and gusto, I wanted to move on the proposition as soon as possible. We were in the final stages of opening a boutique operation in London, but I exhibited more passion for my new mission to go back to college. I wondered if I was too preoccupied with my own personal stuff. Perhaps it would have been better if I had a husband and children, an alternate family life to my own solitary one. But I had always dealt with the here and now, not allowing myself to think of what would never be. The past could not be changed, but the future could be life changing. Going after what I want is my modus operandi and how I function best. I never take NO for an answer. Most highly successful people don't. I am always on to the next big thing.

It was almost four o'clock in the afternoon when Teresa finally traipsed in, plopping herself on the leather sofa in my large office.

"Excuse me. Would you like to come in and make yourself comfortable?"

"I've been on the phone for you all day. Not doing work, mind you—just trying to figure out this whole going-back-to-school-nonsense of yours." She feigned exhaustion.

"And?"

She shook her head from side to side, pursing her lips. She was ecstatic about the information she'd uncovered.

"You're not going to be happy. It's a hell of a lot more complicated than you thought. I would say it's down-right impossible." Teresa practically wallowed in her "I told you so" attitude.

"Really?" I asked, deflating like a balloon.

"Yup. But there's good news as well as bad news. Which do you want first?"

"The good," I said, crossing my fingers.

"Well, your past credits from the first three years are still good. Since you were pursuing a Bachelor of Science degree in design and merchandising, the majority of your requirements haven't changed and are still valid. However, the technology in terms of computer software has advanced since you departed in the Stone Age."

"Very funny. What's the bad news?"

"Here's the kicker. And it makes this impossible for you to do.

Ready?"

"Cut to the chase, Teresa." Her smug demeanor was beginning to annoy me.

"Your final classes MUST be completed at your home institution. That means you would have to take ALL your remaining credits to get the degree at the actual Pennwood University campus. In Philadelphia, Pennsylvania. So therefore: NO CAN DO." She gloated. Like she had won. Like this was a done deal.

"Wait. You mean I couldn't get an exemption or some kind of dispensation to transfer them from here—even from NYU or Columbia? What about completing them online? That can't be!"

"Do you think this is like getting permission from the Pope to eat meat on Good Friday or take communion after a divorce? These are the rules of your academic institution. I even researched other colleges, and they all have the same policy, although you may be able to do some of it online but you would have to ask the college. Even if that is the case, the final credits for a degree must be taken at the home institution. It's some kind of residency requirement. I even printed it out from the catalog web page because I knew you wouldn't believe me." Teresa handed me the copy.

I scanned the page. There it was, in black and white. She wasn't lying.

"Damn!" I was annoyed. "There must be a way around this. People go back to school every day in this country. I thought most colleges and universities try to make it easier for adults to earn their degrees."

"They do if you're just starting out or have a few credits under your belt. Your problem is that you were almost done. You needed around thirty more credits to graduate?" Teresa asked.

"Not even that many. I was a little bit ahead when I entered as a freshman because I had taken three advanced placement courses in high school and scored high enough on the exams to earn some college credit. Crap. This throws a huge roadblock in my plan."

"Yup. Oh, well. So can we please forget about your hair-brained, unrealistic scheme and get back to the business of running MD Shoes?" She was triumphant.

I sat there, staring at the piece of paper with the rules for transferable credit in front of me. Never one to walk away from a challenge, nor let myself go down without a fight, I looked at Teresa who was relishing my predicament.

Narrowing my eyes, I glared at her. "I realize you are overjoyed about this unfortunate turn of events, but I'm not throwing in the towel yet. What does my schedule look like next week?"

"Why?"

"Just go look, please," I asked.

Teresa walked to her desk and pulled up my schedule on her computer. After a few minutes, she came back.

"You never have any free time in your schedule, you already know that. There are meetings and events you have to attend almost every day next week. And the London launch is closing in on us."

"Listen to me." I pointed my finger at her and squinted, treating her like a petulant child. "With no attitude and no fighting me, find my least busy day next week and reschedule whatever is on the calendar. Then, Mrs. Jenks, I want you to call Pennwood University and make an appointment for me to see the Dean of the College of Art and Design. Maybe if I meet him or her face to face, I will get them to bend the rules. I'll go to Philadelphia and give them some Melinda Drake charm, and I'm sure I'll be able to strike some kind of compromise. There has to be a way around this."

I knew if I wormed my way into the dean's office, I would be able to argue my case. After all, I was a skilled negotiator and a shrewd businesswoman. I could throw in my newest accolade as Woman of the Year for *Wealth and Success* magazine as a sweetener. It would be great publicity for the university, I would explain, having one of their alumni on the cover of a nationally recognized magazine. I could do this! They would see my side and I was positive they would work with me. Eventually, I always won.

A little begging, pleading, and maybe tears wouldn't hurt, either.

CHAPTER FOUR

On Tuesday I had an appointment at eleven with Dean Walter Samuels. Dressed in my most conservative black suit, starched white blouse, and the most understated heels in my latest collection, I was ready for battle. Actually, I was planning on killing the man with kindness and compliments because my mom taught me that a little honey, rather than vinegar, was much more effective in getting what you wanted. I knew how to charm the pants off most men, professionally, of course. I mean, how hard could it be to convince him that the rules should be bent just a bit? I wasn't that far off from graduating. Surely, he would understand that a woman of my stature couldn't up and leave running a multi-million-dollar corporation just to take a few classes.

I mentioned I am far from shy and reserved and possess complete confidence in myself. I don't think I've ever truly feared anything in my life, and I don't get nervous. Having this core of inner strength is something I've been blessed with and I don't understand why a person would ever feel insecure and doubt their talents and abilities. If God made each and every one of us unique and in his image, then we too, are like mini-gods. No one questions the greatness of God, so each of us should never doubt that we can do whatever we put our minds to. Some critics have labeled me an egoist, but that comes from a place of jealousy. We all have strengths and weaknesses, and my strength is being self-assured.

My weakness: chocolate, of course.

I grew up in New Jersey, in a family where I was the proverbial, rebellious middle child. My older brother was the spirited one—smart, athletic, yet often, a pest, as my mother lovingly described him. My little sister was the angel with a sweet personality. Me? I was the cayenne pepper of the family; too hot to handle and full of spice. For Marion and Fred Drake, I was the kid who kept them on their toes.

Each member of our family relished the roles we played and how we fit in the fabric of the Drake tapestry. We accepted each other for who we were and what we brought to our crazy, wonderful house. My parents, the two most wonderful, patient humans on the planet, never made one of us feel more special than the other. My dad told us God picked each one of our personalities special for the Drake family, and I always took my father's word as gospel.

Dean Samuels stepped out of his office to greet me after I had been waiting for a few minutes. I liked punctuality. It showed respect for one's time and consideration. We would get along fine.

"Good morning, Ms. Drake. It is a pleasure to meet you. Won't you please have a seat in my office?" He gestured toward the open door.

The dean was on the short side, perhaps five-seven, eight at the most. I guessed his age to be mid-sixties. Dressed in a charcoal suit and paisley tie, he looked quite fashionable.

"Why thank you, Dean Samuels. I appreciate your seeing me today."

He closed his door. I took a seat in front of his large desk that was piled with papers and journals.

"I am always happy to speak with students, alumni, and those from outside the academic community. I must say, I am rather curious as to the nature of your visit to Pennwood University today, Ms. Drake. It is an honor to have you here on campus. Your company has an outstanding reputation in the business world."

"Why, thank you for the wonderful compliment. I am extremely proud of what we have built at MD Shoes. We work hard to maintain high standards and produce quality products. And I must tell you, many of the principles I learned to run a successful business were obtained right here in the hallowed halls of Pennwood."

I would be laying it on thick.

"I apologize—I probably should have checked, but I wasn't aware that you were an alumna. What year did you graduate?" he asked.

"Well, Dean Samuels, as a matter of fact, I did not graduate from Pennwood—yet. But I certainly would like to. It's actually the reason for my coming here today, to speak with you, specifically. I was a student on campus back in the late nineties. I was planning on graduating spring of 1999, with my degree in design and merchandising, but a near-fatal car accident derailed my plans and intentions."

"I'm so sorry to hear that. What a terrible trauma you must have been through. Do you feel comfortable enough to tell me about it?" He asked, his eyes laser focused on me.

"It was a horrible experience. I was on my way home for the long Columbus Day weekend. Luckily, if there was to be any luck in this situation, I was alone in my car in the right lane. It was raining hard, and the road was slick. I lost control of the vehicle and crashed into the center median. Thank God for the air bag, or I would have been killed instantly." I was making my voice sound serious to appeal to his sympathies. And yet, it was deadly serious that day. I could not tell him why.

"Oh, my. How terrible."

"After being extricated from the mangled wreckage, I was taken to the hospital's trauma center where I was in a coma for forty-eight hours."

"My goodness. What an ordeal. Some of these local roads are an abomination. So many accidents happen every day." He shook his head in disgust.

"I couldn't agree with you more. And when I finally awoke from my coma, I was bedridden for weeks. I had to withdraw from Pennwood and take a medical leave of absence. I was in my senior year of college, with graduation in my sights."

"That is heart-wrenching. When were you finally released from the hospital? Your injuries must have been quite extensive," he said.

"I was in the hospital, followed by rehabilitation for several months afterward. Needless to say, this put a hold on my studies and the pursuit of my degree, as I'm certain, you can understand."

"Quite," he agreed.

"By the time I finished my physical rehab, my wonderful parents decided that I needed a positive distraction, a change of scenery." I clenched my fists at the memory and the reason why my parents made the decision to send me away, a decision that would save my life.

"Absolutely. They must have been devastated by your accident and wanted to see you get well and take some much needed time to regroup. I can imagine, being a parent myself."

"You are a perceptive man, Dean Samuels. Seeing how distressed I was over this huge interruption in my educational pursuits, they sent me to France to further recuperate. I was offered an apprenticeship that led to the creation of my business, MD Shoes. Yet, the book of my life, remains unfinished. There is a missing chapter, and being the astute man that you are, I believe you know what I mean."

"Your degree." He looked rather pleased with himself that he had all the answers. I continued.

"Precisely. And that is what brings me to you today. All the way from New York City." It was imperative that I stressed the distance factor. I knew he was beginning to see my point. "I was hoping you could provide me with some assistance and guidance on finishing my degree. After having my assistant look into this, I found there are roadblocks in the way of pursuing my dream. After speaking with several offices on campus, she was informed by someone in the registrar's office that the remaining classes I would need to graduate must be taken here at Pennwood. Please tell me that the school would be flexible with this rule." I made it sound like this was the most ridiculous regulation ever invented in the history of the world.

He looked at me, and I realized he now understood why I had traveled to speak with him in person, rather than call or email his office.

"Ah, I see. Let's take this one step at a time. Why don't we pull up your transcript and take a look." He lifted his phone and asked his assistant to retrieve my record from the archives. While waiting, we discussed the weather, the improvements to the campus since I was enrolled, and how I had come up with the concept for my shoes. I believed he was leaning toward granting me an exception!

It took about fifteen minutes for his secretary to obtain my transcript. As she handed the sheet of paper to him, I realized the dean literally held my fate in his hands. This whole thing had taken on a life of its own, and I was determined to see it to the finish line. That's how I was wired: driven and focused, obsessed with getting my way.

"Let's see what we have here," he said, studying the list of my completed requirements. "Excellent grades, Ms. Drake. You were a fine student, definitely on track to graduate with honors, had you continued with such admirable work habits."

"Thank you. I have always given one-hundred percent effort in everything I do, knowing that hard work translates into success."

"Your transcript shows you withdrew from the University in October 1998," he said.

"Yes, and my parents were able to get a refund of my tuition, thanks to the generosity of Pennwood University."

"Actually, it's standard policy."

"Oh," I said.

With the flip of a switch, Dean Samuels seemed to revert from understanding, grandfatherly type to head rule enforcer. I could feel my armpits begin to dampen. I sat straight, my back pressed against the wooden chair like a defendant in court awaiting sentencing from a judge. Maybe the tide was about to turn on me.

"Based on what I see, you need to complete twenty-four additional credits to earn your degree in design and merchandising. The Advanced Placement course exams you took in high school transferred..."

"Yes. I wanted to have a reduced course load my senior year so I could do a six credit internship in the field."

He glanced at me, brow furrowed. Interrupting the dean was not a smart thing to do.

"As I was saying," he looked directly at me from under his wire-frame glasses, "the AP credit enabled you some flexibility, but you need the remaining twenty-four credits to graduate. The good news is that your previous coursework is all still valid, and you don't lose anything there. But yes, students are required to be matriculated, or enrolled in the College of Art and Design at Pennwood University in order to complete the final credit hours required for a degree."

There it was, straight from the horse's mouth.

Defeated.

Doomed.

Teresa was right. It was a devastating blow both to my master plan and my ego.

"But, Dean Samuels. Surely there must be some exception you could make in my situation. As you can imagine, it would be difficult, if not impossible for me to attend classes here in Philadelphia when I live in New York and run a million-dollar business operation there. I can't commute back and forth, but I would be fully dedicated to completing my coursework at say, NYU or Columbia and transferring the courses back here. I don't understand why that isn't a viable possibility. Aren't those two of the best colleges in the country?" Now I was irritated.

"They are, without question. And they would have been approved for transfer when you were a freshman or sophomore. But these are the rules of this institution, and they are firm and finite. In fact, most colleges and universities adhere to the same rigorous standards and requirements. I cannot bend the rules for you, Ms. Drake. If I did, I would have to for everyone. Besides, I don't have the authority to do it. I must answer to the President of the University, the Provost, and the Board of Trustees, and I would never compromise the integrity of this institution."

I slumped in my chair, feeling like I was being scolded for asking for an extra piece of candy, for God's sake! This was much tougher than I anticipated. But I wasn't about to give up.

"So you are telling me that my college is making the attainment of a life-long dream impossible? Isn't that a little bit un-American? The pursuit of happiness, an American ideal, is being thwarted in this situation by sheer bureaucracy. I find that ludicrous and unfair. Here I am, now a non-traditional student trying to reach my goal, and my home institution is blocking my way!"

He crossed his arms and curled his lip. Perhaps I was being a bit melodramatic. Okay—I was—but who cared? I decided to pursue a different tactic.

"What if I were to make a sizeable donation to the University? Better yet, maybe the College of Art and Design could use a new building or equipment or upgraded technology?" I was a businesswoman, attempting to negotiate a deal. Money always talks, at least in my world.

"Ms. Drake, are you attempting to bribe your way into a degree?" He laughed.

"Not at all. I would simply be happy to provide my future alma mater with such a philanthropic gift."

"Well, that would be magnanimous of you, but I'm sorry. The rules for you and every student at this University still stand. If you would like to discuss a plan for you to move ahead with, we can. Pennwood would be thrilled to have an alumna like you in our roster of graduates. But you will need to be the flexible one in this situation. That is simply the reality of it, I'm afraid."

Was that it? I was shot down, put in my place. This was new for me, and it sucked.

"Okay. I guess I have no choice," I said, reluctantly. "What would you suggest I do?"

"Well, it's not all that terrible. As a matter of fact, you will be pleased to hear that of the twenty-four credits remaining, we could allow three credits using your present work experience to count for your internship, provided you work with an assigned faculty member and submit a research paper or journal based on an selected topic. I would also approve three additional credits for an independent study related to your job that we could use to fulfill one of the required upper level courses in the major program. This would leave eighteen credits—six classes—that would have to be taken here at Pennwood. How and when you complete them would be your choice."

I sat there contemplating my fate. "So what you are saying is I could either take the next couple of years to slowly finish or I could go one full semester and knock out the whole thing?"

"I would strongly suggest the slower pace, particularly in light of the fact you have been out of the classroom for a long time and how it is better often to ease back into being a student again. But it is entirely up to you. I can see you are a strong, determined person, and I would not underestimate your ability to overcome any challenge based on the history of your success. The decision is yours. Whatever you decide, we can work together. I will help you with whatever you need to make this goal of yours a reality.

"Deal?" he asked, extending his hand with a sly smile.

"Dean Samuels, you run a tight ship, but I fully respect your integrity and authority. I also appreciate the idea that I can use my work experience for actual college credit, and I thank you for allowing me that much. Let me give this some thought as to the pace I want to proceed, but yes, we have a deal," I said, and shook his hand. "Now if you wouldn't mind, could you please tell me how I get the ball rolling to matriculate again?"

"I will set you up with one of the staff here to get as much paperwork done as you can while you are on campus today. I know how busy you are," he said.

Obviously a dig at my failed attempt to get one over on him, not realizing that in all his years of dealing with students, he has probably seen every trick in the book.

"I appreciate your help, time, and consideration. Eventually, I hope we might even become friends after this is over."

He smiled. "What I hope to see are internships and job placements for our students and graduates at MD Shoes. How does that sound, my future friend?"

"As we say in the shoe business, Dean Samuels, you're a good sole."

"Shoe pun?"

"Occupational hazard," I nodded.

We laughed, as he walked me out to the larger office to find someone to assist me with the necessary forms.

"Thank you again, Dean. I'll be in touch if I have any further questions."

"You're welcome. Oh, and one last thing, Ms. Drake?"

"Yes?"

"After you graduate, a building with your name on it would be a nice legacy. Don't you agree?"

I took a deep breath, repeating the same words he said to me just minutes before. "Let's take this one step at a time."

CHAPTER FIVE

My staff assembled in our largest conference room, milling about, questioning why I called an emergency meeting. To calm their nerves, I made certain there were plenty of doughnuts and coffee to appease the hungry hoard. Teresa was the only one, aside from Alyce Cumberland, the president of my company, who knew what I was about to say.

Alyce was hand selected by me when we first started MD Shoes. A smart, forty-five-year-old executive who worked many years in the field, Alyce knew the business inside and out, and I trusted her with my life. A week ago, we spent a long night at my home over dinner and several cocktails where I outlined my latest plan to her. As usual, she was supportive and encouraging, assuring me that MD Shoes would run smoothly in my absence. When she had been out on maternity leave a few years ago with her second child, we set-up an arrangement for her to work from home, easing back into the office when she was physically and emotionally ready to separate from her newborn and return to her job. I held her as she cried buckets of tears on her first day back, heartbroken at having to leave her kids.

"Good morning!" I said, entering the crowded room. Teresa gave me a nod, indicating that all was under control and ready for me. In addition to meeting with Alyce, I had to break the news to my reluctant assistant that things would be business as usual while I pursued this crazy dream, and that she too would play a pivotal role. It helped that I took her to one of the finest restaurants in New York City and ordered a bottle of their best champagne. Teresa was tough, but she could so easily be swayed by the prospect of a girl's night out with me.

"I'm sure you are curious as to why I called this impromptu meeting. I have some news to share with you, which will involve a few tweaks here at MD Shoes. Luckily, none of these changes will affect you, your jobs, or your security here, so you can rest easy."

An audible sigh spread across the room as my employees relaxed with nervous relief.

"After a great deal of thought and discussion with family, friends, and key personnel here at our company, I have decided to pursue the goal of completing my college degree. Normally, this would not necessitate a staff meeting for my employees, but in my situation it does. For those of you who don't know my personal history, I was forced to drop out of college in my senior year due to a medical situation. I never returned because I started this wonderful place we now call home, and I put all my energy and focus into it. After investigating the procedures of going back, I discovered that oftentimes, getting what we desire is never easy. What I thought would be a simple plan is, unfortunately, more complicated and will involve some significant changes for me. Therefore, beginning in September, I will be out of the office on Tuesdays because I will be at Pennwood University in Philadelphia, meeting with one of my professors to complete an independent study. I will also meet with my faculty advisor on another required project. The more significant changes will happen in January, when I will be enrolled as a full-time student and take a six-month leave of absence here at MD Shoes so that I can graduate from the university next June."

Several of my employees gasped, looking back and forth at each other, obviously surprised at my decision to do such a strange and, in their opinion, useless thing. I could see many of them shared Teresa's initial sentiment that this was a foolish pipe dream, an unnecessary distraction for a nice lady with too much money. Yet there were others who were excited for me, understanding the value of a formal education and how much it meant.

"In my absence, the day-to-day operations will continue without interruption and without any change, and our capable president, Alyce Cumberland will stand in for me as chief operating officer. If you have any concerns or issues while I am out of the office, please see my executive assistant, Teresa Jenks, who will bring it to my attention. I will be in constant communication with Alyce, my capable department directors, and Teresa, so I don't anticipate any problems. I am thrilled to have the greatest employees on the planet here at MD Shoes, and I hope you will continue to make us the fastest growing manufacturer of quality women's footwear in the industry. I would like to open the floor to any questions you may have regarding this announcement or anything else."

I knew the first question would come from Ed Ross, a manager in the accounting department. Great with numbers, but he could use a lesson in diplomacy. Ed loved gossip and rumors and was often a pain in the ass.

"Hey Melinda, I have a question."

Of course, you do.

"Yes, Ed?"

"Like, why? Why on earth would you want to go sit in a classroom for hours? It's not like you need a college degree. You can buy anything you want. It doesn't make sense. And why can't you do it here in New York? Schools not good enough here?"

Most of my staff rolled their eyes. One whispered: "Shut up, Ed."

"Well, let's see, Ed. That's several questions, but I will still answer them." I would love to hurl a doughnut at your face, you insubordinate boor. "To begin with, University policy requires that all final credits be completed at the home institution, so physically, I must be in Philadelphia. As to the value of a degree in higher education, I'm certain that even you can understand the aspiration to better oneself in light of personal shortcomings. Isn't that right?"

My retort elicited a group chuckle and a round of applause at his expense. His face turned red as he slinked into the depths of his chair.

"Anyone else have a question or concern?" I asked, my eyes scanning the crowd. But after putting the annoying Ed in his place, no one dared. I was known around the company as a fair and generous boss, but my employees respected that I was still the boss.

"Very well, then. Thank you all for your time this morning. Please take another doughnut and a coffee before you go back to work and have a great day." Flashing a broad smile, I returned to my office with Teresa and Alyce.

"That went fine, I thought," Alyce said. "You handled it perfectly, even with you-know-who."

"You mean Ed, the village idiot?" Teresa asked.

"Well, you thought the same thing, remember?" I said.

"Yes, but I'm your mini-me. I'm allowed to question your motives, not that piss-ant. He had some nerve." Teresa shook her head in disbelief.

"Whatever. It's expected with him, but I took care of it," I sat at my desk.

"Seems like you are all set, my dear," Alyce said.

"Looks that way. We need to get through the London launch this summer and then I can breathe. Thank God, the timing worked out. Teresa, are all the arrangements finalized for London—flights, hotel, meetings, etc.?" I asked.

"Yes, Boss. All done." When the phone rang, she left my office to run to her desk.

"Mel, I've been meaning to ask: what do your parents think of all this college stuff? Were they excited or did you get an Ed-type response?" Alyce asked.

"Are you kidding? My parents are the best: full support and go-for-it attitude, as usual."

"And what about Steven? How does he feel?"

"As much as I like Steven, he would never factor into my decision whether or not I would do this. We are friends; we are not in any sort of committed relationship. We both do our own thing."

"You have been seeing each other exclusively for, what, a couple of years?"

"Almost three. But not so exclusively, I recently learned."

"What? I thought he'd be concerned about you living in Philly next year."

"He's fine with it. When I told him I had finalized my plans, he admitted he'd met someone and wanted to ask her out. They met in a clothing store, in the men's department, while he was trying on shoes, if you can believe it. Of all things, she sells men's shoes, for Christ's sake! The irony of that is hilarious, don't you think?"

Alyce looked at me, apparently not getting the joke. "That doesn't bother you? He's interested in another woman and you aren't the least bit jealous or even pissed off?"

"No. Sure, I like Steven and we have a lot of fun together, but I'm not in love with him or anything. He's been great to me, but he is a player and it wasn't destined to last." It was sad, but true.

"Have you ever been in love, Mel?"

This was an easy question. "No, I haven't. Not even close—lots of lovers, always friends, but never the real thing. I honestly believe I wasn't meant to have that sort of life, being madly in love, with a husband and kids and a house in the country. It would have diverted my focus, and I never would've created what I have today. But I'm happy and totally content with my life. It's a good life."

"I know. But don't be surprised if some day, love sneaks up and kicks you in the butt. You are quite loveable. But only a special, unique man can handle the authentic you. Someday, I bet I'll meet him," she said.

"Well, when you do, introduce him to me, will you?"

CHAPTER SIX

The remainder of spring and the majority of the summer flew as I prepared to shift my focus from CEO to college student. My home in New York looked like an advertisement for one of those travel tech companies, appearing as though I was packing to go on vacation. I assembled a huge pile of stuff in one of my extra bedrooms, in preparation for getting a place to stay while I was in Philly. It was reminiscent of the days long ago my mother and I would run from store to store to store stocking up on twin XL sheets for the dreaded, paper-thin mattress, several big pillows for the bed, towels that would coordinate with my roommate's junk, and, naturally, tons of snack food and toiletries. I felt like a teenager again, giddy with the prospect of going back in time. I wouldn't be staying in a dorm, obviously, but the hilarious thought did cross my mind. Can you imagine being eighteen-years-old, scared out of your mind starting at a huge university, and in walks your roommate who is twice your age, with red hair and gorgeous, high-heeled stilettos, sporting a big mouth to boot? The poor kid would either faint in her parents' arms or run screaming from the building.

Flash forward twenty years: I was purchasing 800 thread count sheets and expensive cookware for the luxury apartment I was sure I could find with the help of a realtor.

I hadn't started the process of finding a place to stay while at Pennwood. The opening of the London store was intensely time-consuming, but it all fell into place as planned. I hired a terrific staff there, and they spent quite a bit of time here in New York, learning how I wanted the business to run. I discovered early on in my career that if you hired the right people to work for you, things functioned as they should. My shoes were popular in Great Britain. Women across the pond appreciated fashion on a budget and had a great sense of style.

Through Dean Samuels, I was assigned a faculty advisor who sat with me in early August and mapped out an academic roadmap to graduation. My advisor was a no nonsense type, all business and no warm fuzzies. I appreciated this; I was a woman on a mission, and I needed quick answers to my many questions. She told me exactly what to do, and I did it.

Going back to college didn't scare me in terms of fitting in with younger students. I couldn't have cared less if they ignored me or dismissed my goals in being there. And I knew I could handle the academic requirements because I was a CEO accustomed to multitasking, analyzing data, and writing reports. I was proficient in the latest technology. My greatest challenge would be making sure MD Shoes wasn't affected in the least by this decision to return to school.

The three credits for my work experience turned out to be fun. I wrote a ten-page paper detailing the London launch of my business, incorporating the elements of fashion, retail merchandising, promotions, and product development and how they relate to and affect the global marketplace. My supervising professor was impressed with my business acumen. We went off topic countless times, discussing fashion trends, textiles, and media influences. My chest swelled with pride when I received an **A** for that paper and the internship. I knew then: I was back! I still had what it took to succeed in the academic world. My brain didn't go to mush as I had feared. On the contrary, I think I was actually smarter now. Experience and maturity were assets, not liabilities.

For one of my upper-level courses in my major, problems in design and merchandising, I did a presentation and a paper on how I developed the technology for my footwear: basically, the patent I had secured for my comfort design in a high-heeled shoe. I deduced at the beginning, if I could take the comfort that a platform shoe afforded and combine it with the technology of a stiletto heel, I could revolutionize the shoe industry. I came up with a design, had several podiatrists and footwear experts critique it, and made a prototype. I walked in the shoes for a week. It's a ritual I continue today, road testing my latest designs on the streets of Manhattan.

I created a sleek, sexy shoe and realized I had something special when women on the subway and streets stopped me to ask where my shoes were from. I was brazen enough to invite them back to our corporate office and allow the test group to try on the shoes and walk in them. The feedback I received from these ladies and other focus groups was electric. I knew I created something fabulous women would love.

My ego was further boosted when the panel of faculty adored my presentation and gave me a rousing ovation. My grade was another **A**. After the semester was over, I would be sure to invite these professors to New York to see my operation, and I would treat them to lunch. I was floating on cloud nine. I became quite the celebrity around the department. They liked me, and I ate up every glorious minute. At home among the faculty, staff, and students, I was certain this was going to be an unforgettable adventure.

One afternoon, I was in visiting with Dean Samuels. I had been stopping by on a regular basis during the fall semester and was on a first-name basis with his secretary, Rose. The dean would make sure that upon my graduation, Pennwood students would be placed in internships and co-ops at MD Shoes. Of course I was planning on doing this, but it was fun to watch him grovel.

He summoned me to his office via Rose one day in late September. As I walked into the room, I saw a young student sitting by the window. He stood as I entered.

"Melinda Drake, this is Aiden Flanagan. Aiden is the graduate assistant in our office."

"Nice to meet you, Ms. Drake," Aiden smiled.

Oh, boy.

"Likewise. Please, call me Melinda."

Aiden was obviously pleased with meeting me, gazing with puppy-dog eyes. I attained the reputation around campus for being some sort of VIP.

"Aiden, Ms. Drake is here through the end of the year, finishing her degree in design and merchandising."

"That's great," He said, probably thinking how ancient I appeared, apparently another adult student finally getting it done.

The dean turned to me. "Aiden received his undergraduate degree in game art and production, with honors, and is pursuing his masters in digital media. He is talented, and I'm expecting great things from him in the future."

"Thanks, Dean. I appreciate your inflated hopes for my career."

"At the risk of sounding like a dinosaur, what does one do with a degree in game art, Aiden? I'm sure it's a noble profession, but I'm a tad clueless when it comes to those things," I asked.

His eyes roamed from the top of my head to my feet, which of course were adorned with a pair of my MD shoes. It was subtle, and he was attempting to play the whole thing cool. His face lit up with excitement, surprised and delighted that I was inquiring about his plan for the future and that I was genuinely interested in hearing what he had to say. He couldn't have been more than twenty-four. I was close to forty. The fact that I was not one of the faculty or administration but a fellow student asking him to elucidate the details of his career path, seemed to ignite a fire of youthful enthusiasm in him to talk.

"Digital media is more than playing video games, Ms. Drake."

Ms. Drake? Are you kidding me? Now I felt like a dinosaur.

"Aiden, please call me Melinda," I repeated. "I realize that gaming is big business, but what are you seeking to do with this? What exactly does it entail?"

"It basically combines the principles of technology and art in a way that they can be used for different mediums like animation, gaming, theme park design, and interactive educational methods. It's the ultimate mix of science, art, and computers for the next century. Eventually, my goal is to get a job with one of the major animation studios, designing for them."

"I think that would be the coolest job ever." I turned to Dean Samuels and remarked, "Can you imagine working each day at a place like that? I wonder if you ever get frustrated or bored when those are your daily surroundings, right?"

He laughed. "I imagine it must be better than the average working environment. Being in the same building as super heroes and cartoon characters has to have its advantages."

Aiden looked right into my eyes and winked at me. This kid—I mean guy—was charming.

The dean shifted gears. "All jocularity aside, I need to discuss a department matter with the two of you. As you may be aware, Pennwood

University will be losing our current president at the end of this semester. I have been asked to chair the search committee for his replacement. I am in the process of assembling a group of campus representatives from several different areas. I would like to have you, Melinda, represent the undergraduate and non-traditional population and you, Aiden as a graduate student, serve on the search committee. We realize, Melinda, with your business experience and retention record at your company, you would be a huge asset in this effort. Aiden, you would bring a fresh perspective to the table. I consider myself lucky to have two gems right here in this part of the university. So how about it? Can I count on both of you in this important endeavor?"

I relished the compliment and would have been an absolute fool to turn him down. Besides, it would be fun to show how much I knew about hiring the right candidate for the job and getting to know Aiden and spend some time with him.

"Thank you. I would be honored to serve," I said.

"Same. I would do anything to help you out after all you've done for me," Aiden added.

"Wonderful. Thank you. Rose will email you with the details when we have them. Résumés are already flooding in, so we will have our job cut out for us examining all these potential candidates."

"Will this be a large search committee?" I asked.

"I have asked two faculty members, two administrators, and one alumnus, plus the two of you. I think we have a good mix. We will meet sometime in January." Dean Samuels rose from his chair, a sign that it was time for Aiden and I to leave so he could get back to work.

As we walked out of his office, Aiden held the door open for me, and I waved good-bye to Rose.

"I'm headed over to get coffee before my class. Can I interest you in joining me?" he asked.

"God, I would love to. I have to make the drive back to New York, and a caffeine fix is just what I need. Let's go."

It was a lovely fall day on campus, with the leaves turning gold and red. My eyes scanned the landscape; I was so lucky to be here. I tried to do this more often these days: take in my surroundings, smell the roses. My sister called me the other day to tell me her forty-six-year-old neighbor dropped dead at work from a heart attack. It forced me to stop and take stock of my own life and appreciate how fast it can be snatched away. My career was everything, and maybe this whole going back to school was the best thing to happen at this stage of my life. I looked at the handsome, carefree young man walking beside me. Life was good, I was having fun, and all the sights around me were appealing.

The campus of Pennwood University was stunning. Nestled in the heart of Philadelphia, it possessed old-world charm together with the best of technological advances and improvements in its basic infrastructure. The school was a perfect fit in the City of Brotherly Love, standing as a beacon of free expression and intellectual pursuits for generations of students. The late October chill warranted a warm sweater, hoodie or vest over a pair of comfortable jeans, sweats, or yoga pants, the uniform of choice on campus. I loved this time of year and excitedly looked forward to the even colder days November would bring. The crunch of walking through leaves, the scent of autumn in the air coupled with local coffee shops brewing dark roast beans and baking seasonal apple cider doughnuts was intoxicating.

We walked into the student center and ordered lattes, and Aiden opted for a chocolate chip cookie. Before I could reach in to my bag for my wallet, he paid the cashier.

"Thank you. But I should be the one buying. You're probably a poor, starving graduate student, and I wanted to treat you."

"Nope, sorry. I was the one who extended the invitation, so you have no say in the matter," he said, leading me through the crowd as we found a table.

"Well, maybe you'll come to my place so I can make you a nice dinner sometime. That is, if I ever find a place."

"I've gotten bits and pieces of why you're here. I'm dying to hear how you're planning to pull this off. It's like that old movie from the 1980s when the dad goes back to college with his son and basically rules the school. Do you have the same sort of plan?"

"You are way too young to even know about that movie."

"Ever heard of streaming services? Great new thing," he grinned.

"Very funny. And, yes, my executive assistant reminded me of that movie when I first proposed this scheme, as she called it."

Aiden laughed.

"Yeah, my assistant is one of a kind. However, I'm here to finish what I started, bottom line. Better late than never. Since I am the CEO at my own company, I can do whatever the hell I want. I had to ensure my employees that the business would not be impacted in any way, and Dean Samuels was instrumental in helping me iron out the details. This semester I am here one day a week, commuting from New York, completing my internship and an independent study. I need to find an apartment because I will live here in Philly for the spring term taking eighteen credits so I can graduate with my degree."

"Wow. Impressive. Going back with a full load after being out for so long. Are you sure you'll be able to juggle it?"

"If you saw what I am able to juggle at one time in my job, it would make your head spin. I thrive on pressure, deadlines, and stress. I'm finding this whole academia thing a welcome distraction from the demands of my business. I'm relishing the opportunity to think and create again and be mentally challenged. Excuse me, but your generation has gotten whiny and complacent. A little hard work is good for the mind and body, Mr. Flanagan."

"I couldn't agree more. I think it's great that you're doing this. Probably the best day of my life to date was the day I graduated with my bachelor's degree. It feels like a total personal accomplishment, because you alone make it happen."

"You along with your parents who pay for it."

"Not all of us. I put myself through undergraduate school working several jobs, and I have a graduate assistantship that covers tuition and gives me a small stipend to pay for books and meals. Mac and cheese and ramen noodles meals, but meals nonetheless." He winked.

I wish he would stop doing that. It was kind of cute and way too flirty. "Sorry, I guess it was wrong to assume that…"

"It's ok. My father is a real douche, and I'm happy I don't owe him a damn thing. All his money went to the ponies and Atlantic City when I was little, so if I wanted anything, I had to make it happen myself."

I felt horrible. "Well, then, I take back what I said about your generation. You are obviously the exception to the rule. I apologize. I admire that kind of drive. You'll be successful some day; I can tell. I am an expert at spotting talent and potential, and you seem to have both. You'll forever appreciate all you achieve because when you work hard and don't have things handed to you, they mean so much more. I like you, Aiden Flanagan."

"Thank you. So now that we have a brief overview of each other, maybe I can help with your apartment search. I assume money isn't an issue, right?"

"No, it isn't," I said, embarrassed in light of what Aiden had just revealed about his own financial situation.

"Because my cousin Ellie is a realtor here in the city. She found my small studio, even though it's a dive. I could call her if you want. She handles nicer, uptown stuff, too."

"That would be great. I need all the help I can get. When I was here all those years ago, I lived on campus so it was easy. But I am familiar with the city, so I need to have someone find what's available."

"I'll call her tonight. How often are you on campus?"

"I'll be here on Tuesdays. But I could meet on Saturday or Sunday, if that works for her."

"Won't that interfere with your family time, you know hubby and kids?" he asked, before taking a sip of his coffee.

"No, since I possess neither. It's me, along with my parents, siblings, and a few close friends. And you? Is there a significant other in your life?"

"No. No time, energy, or finances for that, I'm afraid. "But I am all about having a good time and enjoying the company of a pretty lady."

Okay, then.

"Well, if anything, we've made a great connection today. I have a good feeling you and I will become great friends, despite the gap in our age. We certainly will be spending some time together on the presidential search committee, and I'll be counting on you and your cousin to find me an apartment and a social life here in Philly."

"You've got yourself a new friend, Melinda. My one requirement is that you ignore our age difference and treat me like an equal. I think we're gonna get along fine. In fact, I'm absolutely sure." He winked.

This is going to be so much fun.

CHAPTER SEVEN

Teresa was acting weird even for Teresa. Each time she came into my office, she would stare at me for a few seconds without saying a word, make a loud sighing noise, then limp out with her head down like a wounded fawn. Finally, I couldn't take it anymore.

"Teresa—what the hell are you doing?"

"I don't know what you mean."

"Are you crying?"

"What makes you think that?" she asked.

"Because you've been moping around here for the last week like you lost your best friend…"

Oh, crap.

"Is that it? Are you upset…about me? About me not being around here everyday?" My eyes widened. I was taken aback by her emotional state.

"Maybe."

"Oh, Teresa. That's so sweet! You actually have a soft side after all. Who would have guessed this side of you existed?" I opened my arms to give her a hug.

She embraced me. "If you breathe a word of this to anyone in the company, I'll sue you for harassment or make up some other stuff like there's a sex tape of you floating around the mailroom."

"Calm down. I promise I won't repeat a word of this. Your secret is safe with me. Teresa Jenks is nothing more than a sentimental fool."

"You know, Mel, things will be strange—terrifying around here without you for six months. I hope we don't crumble from lack of leadership. I'm nervous about the whole situation. Oh, and by the way: a lot of employees have approached me about throwing you a going off to college party. Nothing major, just another excuse for cake and time off from the usual grind."

"NO. No party. I want to draw the least bit of attention as possible. Six months will fly by if we all go about our daily, normal routine. Give them a cake for birthdays or employee of the month, anything along those lines would be fine. But leave my personal business to me and me alone."

"All right, you're the boss." Waterworks formed in the corners of her eyes again, coupled with a semi-quivering lip.

"Teresa, I need you to be strong. It's not like I'm going to the moon or even out of the country. I'll be in Philadelphia, for God's sake. Less than two hours away. This is not a big deal."

"It is for me. We're a team: always have been, always will be. It's going to suck not having you here, and I'm gonna miss you. Let me wallow in my misery, okay?"

I shot a slow, lazy smile at my loyal, wonderful assistant.

"I bet I know what would make you feel all better."

"Yeah, what?" She asked, using a tissue to dab her tears, understanding exactly what I was about to say.

"Tell your husband I'm taking my favorite employee to dinner and the show of her choice on Friday. For old time's sake and to cheer her up."

"Are you sure?"

"Yes, Mama. But you have to promise there will be no more moping around. I need to take a couple of days to organize my apartment at school, and I can't be worrying about you and this place, which I am putting in the capable hands of Alyce. Are we clear?"

"Crystal clear, boss. And thank you: for the talk, the tickets, and dinner. I'm sorry, but I'm going to miss you. As it gets closer, I'm getting sadder. Cut me some slack."

"Done. Let's get back to work."

I had Teresa clear my calendar so I could take a long weekend and move some things into my new apartment. Aiden's cousin Ellie found me a great place, a mere ten minutes from campus. It was a luxury apartment, overlooking a beautiful tree-lined park surrounded by restaurants, boutiques, and historical landmarks. Aiden whistled when he walked in the vacant apartment, clearly impressed.

"Just so you know, Melinda, I will be coming here a lot. This is pure paradise compared to my dump. Thanks, El, BTW."

"You could only afford this in your dreams, cuz," Ellie joked, gently punching his arm.

"You're both welcome any time." I walked around, opening doors and drawers, feeling instantly like it was home. I would have to sign a year lease on the place, but that was fine. After I graduated, it would be nice to have a place to stay in Philly when I visited all the people I planned on meeting while being a student. It felt so right, so exciting. I couldn't wait to be back here at college again. This was going to be excellent.

"Ellie, tell them I'll take it. Forward me the paperwork ASAP. I don't want to lose this place. It's perfect: it has charm, it's close to campus, and there's so much to do in the surrounding area. Well done. Thanks for all your help."

"My pleasure, Melinda. Don't worry. I'll take care of everything. I agree—this place is terrific!"

"Let's go. I'm taking you miracle workers out to lunch to celebrate," I said.

Aiden and Ellie looked at each other.

"Is there a problem?"

"It's just that I promised my husband I would meet him today. Can I take a rain check? Ellie asked.

"Sure. Your hubby is welcome to join us, unless you were planning a romantic lunch. I'll just have to treat Aiden." He wrinkled his nose, apparently not comfortable having a woman pay. He would need to become accustomed to the Melinda Drake way of generosity.

"Stop making a face, Aiden, and get used to it. I have a lot of money and I like to spend it, particularly on people and things I like. I am a wealthy woman, and although I appreciate your chivalry and respect for me, I'll need to treat you every now and then. After all, you are my first friend I met coming back here, which should count for something. Don't you agree?"

He shrugged his shoulders in submission. Then, he raised an index finger, rummaging around in his messenger bag. Aiden pulled out a magazine, displaying it for Ellie and me.

"How could I possibly disagree with the Woman of the Year?"

"What are you doing with that? That issue came out months ago!" I howled.

There I was, in all my glory, gracing the cover of *Wealth and Success* magazine.

"I stole it from the library. I couldn't resist."

Maybe I couldn't resist either.

Life was good. And Aiden Flanagan was sublime.

My parents insisted on helping me move into what would essentially be my home for the next few months. Still treating me like a little girl, I was touched at their concern for my welfare. I deduced this was due to the fact I was the only one of their children who was not married. It didn't matter I was a millionaire several times over and could well afford a moving company with handlers to take care of my things. Mommy and Daddy had to "get Melinda settled." I loved them dearly, and if it made them feel better to do this, I would not deny them. They were both in their mid-sixties and were not going to be doing any heavy lifting or moving of furniture. But Dad would make sure he was outside supervising the movers and Mom remained inside, telling me where things should be placed. They needed to hover over me, but I guess it's what parents do. Since I assumed I would never have children of my own, I tried to understand as best I could and accept it. So many times I would watch them with so much love, grateful that they have always been there for me in the best and worst of times.

I had hired a local interior designer Ellie recommended to fill the apartment with furniture, window treatments, and accessories. Hours later, all of my things were moved in, the kitchen and bathrooms were stocked, and we collapsed in the big, comfortable couch in my new living room. All I had to do was unpack the few clothes and toiletries I lugged this trip. I would bring additional stuff from my Manhattan apartment as needed.

"I'm starving. Should we order in or would you guys like to go out?" I asked, slouching against the living room wall.

"Let's stay in. I'm beat." My father yawned. Ellie had left a bunch of take-out menus on my kitchen counter, leaving me a note: *These are the best in the neighborhood.* She was a fantastic realtor, and someday I would repay her for all she had done. Whenever someone went the extra mile on my behalf, I made sure they were properly thanked. I had some ideas on the subject, and, I would make a few phone calls after I left here in June.

"Do you guys want pizza, cheesesteaks?"

My intercom buzzed. I was in a secure building with a doorman who announced all visitors. I needed to provide him with a list of approved guests in the next week, folks who did not need to show ID when they came to see me.

"Yes?"

"Ms. Drake, I have a delivery for you downstairs. Shall I send him up?"

"Absolutely, thank you."

"I wonder what it is?" I said to my mom. Minutes later, there was a knock at my door. When I opened it, the entire doorway was filled with the largest arrangement of flowers I have ever seen.

"Holy cow!" My father said.

"Melinda Drake?" The guy asked.

"That would be me. Oh, my God!"

He handed me the delivery. I placed the hefty bouquet on my coffee table. Palming him a tip, I closed the door. I dug the card out from the massive arrangement, blushing as I read the note, holding the card to my heart.

"Who are they from?" My mother asked.

"Steven Hill." I smiled.

"How sweet of him to think of you."

Even though we weren't a couple anymore, he was still one of my dearest male friends and probably one of my biggest supporters in my decision to go back to school. He was the one who encouraged me, assuring me my shoe company would be fine with my temporary hiatus and that I needed to do this purely for my own satisfaction. Steven understood me; I was happy we decided to continue being a part of each other's lives.

The card read: *My dear Melinda. Wishing you all the best in your new venture. I know you will take that university by storm and accomplish great things while you are there. Remember: you have a friend cheering you on from New York, and if you need anything, I'm a phone call or email away. Love you. Steven*

Later, after my parents went to sleep in my guestroom, I called Steven to thank him. I needed a pep talk before I was to begin this new college adventure. I wasn't nervous; I simply needed to commiserate with someone closer to my age concerning my leap into Generation Z hell. Here I was, about to compete with the best and the brightest, and I wanted emotional support.

The next morning, I headed back to Manhattan with my parents. My driver, Buddy, dropped me off in the city and drove my parents home to New Jersey. I was grateful they helped so much with the move, but I was a grown woman and needed my space and privacy. I spent most of Saturday locked in my corporate office, catching up on emails and other pressing issues. I called my childhood girlfriends, Chelsea and Gina and asked if they wanted to come into the city to go to a couple of clubs. As I had told Aiden, I loved to treat my friends to a night out. I enjoyed spending my money on the people I cared about. Chelsea was divorced with two tween kids, and Gina was between girlfriends. I promised Gina I would go to the bar of her choice if she gave me a quick haircut. I could afford a top salon and stylist in New York, but Gina was unbelievably talented in the hair department and made me look and feel like a new woman.

My friends arrived at six that night, and after my beauty treatment and several pink drinks, we were ready to hit the town. With so much to do in the next week in preparation for my new life between work, personal stuff, buying last-minute items, checking in with Dean Samuels, Alyce, and Teresa, my head was spinning. Tonight I wanted to have fun, relax, and forget about my to-do list.

Our first stop was a restaurant in Tribeca, where we commandeered a booth, catching up on our busy lives. Of course, my upcoming venture was the main topic of conversation, because they considered this daring and exciting. I decided to tell them all about my new found friend, the handsome and beguiling Aiden Flanagan.

"How old is he?" Gina asked, sipping her martini.

"I would guess around twenty-four," I said, "and totally adorable. I think we'll become good friends."

"Would you stop the friend BS with all these men you get involved with Mel? You need to fall in love, find someone. Someone who will make your heart race and your palms sweat and who will want no one but you," Chelsea said.

"First of all, you guys know my palms always sweat." Along with my damn sweaty feet, it was one of my annoying flaws I had zero control over. "Second, we are not involved—at all. Third, he is way too young, and, aside from school, I'm sure we'd have nothing in common. We like to goof on each other and flirt. I am the older, successful woman, and he is intrigued. The kid is nice and helpful, and we laugh a lot. Someday, he'll be a huge success, and right now he is my only social life. His cousin is my realtor and found me a great place, so I owe him."

"Does he have any idea that you are the most generous person in the world and that you will probably help him more in his career than anyone he will ever meet?" Gina asked.

It was true. I have always felt a need to repay anyone in my life who helps me, and Aiden would be no exception. This is the reason being wealthy is so much fun: I am able to lavish gifts and favors on anyone I choose. I take care of the people in my life, these two especially— jobs, cars, clothes, contacts—whatever. Cross me and I will crush you; help me and I will forever be in your debt.

"Aiden's a good guy. And we're on the presidential search committee for the university, which will be a fun diversion from schoolwork. Our first meeting is this week."

Chelsea laughed. "You're going to have to control yourself and try to not take over the dean's authority. You're used to being in charge, and I can't see you taking a backseat to anything."

Gina nodded in agreement.

"True, but I'll be a huge help. He even mentioned this when he asked me to serve on the committee. Dean Samuels understands I'm an expert on hiring the right people. I'll find him the perfect replacement."

"You and a committee of several others," Chelsea said.

"We'll see. Are things good with both of you, I hope? Fill me in," I instructed. As busy as I always was, I needed to know my friends and family were status quo and happy.

"I went on a dating app this past week," Chelsea reported, making a face like she had just sucked a lemon. "Not much out there. And I bet the few cute guys that I saw are either liars or psychopaths or momma's boys. Doesn't either of you know of anyone who is unattached and normal? I think I'm almost at that desperate stage."

"I think you need to get out more. I meet girls through other friends and the gym and work functions," Gina said.

Chelsea took a sip of her drink. "I think it's less complicated for you."

"Oh, and why is that?"

"There is less of a game to play. You are a woman seeking another woman. We understand how to cut through all the bull and be ourselves. What you see is what you get, and you either take it or leave it. I think men are a whole different dance, and maybe because it involves the opposite sex, we never quite seem to get each other. Right?"

Gina bobbed her head in agreement. "That may be true."

"By the way, Mel. Have you heard from Steven?" Chelsea asked. "I honestly thought he was the one."

"As a matter of fact, I did. He sent a beautiful arrangement of flowers to my Philly apartment to wish me luck. He's a sweetheart. But it was always just fun and friendship with Steven, nothing more."

"Is he still seeing that woman from the shoe department? What a kick in the pants that must have been, Mel. Kind of a heel, right?"

The three of us looked at each other and giggled.

"I don't know, and I don't ask. That's his business. Steven will never be one to tie himself down again to one woman. It's not in his DNA," I said.

"That's why you were so perfect for each other. You are the same way, Melinda. Whenever you get close with a guy and begin to get serious, something happens, and it inevitably ends. Why is that?" Chelsea asked, stirring her cocktail.

"Oh, for God's sake. That's how I like it. I don't have the time to invest in a full-time, long-term relationship. I will never stretch myself so thin like that because of my career. I live the life I want and men have always been an addendum, nothing more. And I'm fine with that."

"I know. I just like to tease you now and then. So, when will we get to see this new place and get to meet all your new, hip Philly friends?"

"When I actually get some. I want to get this degree, close this chapter of my life, and get back to running my company. Yet, I'm looking forward to this change. I'm going to make it fun, even if it takes every last ounce of my energy to do it," I laughed, signaling for our waitress.

"Well, Melly Belly," Gina warned, "make sure that it's just the papers and projects and exams that wear you out, not some twenty-four-year-old dude."

"Oh, yeah," Chelsea said. "This is going to be so much fun to watch you navigate the ins and outs of being a college student again. I can't imagine going back after all this time—I give you a whole lot of credit. Things have changed considerably since the '90s. College feels like a million years ago."

It does. And I guess that makes me prehistoric. What the hell am I doing here?

CHAPTER EIGHT

Standing in front of my living room window, I notice a layer of frost clinging to the car windows parked on the street below. The cup of coffee warming my hands reminds me that I will momentarily have to brave the cold reality when I exit my balmy cocoon of a house. January in Philadelphia is brutal. Why I didn't plan this with more thought is beyond my comprehension. I should have finished the independent study and other work over the summer and done my eighteen credits in the fall. At least the weather would have been bearable, for God's sake. But with the London launch, I couldn't have pulled it off. I whip out my phone and examine my schedule of for the millionth time. There are many new buildings on campus since I left years ago. Yesterday, Aiden and his friend Brett walked with me to where my classes are located, so at least I'll be sure of where I'm going. I have three classes on Monday, Wednesday and Friday, which finish early in the afternoon. I have two classes on Tuesday and Thursday and one three-hour course on Tuesday evening. I have most late afternoons free for search committee meetings and conference calls and to video chat with my office. Giddy with excitement, I grab my sturdy designer backpack and fling it over my shoulder. Bracing the cold, I head out the door into the unknown.

Put one foot in front of the other. That's how I operate.

I have no idea how to dress for my brief tenure here. Should I try to act my age or should I make some kind of an attempt to look young and relevant, assimilating into the crowd? But then again, a tall, middle-aged woman with red hair doesn't exactly blend in with a bunch of fresh-faced undergrads in boxy sweaters and leggings. I opted for jeans, knee-length boots and a warm coat.

My first class was one of those general education requirements conveniently ignored until the last possible semester. I needed a social science course and registered for political science. Politics amused me, so I thought it would be fun to spar with my fellow students and professor, since I read at least two or three newspapers a day and kept abreast of the current political climate. As I approached the building, I froze, keenly aware of the fact that this was my first foray back into classroom life. Hoisting the bag over my shoulder, I took in a deep breath, praying my college socializing skills hadn't rusted over like the copper drainpipe jutting out from Patriot Hall.

Opening the door to Room 312, I scanned the space to discover I was the sole non-traditional student in the class, and everyone was looking at me like I had two heads or spinach stuck in my teeth. Instead of acting like the old fart they probably think I am, I decided to forgo my preferred seat in front, sliding into an arm desk toward the back near the window. When I left my apartment this morning, I made a vow to ratchet my personality down a notch so as not to intimidate and scare people away. I would be a student, not a CEO.

"Good morning all, and welcome. This is Introduction to American Government, so if you didn't sign up for this you are officially in the wrong class. However, if you would like to stay, I'd be more than happy to have you join us. My name is Dr. Gregory Kramer and..."

The door squeaked open, and a frazzled, mature woman like myself (and certainly more nervous) slid into the room and mouthed "sorry" in the direction of Dr. Kramer. She hurried in and slumped into the seat next to me, cringing. Now *she* was the center of attention in a class of approximately twenty students. Is it wrong I am thrilled to not be the only relic in this class of Gen Z kids?

Unfazed, Dr. Kramer continued his introduction, informing us we would be examining and analyzing the different branches of the federal government and their political processes. He reviewed the syllabus we were able to preview online, while displaying the large textbook I had purchased at the university bookstore. After a short lecture, Dr. Kramer gave us a reading assignment, dismissing the class early.

That was it. I had stressed and obsessed over nothing.

Stuffing the text and a notebook in my bag, I glanced over to the woman next to me. Brows crumpled together in a frown, she read a printout of her schedule, sighing in frustration.

"You look like you could use some help," I said.

"More like I am desperate. I feel like a fish out of water. This is my first day and first class, and I have no idea what the hell I'm doing." She stood to gather her things as the last of the students along with Dr. Kramer exited the room.

"Well, if I can be of any assistance, I know my way around the campus pretty well. Maybe I can point you in the right direction."

Her eyes widened. "You can?"

"I'm a senior. Back after a bit of a hiatus, but back nonetheless." I held out my hand and introduced myself. "Melinda Drake—nice to meet a fellow student who undoubtedly agrees that the 1980s produced *the* best movies of all time.

She busted out a grateful laugh. "You have no idea. Heidi Larson—nice to meet you, too. Ugh. I stick out like a sore thumb. I didn't think it would be this hard. I hope it gets easier."

"It will. New is always difficult, but you'll get the hang of it. What time is your next class?" I asked.

"Not until 11:30. What about you?"

"I'm free until then also. Would you like to go grab a coffee? There's a cafe right in the next building. We can sit, and I can help you map out your daily routes if you want."

"Perfect," she said.

Heidi and I bundled in our coats. Walking next door, we braved the crowd of students and faculty who swarmed like flies into the spacious lounge for coffee and hot chocolate. It took about ten minutes to be served and locate two seats.

"Thanks, Melinda. It's nice to have someone to talk to. I've been so nervous for weeks, and I can't believe I'm doing this, hoping it's all worth the effort," she said, sipping her coffee.

"Well, I think pursuing higher education is a noble, worthy endeavor and if you've made it this far, you can relax. It'll be challenging, but you'll see how exciting it is."

"I guess. I just need to settle in, and now that the semester has finally started, I'm relieved."

"What are you planning to major in?" I asked.

"I want to get my degree in business. I had originally thought accounting, but to be a CPA requires five years, and that's not in the cards at this point in my life. I'm forty-two. I'll be in school for the next few years. I have my associate degree from community college, but I need a four-year degree to get a decent job. I have two kids who are old enough to semi-function on their own, and my husband is encouraging me to finish, so here I am. What about you?"

I proceeded to fill her in on my personal plan, and her eyes illuminated like a Christmas tree when I told her that I was the founder of MD Shoes.

"Oh my God! I love your shoes. They are the most comfortable shoes I own when I'm not in my usual flats and sneakers. My husband loves your heels on me. I have the turquoise pumps with the pink design on the soles and the patent leather, beige stilettos. Love them. I can't believe I'm actually sitting here with you."

"Why thank you. Always happy to meet another satisfied customer," I said, stirring my coffee.

She looked quizzically at me. "Um, excuse me for asking but why are you even here? You obviously made it big, huge, as a matter of fact. Do you even need a college degree? You are already a successful businesswoman. I don't get it."

"That's what everyone asks me. I was twenty-four credits short of graduation in the fall of my senior year back in 1998 when a car accident derailed my plans. Life crept in, and I never went back. Things changed and the time was right, so here I am. Simple as that."

"Wow. That must have been terrible. I guess I can understand why you would want to finish. I admire you more than ever."

"Thank you. Working out the logistics was difficult, but I have a place nearby, so if you ever need to crash somewhere, you're more than welcome."

As I looked around the room, I spotted a few people in our age group, but they were dressed more formally than we were so I assumed they were faculty and staff who worked at the university.

"I may need to take a nap in your apartment with this crazy schedule of mine, so thanks. Tell me, what degree are you pursuing?

"Design and merchandising. My biggest challenge will be keeping a handle on my schoolwork while running my company from here."

"And my greatest challenge will be juggling two kids, a house, a part-time job, and a husband. Talk about spreading yourself too thin. But like you said, it's now or never, before we get really old." Heidi tilted her head in the direction of three gorgeous co-eds who stood in line reading their phones. Every male with a pulse in the lounge was transfixed. Our eyes rolled skyward.

Deciding this would be a regular thing for the two of us to meet for coffee after our class, I had Heidi display her schedule for me as I grabbed a campus directory sheet from the help desk in the building. I mapped out the rest of her courses for her, and we parted ways. My next two classes were back-to-back in the media building, so I headed across campus.

The day flew, and I couldn't wait to get back to my warm apartment. I was too tired to cook myself dinner, so I decided to order in food. As I pulled out my phone, the doorman buzzed me.

"Ms. Drake, there is a Mr. Flanagan here to see you. Would you like me to send him up?"

Surprised, I happily replied, "Please do, thanks." Even though I was exhausted, my apartment was too quiet and I was lonely. I missed my life in New York.

I opened my front door to a grinning Aiden holding a large pizza box.

"Dinner is served!" he said with that utterly adorable face of his.

"You didn't have to do this. You're a struggling graduate student. My mother stocked this place with enough food to last me through three blizzards. I have enough to feed you and probably most of your friends."

"Well, Ms. Drake, I may take you up on that. My friends would freak if they ever saw this place—and the gorgeous woman who lives here." Aiden was a charmer, and this was only a small part of his overall appeal.

"Nonetheless, you are such a sweetheart for doing this. I was just about to order take-out."

"Rough first day?"

"Not at all. Just different from what I'm used to on a daily basis. Normally, I start at eight in my office and go from meeting to meeting, with working lunches and dinners thrown in as part of my day. I love the frenetic pace of it. Things move a whole lot slower in academia."

"I can't wait to be out in the real world. I'm so sick of going to school. When we both graduate in June, we should have a huge party to celebrate. Great idea, right?"

"That could certainly be a possibility, my new friend. Come on. I'm starved," I said as I opened the lid and exclaimed, "and sweet Jesus, it's pepperoni! I could kiss you, Aiden."

He stared at me.

Was he waiting for me to deliver?

CHAPTER NINE

The first official meeting of the presidential search committee was immediately following my senior seminar class. I rushed to the other side of campus to arrive on time to Dean Samuels' stately conference room in the historic Adams Building, donning a conservative suit and pair of pumps from my executive line. Rose sent us an email, where I was finally able to see the names of the other participants on the committee. Listed were the two administrators, Margaret Garren, director of admissions, and Levi Stone, director of residential life; two faculty members, Jack Sweeney, professor of American history and Ruth Forrester, assistant professor of psychology; and Gavin Beck, CEO of Beck Industries in nearby Conshohocken.

As I entered the room, everyone was settling into their seats after helping themselves to the hot coffee and tray of fresh pastries Rose had ordered. Aiden saved the chair next to him for me, and I placed my coat and backpack on it before heading to the welcome refreshments. Out of the corner of my eye, I noticed another set of eyes fixated on me—on my behind to be exact. I admit: my fitted skirt did make my butt look pretty darn good.

Gavin stood and walked over to join me as I was pouring the steaming coffee into a porcelain mug.

"Sugar?" he asked.

"I beg your pardon?" My eyes widened.

"Sugar. For your coffee," he answered, holding aloft the container of sugar packets.

"No, thank you, just a touch of cream. But thanks for offering."

"My absolute pleasure. I'm Gavin Beck," he said, extending a hand with long, slender fingers. With no wedding ring, I might add.

"Nice to meet you. I'm Melinda Drake." I extended my free hand,

and he shook it gently, yet firmly. He was handsome. He was smooth. I was intrigued.

At the same time we were introducing ourselves, Dean Samuels entered and placed a file folder at his seat at the head of the conference table. "Hello all, and welcome. If you haven't already, please help yourself to coffee and a bite to eat," he said, as he proceeded to grab a mug and a cheese pastry for himself.

The members of the committee took their seats around the table. Everyone seemed to know or be familiar with each other except for Gavin and me. The mood was jovial and cooperative, and the group seemed eager to be involved in such an important process. With the exception of Dr. Jack Sweeney. The man had to be at least six-foot-three inches tall. Arriving at the last minute, huffing and puffing, he looked like he wanted to be anyplace but here. Annoyed and distracted, he tapped his pen on his leg, annoying me. I saw this sometimes in my own meetings at MD Shoes. This guy probably loathed the fact that one of his many requirements as a tenured faculty member was to serve on committees at the request of the dean of the university. Suck it up, professor.

"Since we are all here, let's get started. I appreciate that you have agreed to serve on this important committee to find the next president of our beloved Pennwood University. We have conducted a nationwide call for résumés and have gotten an overwhelming response from all over the country and abroad. I would like to spend this first meeting weeding through candidates and selecting a pool that we can call in for interviews. Please take a few CVs and start reading, placing anyone you think we should consider in the center of the table. Then, we will select our top choices. But first, I would like to go around and have you each introduce yourself. Melinda, would you please go first?"

Leaning forward, I made sure to make eye contact with each person in the group, Sweeney included. "Why, certainly, Dean Samuels. Good afternoon. My name is Melinda Drake. I am Chief Executive Officer and owner of my own footwear company, MD Shoes."

Margaret and Ruth perked up, obviously former or current customers who liked my product. They gawked at me like I was famous.

Gavin was also attentive, but I had the distinct impression the dean had already informed him that I would be serving with him on the committee.

Jack Sweeney was not impressed the least bit, barely acknowledging the fact I was speaking.

"In addition, I have returned to Pennwood as a student in order to complete my undergraduate degree, and I plan to graduate in June. I'm thrilled to be back after a long absence, and I am excited to serve on this committee."

The introductions continued, and Jack Sweeney went last. It was short and terse.

"Jack Sweeney, history department."

That was it. Nice curriculum vitae, Jack Sweeny, an apparent jerk.

Rose had placed the stack of résumés in the corner of the conference table before we arrived. I stood, leaning forward to grab several. Gavin, sitting across from me, smiled as I reached in, while Jack Sweeney sneered at me and everyone else in the room. Aiden, in his youthful zeal, took a few, skimming over them.

I loved being part of a team. In high school, I participated in the annual play and was a member of the cast in several productions. I understood how important it was to have the right players and that every member played an important role, no matter how small. I was going to give this effort my undivided attention and take it seriously. I observed as the committee sat munching their pastries, flipping pages. All but Jack Sweeney. Brooding, obviously annoyed, he would scan a résumé, grunting in disgust as if it were a joke the candidate had even applied.

After about a half hour of reading curricula, we had thrown several outstanding candidates into the contact pile. The committee members voiced valid input while enjoying spirited conversation. We were excited to meet these candidates who had such monumental academic and professional credentials.

Margaret and Levi were delightful, Ruth was witty as hell, Dean Samuels was charming as ever, Aiden was candid and insightful, and Gavin was surprisingly bright and creative. Jack Sweeney was, well, grumpy and monosyllabic. I was my usual burst of enthusiastic energy. This was a welcome diversion from classwork, projects, and work responsibilities. I was in my element, used to having people hear what I had to say, a mover and shaker. A shrinking violet, I was not. Haven't I made that clear? I would make my mark on this committee and this university.

At four thirty, the dean closed his file and looked across the long table. "Okay, folks, I think we're done for today. Next time we will go through your individual choices and come up with a list. Thank you again for sacrificing your valuable time to do this. I will see you next week."

Aiden stood and stretched his lean frame. Margaret, Levi, Ruth, the dean, and I rose from our chairs and flexed a few middle-aged muscles. Gavin, about my age, showed no signs of being fortyish and looked mighty fine in an expensive, custom-made fitted suit.

Jack Sweeney glanced at his watch, pulled on a ratty overcoat, grabbed his worn, brown messenger bag, nodded to the group without smiling and hightailed it out of the conference room like he was being chased by a pack of wolves.

"What is the deal with him?" I whispered to Ruth.

She laughed. "That's Jack. Man of few words and even less emotions. I think he has to run and pick up his kid at school. Honestly, he doesn't say much. Unless you want to discuss the Civil War or Abraham Lincoln."

"Gotcha. Absent-minded professor. How stereotypical of him," I judged, maybe unfairly. I wasn't sure yet.

As we prepared to leave, Gavin approached, taking my elbow and leading me away from the group.

"Melinda, would you like to have dinner with me tonight? I realize it's last minute, but I would love to hear all about your company and compare notes."

He had a million-dollar smile and probably a stock portfolio to match.

Aiden was a few feet away, watching Gavin with suspicion. I had promised him homemade penne vodka and ice cream sundaes back at my place tonight. He had helped me with my new computer, and I owed him.

"Thank you, but I have plans. Rain check?"

"Sure thing. Can I get your number?" He took out his phone and tapped the numbers into his contacts. Then he called my cell. "There—

now you have me, too."

I certainly do. And I don't think I would mind that too much. He was an attractive guy and my contemporary. It was a welcome change from the kids I was surrounded by on campus. I hoped he would call. It would be a nice diversion.

Gavin walked over and shook the dean's hand. I turned to find a dejected Aiden, still looking at me with those big, puppy dog brown eyes. I decided tonight I would set him straight on our relationship.

I needed a friend, nothing more.

CHAPTER TEN

The temperature had plummeted, so we grabbed an Uber instead of walking back to my apartment. I hoped Aiden didn't mind hanging around with a woman of my financial means. He always offered to pay, but he also seemed to understand I was used to a certain lifestyle. The fact that I was a student wasn't going to change how I liked to live. In the future I would allow him to pick up the check once in a while for an inexpensive lunch or coffee, so as not to completely bruise his male ego. He genuinely appreciated my generosity, and I, in turn, had someone to go out with so I wasn't alone in a sea of undergraduates in a new city.

I came to the sobering realization it would not be right to get involved with Aiden or use him for my own needs or pleasure. Believe me, the temptation was there, and I knew he had developed a bit of a crush on me. I also knew we could last forever as friends, and that seemed like a much smarter direction. Perhaps I was getting older and wiser, or maybe I was looking for something more at this point in my life.

Aiden reminded me of how important it was to have platonic male friends, and I had plenty in my younger days. I loved hearing the male perspective on everything from fashion to dating. He was beginning to feel at home here in my luxury apartment, and I liked that I could provide him with the added comforts that were unavailable to him in that hovel of a dive he told me he occupied near campus.

We entered my apartment where I immediately jacked the heat up a notch. My dad taught me to lower the thermostat when I left to go out, explaining I would enjoy a burst of heat or air conditioning when I needed it most. I'm certain he told me that so that it would save me a few dollars each month. To this day, my daddy has not grasped the fact that I take in millions of dollars each year from my business. He still thinks I sell women pretty shoes and make a decent profit from it.

"So what did you think about the meeting?" Aiden asked.

I knew this was a fishing expedition on his part, to see what I thought of Gavin Beck.

"I thought it was good. Well run, organized, hot coffee and pastries, what more could you ask for?"

"Not that part. The participants—what'd you think of the other committee members?"

"Oh. Well, I liked Maggie and Levi, and Ruth's a pistol!" I laughed. "But what's with that Jack Sweeney? What a negative attitude. He's got a huge stick up his…"

"What'd you think of that Beck guy? He's slick as an oil spill and tried to hit on you the whole time. I could take him out if he bothered you or made you uncomfortable."

Aiden's chivalry was admirable, but his jealousy had to be dealt with, beginning now. If there was one thing I disliked in a man it was possessiveness, and although I would never be a girlfriend to Aiden, I felt it necessary to teach him that most women shared the same sentiment.

"I actually thought he was nice. Probably a player, but smart, good-looking, and he brings a lot to the group in terms of his ability to hire the right candidate. We both run corporations. We have to develop the skill of finding the right people for jobs. A CEO is nothing without good people to support her or him.

"Yeah, but he kept sucking up to you. It was pathetic and annoying." His jaw clenched.

I walked in from the kitchen holding a beer for Aiden and a glass of wine for myself. Sitting on the couch, I turned to face him, sucking in a deep breath.

"Aiden, we need to talk."

His angered expression faded, and he sat back, sipping his beer. I was under the impression that someone in his past had possibly uttered similar words to him—based on his reaction—and he became suddenly nervous.

"Is something wrong?" he asked.

"No, nothing is wrong. I need to clarify something. You are the first person I met when I came back here, and you are fabulous. You helped me when I didn't even ask for help, and you and Ellie have been a godsend. I love having you here and you make me laugh. In short, we are friends. Really good friends, and I want to keep it that way. Friends are forever. Other stuff becomes, well, complicated, and I have no room in my life right now for complications. I don't want you getting the wrong idea about us or where our relationship stands."

Aiden leaned forward, placing his bottle on the glass coffee table. "I realize you are a little older than me."

I snorted. "A little? You think?"

"But you and I could be good together. I've never met anyone like you. Girls my age are wacked and super needy and want to get married and have babies."

"Not all, girls. Don't stereotype like that. It's unbecoming of you."

"You know what I mean. Most girls out there aren't as confident and worldly, like you. It's super hot; you have no idea," he said, shaking his head.

"Well, thank you. I'll take the awesome compliment. But here's the thing. I am not in the market for a boyfriend, husband, or partner of any kind at this point in my life. And I like you too much to lose you. And being together would be a mistake."

Aiden blinked his eyes, contemplating my statement. Although we had been acquainted for a short time, I had to make it clear that I didn't play games and that once my mind was made up, there was no way to change it. He admired the things about me I liked the most about myself. It was what a good friend did.

Smirking, he asked, "How about we just hook-up, like once, so that I can fulfill the greatest fantasy of my lifetime. I promise I'll leave you alone after that. I mean, that crazy red hair of yours, those..."

I punched him in the arm and pushed him off the sofa. Let me repeat: I'm not a little wisp of a thing. I have a lot in me, including the ability to put a guy in his place. But this was all said in jest, and Aiden appreciated the fact I had broken the seriousness of the conversation.

He hoisted himself back on the couch, running his hand through his shoulder-length hair. I knew I had done the right thing with Aiden, although I lamented the realization that my own younger-man fantasy had been extinguished. In the back of my mind, I harbored the fear that if Dean Samuels had ever discovered that Aiden and I were involved, it would have caused my professional reputation to suffer. I didn't want him to think less of me. I had too much respect for the dean to risk it. I was the adult in the room here, and I had to make the mature, right decision.

But damn. It would have been fun.

Proving true that the way to a man's heart is through his stomach, Aiden recovered quickly from his perceived rejection, inquiring whether or not I still planned to provide a meal for him.

"Only if you come in the kitchen and help. Or at least keep me company." I loved to cook, and I relished the fact that I had a hungry young man who would enjoy and appreciate a home-cooked meal. He grabbed my glass and his beer bottle and followed me, opening the refrigerator to take out the wine.

"Okay, Melinda."

"Aiden, call me Mel. All my closest friends do." I winked.

"Okay, Mel—and ouch, BTW. So, as your friend, I think you need to watch out for this Beck asshole. I meant what I said about him before you went and broke my heart."

I smiled. "Don't worry about me. I can handle him. He's pretty predictable, and I've dealt with his type before. The one I can't figure out is the professor."

"Who? Sweeney?"

"Yes. Sweeney. I mean what was his deal? He obviously didn't want to be there. I wonder why Samuels put him on the committee over so many great faculty members he could have chosen. Did you ever have him for a class?"

"No. I took ancient world history to satisfy my requirement. He teaches American history, and he is a pretty recognized dude in the field. He's written a ton of books and articles and was a consultant to Thomas Clark on his award-winning Civil War series."

Cocking my head, I asked, "No kidding?"

"Yup. My friend, who's an education/history major, told me Sweeney has a framed, autographed picture of the two of them on his desk. I think he won an Emmy, along with Clark. It's pretty cool."

"Well, well. Wonders never cease."

"My friend also told me that he's one of the best teachers she's ever had and his classes are great."

"Are we talking about the same Jack Sweeney? The guy who grunted and snorted through the entire meeting? He seems like the biggest jerk on the planet, and I would've wagered good money he was a total bore in class. Let's face it, Aiden. That man has the personality of a rock."

"Maybe he's the kind who saves it all for class and his students. I have no idea, and I couldn't care less. But you know what I do care about?" he asked.

Distracted, I answered. "What's that?"

"I care about that penne vodka you promised me. Now get to work, missy." He grinned.

Coming out of my momentary fog, I gasped. "What did you call me? Did you say *missy*?"

"I did. Friends can joke around with each other. Isn't that right, Mel?" Aiden flashed his stellar smile.

"Yes, they can. But if you ever utter that word again in regards to me or any other female, I'll lay you out on the floor, and this time you won't get up."

CHAPTER ELEVEN

It was almost noon, and I was starving. Heidi was home with her daughter, who was sick, so I was on my own for lunch. I opened the heavy glass door to the student center, forcing a blast of cold air to follow me into the building. A couple of students in T-shirts were sitting close to the entrance and shot me a dirty look. The place was a mob scene—people yelling over one another, rushing in and out. I was hoping to grab something quick before heading over to the library. But I realized I had to sit and consume an entire meal in order to make it through the rest of my schedule.

Looking around, I spotted a group of kids (yes, this is how I sometimes viewed most of my younger, undergraduate counterparts) getting ready to leave and abandon one of the larger tables in the room. Since there were no other seats in the entire place and I was dying of hunger so much my stomach was growling, I turned to a group of young women who had entered the building and asked if they would like to share the table. They were young and bubbly and with a resounding YASS! (BTW that meant totally yes!) dashed over and secured the seats before several members of the men's lacrosse team beat us there. Piling the top with backpacks and flinging our coats over the backs of chairs to indicate rightful possession, we headed toward the cafeteria portion of the student center, most of us carrying along our purses and the ever-present third appendage, our phones.

Walking through the food line, I selected a turkey and cheese sub (not a hoagie, as the Philly natives incorrectly dubbed it) a bag of chips, an apple, a chocolate chip cookie, a large coffee, and a bottle of water. I wouldn't get dinner until much later in the evening, as this was Tuesday, and I had my three-hour night class. I needed basic sustenance—fuel, in the form of a rib-sticking meal.

The young women I would be lunching with looked at my tray in amazement and horror as they had selected bird food—yogurt, soup, and small salads to eat. I don't think I ever ate like these college students today do, even when I was their age. My mom is Polish, and I was raised on pierogies, kielbasa, and stuffed cabbage. Since we walk a couple of miles each day around this large campus, I couldn't understand the logic of starving and depriving yourself. Any calories consumed would soon be gone simply by getting from place to place. Seven of us sat around the table, as one of them commented on my tray of food, an anomaly compared to the others.

"Um, how do you eat all that and stay skinny?" Katie asked, setting her meager tray next to mine.

"You think I'm skinny?" I laughed.

"Well, for an older..." She caught herself, face flushing with embarrassment. "I mean, you look bomb for your age..."

The poor soul was stuck in an awkward pile of verbal gaffes, so I decided to spare her from any further humiliation.

"It's okay. I think I get what you're trying to say. Thanks for the nice compliment. I'm Melinda Drake, by the way. Nice to meet you ladies."

The amicable group went around the table introducing themselves with effortless enthusiasm, acceptance, and confidence. I discovered they were a circle of close friends, juniors and seniors sharing a house off-campus. Most had partial meal plans, so they could still eat on campus when they needed. They could have saved their parents a ton of money because they barely ate enough to keep a guppy alive. Initially, they assumed I was a faculty member or administrator because one of them asked me what department I worked in.

"Actually, I'm a student here, completing my degree in design and merchandising. I got sidetracked when I was about to graduate years ago in the '90s, and I decided I wanted to come back and fulfill my dream, so here I am," I said, opening my bag of kettle chips, emptying them on the plate beside my sandwich.

"For real, the '90s?"

"I imagine that probably seems like medieval times to you ladies. Wait—were you all even born yet?"

"Yup, 1997. So what are you, a mom or what?" Taylor, the brunette with the messy bun asked.

"No. I run my own company in New York City. Perhaps you've heard of it—MD Shoes?"

Several of my luncheon companions were oblivious, but two of them, Lucy and Blake, bolted upright in surprise.

"OMG! You own MD Shoes? Some of their stuff is so boujee. I mean, some are more for my mother, but some are on fleek and classy. I have to visit classrooms for my major this semester, and my older sister told me to get a pair because I have to stand all day, and flats are so ugly with my outfits. I ordered a pair. Now I'm obsessed," remarked Lucy, a stunning, petite blonde with side swept bangs and thin legs stuffed into a pair of tight jeans.

"Yes, that's my company. And I'm always happy to meet a satisfied customer," I smiled as I bit into my sub.

"Are they, for young people, your shoes?" Taylor asked.

I swallowed. "Well, I'm wearing a pair of my boots right now. You tell me." I stood and circled the table so they could take a peek. They were from my Look Sleek in the Snow collection and had a wedge heel with a lace-up front and a fold over, flannel cuff that went over the knee. I had paired them with my skinny jeans, and if I do say so myself, I looked pretty good.

"Ooh, they're gorge," Morgan said. "Do they cost a lot? My dad said I have to stop ordering so much online because his credit card is on fire. I keep telling him that I have no money, and he keeps telling me to get a job on campus…"

This was dizzying. "Gorge?"

Blake, completely ignoring Morgan, leaned over and clarified. "Gorgeous. Melinda, don't mind me asking, but aren't you a gazillionaire? Why are you here? I mean you are already a successful businesswoman. And BT dubs—can you please give me a job with you when I graduate?"

They howled. Blake was the leader and extrovert of the group. She also had guts, which I admired. She reminded me of, well, me.

"In answer to both your questions: I wanted to finish my degree because education is important, and you should finish what you start. And give me your résumé and we'll talk," I winked.

"Awesome," Blake said.

"Hey Melinda, I just searched you online, and you are kind of famous. I bet you have a ton of stans. Can I follow you?" Morgan asked.

"Stans?"

"Stalker fans."

"Sorry. I have a policy that I am not on any public social media, only with family and close friends. But you can follow MD Shoes on those platforms, along with checking out our website," I said.

"That's crazy AF, big time. But I get it. Do you know any celebrities?" asked Courtney with the big blue eyes.

"A few—but enough about me. How do you ladies like it here at Pennwood? What are you involved with on campus?" I wanted to divert the conversation and stop talking so I could finish eating my lunch.

Blake took the lead. "I'm looking to go into the apparel industry, specifically operations. I have a three-credit internship this semester, and so far, it's pretty interesting, and I like it. Except that my supervisor is sort of a creeper, and some of the people are lame and love to spill the tea about us interns. I have a 4.0 GPA. I'm hoping they offer me a full-time position after I graduate this year. If not, Melinda, I'm hitting you up for a job."

This was fun. I was enjoying the company of these young women. Oh, to not have a care in the world except for what you were going to eat for lunch that day and getting your classwork completed. I felt young again.

"I'm student teaching at a middle school in Berwyn in the fall, and I'm scared," Lucy uttered, biting her bottom lip.

"Why?" I asked.

"Because it's real world. It's scary."

"Nonsense. You can do anything. You're a woman. Consider yourself lucky," I affirmed.

"Easy for you to say, Melinda. You're already a grown-up. Oops! Sorry, I mean that in a good way." Courtney corrected her gaffe.

"It's okay, I'm not easily offended. I get it." I said.

"What do you mean we are lucky to be women? Isn't it a man's world? My parents are divorced and hate each other, and that's what my mom always says to me," Morgan asked, sipping an iced coffee.

"Oh yeah. My boyfriend Tyler told me someday when we get married, I will have to stay home with our kids because he will make more money than I ever will," Katie said.

"I know, my boyfriend told me girls can't survive in business because they always cry, and no guy respects a female boss." Taylor said. "I told him to kiss my…"

"Sorry, but your boyfriends are both so extra," Blake concluded, shaking her head in disgust. "And misogynists."

I clasped my hands over my ears. "Please tell me I didn't hear what I just heard," I uttered in disbelief and annoyance. "Intelligent, contemporary young women don't buy into that kind of BS, do they?"

"No, but my dad says the same thing. My mom stays home with my little brother because she has to drive him everywhere, and he's such a baby. But she says she likes it. All she does is play tennis and go to lunch with her friends. I never want that kind of life."

"I'm sure that's not all she does," I corrected. I knew plenty of women who stayed home, and it's no picnic in the park.

"That's not the life I want, either!" Taylor said.

"I never want to depend on some idiot guy to support me," Blake added.

"Same. This isn't the 1950s. I can't even." Morgan said in disgust.

"Amen, and thank God for that," I replied. I wasn't going to judge any of these young ladies, some of whom were still expressing the views and values of their parents. When they finally got out into the real world, they would see things differently.

"Hey Melinda, are you married?" Lucy asked.

"No."

"Any kids?"

"Nope."

"Why not? You're really p."

"Excuse me?" I asked.

"Pretty."

"Is that a reason to get married?" I laughed.

"No," Lucy said, "but I'm sure a lot of guys would want to be with someone as glamorous and worldly as you."

"Well ladies, here's the deal: I am a busy woman and not many men

72

can handle my success. I date occasionally, but there is no one special in my life right now." I glanced over at Lucy who seemed relieved at my proclamation. What was that about?

"Well, watch out Melinda, because you are a definite bae. Guys on this campus will want to hit on you, you'll see," Blake said.

I decided to call these wonderful ladies my "Bae Watch Crew." What a hoot they were.

"Cougar city!" Morgan laughed.

"Why thank you. But I don't think any young guys will be looking at me with you around. And, BTW, (me trying to be cool here) I'd like to give you all something for having lunch with an old lady like me."

"You're def not an old creeper, Melinda," Taylor confirmed, in between bites of her wrap, "you're so chill."

I reached into my bag and pulled out a bunch of gift cards I kept on hand.

"Here, these are for you." I handed each girl a fifty-dollar gift card to MD Shoes. "Try a pair of shoes or boots, on me. And if you like them, put a review on our website."

They shrieked with delight at the prospect of anything free.

"Thanks, Melinda. You're the GOAT! I'm going to look online right after my next class," Katie said.

"Goat? Translate please," I asked.

"GREATEST OF ALL TIME!" they shouted in unison.

"Oh, well then, enjoy." I gathered my garbage as I finished the last bite of my cookie. As I approached the trashcan, I noticed Jack Sweeney sitting at a table by himself, near the windows. The table could have easily accommodated four people, and this guy had spread his belongings and papers over the surface so no one would be able to share or intrude on his space. He was chewing a bite of sandwich while his fingers flew adroitly over his laptop keyboard.

"Bye, Melinda. You can eat lunch with our squad any time you want. And we are going to invite you to our next party. Would you come if we did?" Blake asked.

"Depends on my schedule." I knew I would never set foot at a party on campus, but I didn't want to disappoint my new young friends.

They gathered their things, bundled in coats and shouted their good-byes. Lucy lagged behind.

"Um, Melinda?"

"Yes, Lucy?"

"I think you know a friend of mine—Aiden? Aiden Flanagan?"

Now I realized the origin of the look on her face about the "worldly woman" remark. It was obvious she had feelings for Aiden, feelings that may or may not be reciprocated.

"I do know Aiden—nice person." Something was up here.

"He's a good friend of my brother's since high school. He was three years ahead of me."

She was obviously smitten with him. "How are you aware we knew each other?"

"He came over last week and told us he was on some search committee with the dean. He mentioned your name and how awesome and gorgeous you were. I almost died when you introduced yourself. I've had a thing for him since middle school."

The poor lovesick girl looked so forlorn, it was depressing. "Well, I can assure you, Lucy. Aiden and I are just friends. He and his cousin helped me when I didn't know anyone here, and I appreciated it. But that's all we are: friends," I smiled.

"I got so nervous. I mean he doesn't even notice I exist, and he's so hot and smart, and I don't stand a chance but…"

"Nonsense. You are a beautiful girl. Does he have any idea you have feelings for him?"

"No way. I wouldn't be able to take the rejection. I just worship him from afar."

"Hang in there. If I've learned anything in all my years on this earth, it's that life is a series of unpredictable events. And you can have anything you want if you work hard enough to get it. So go and get it."

"Okay. Thanks Melinda. And Aiden was hundo p and straight about you, for real."

Lucy turned and walked away. I felt like I was on Mars. What the hell did she just say, and what the hell did that mean? I needed desperately to reconnect with someone from my age group immediately.

Jack Sweeney.

I needed to regain some normalcy. My new Gen Z friends were

wonderful, but I felt like Gilligan on a remote island. Walking over, I stood in front of him.

Nothing. Nada. Not a hello, not a "How are you?" Radio silence.

"Excuse me, Jack, right?

He stopped chewing and typing. He still had his coat on, and he looked older than he probably was with that pair of glasses sitting on his forehead. Annoyed at the interruption, he looked at me.

"Do I know you?"

Are you kidding me?

"Melinda Drake? We are on the presidential search committee together? We met the other day?"

"Oh. You look different."

"I was dressed in a business suit for the meeting. This is my student attire."

He gazed at me with a blank stare. Either he was trying to get rid of me or he was senile. I decided to take the high road and mix it with a little levity.

"Sorry to interrupt, but I just had lunch with a bunch of kids who are much younger than I am, and I was hoping to come back to earth with someone from my generation, so I thought I would come over and say hello…"

"Ms. Drake. I'm on a tight deadline here—do you mind?" he asked, dismissing me.

"Oh, well. Sorry. I'll leave you to your work. Have a nice day, then."

He nodded, and resumed typing. I walked away, zipping my coat. WHAT AN ASS! He was rude as hell. Who did this jerk think he was? I wasn't some insignificant coed making googly eyes at him. In my real life, I was a CEO and businesswoman of the year. I made more money than this guy could ever dream of in his life. I lived in a huge penthouse apartment in Manhattan. I was on the guest list of almost every famous person in New York City. I was Melinda Drake, for Christ's sake!

A blast of cold air smacked me in the face as I left the student center, and it catapulted me back to reality. I was furious, but I must admit, even with the dork glasses and the disheveled clothes, he was handsome in a strange sort of way. He had brown hair and blue eyes, and he was thinner than I was normally attracted to. Dear God—what the hell am I thinking?

Attracted to? If I were still sitting with my new Gen Z girlfriends, they would have agreed with my response to this tool of a guy.

See you later, loser!

The Baes would have def high-fived me. Although, I wasn't sure if high-fiving was even still cool.

CHAPTER TWELVE

After my semi-humiliating confrontation with the exasperating Jack Sweeney, I retreated to the art building until my next class. I needed to call my parents and touch base with them and, after that, I would do my daily check-in with Teresa at work. A dose of normalcy was needed to remind me what mattered in my life. Jack Sweeney made my blood boil. What would make a human being so miserable and nasty?

After a few rings, my mother picked up the phone. Simply hearing her voice was like a sedative for me. She had the power to center me, to calm my frayed nerves, to right my ship on a stormy sea. My mama was a warm hug on a snowy, winter day. I was lucky to have both my parents, and I couldn't entertain the idea of life without them. I decided to mess with her, just a little.

"Hey, Marion. What's going on? Did I interrupt something between you and Fred?"

"First of all, don't call us by our first names. It's disrespectful. I don't care how old you are or what year we're in. Secondly, what your father and I do in this house is none of your business, and I want you to stop watching those dirty shows on cable TV. Are we clear?"

I loved the lilting song of her voice, even when she scolded me. "Yes, Mother."

"How is school? Did you get any grades back yet?"

I swear my father would have still given me a five dollar bill if I told them I got an **A**. Old habits die hard in the Drake house.

"No, Mom. I have a big project due next week in one of my design classes. I'll give you a full report of how I do. I have a poly sci test on Friday, and then I'm going back to my apartment in New York for the weekend."

"Oh, that's nice, dear. Do you want us to come in and meet you? We

77

can take you out to dinner on Saturday if you'd like."

"Thanks for the offer, but I have a lot of schoolwork to do, and I plan on going into my office for a few hours. I need to square away some business there, and meet with Alyce and Teresa. Maybe next time."

"Well, okay. Do you want to say hi to Daddy? He just got back from the super market and is mad because I sent him to get parsley and he came back with cilantro. I asked him how did he mess that up when all he had to do was read the sign, and he told me all the green stuff looks the same and if I didn't like it, next time I should go myself. Can you believe it? I mean, really, Mel. Cilantro has such a distinct fragrance—don't you agree?"

I heard my father yell from the den, "How the hell would I know what it smells like? For cryin' out loud. Get your own groceries from now on!"

My mom covered the phone with her hand, muffling her response. "Fred, relax. It's not a big deal. I won't put any parsley in my sauce. My God, you are becoming so cranky in your old age. Do you hear him Melinda? I told your brother I think he needs to get a part-time job. His retirement is driving me to drink."

I laughed. "Put him on the phone. I'll yell at him for you."

"Thanks, Dolly."

My mother had given her three children pet names. I was Dolly (because of my red hair and white complexion she said I resembled a porcelain figurine, and because of my angelic temperament, of course), my brother was Bug (because he was usually a pest), and my sister was Bunny (because she used to run away from my mother in stores. Marion considered putting her on one of those leashes but feared snide comments from parents who had good kids and therefore, didn't need them). Funny, but she had no name of endearment for my dad. He was just Fred. But she loved him and us. My mother was a saint.

"Hello?"

"Hi, Daddy. Stop yelling at Mom. And read the signs next time."

"Hi, Mel. You make one little mistake, and they let you have it. Don't ever get married. They all become nags."

"Do you mean wives or husbands?"

"What?"

"Nags. Who do you mean?"

"Oh. Wives, of course."

"Oh my God, would you listen to yourself? You sound like an old fart, which you are not. So knock it off. You are driving my sainted mother crazy."

"That's garbage."

"Dad, I think you should get a part-time job. Why don't you go work with Ralphie at the store? I'm sure he could use the help and would enjoy having you around." His friend Ralphie owned the local health food store.

"I hate Ralphie! He's a know-it-all and makes eyes at your mother all the time. And all he sells in that stupid store is hippie food. Pure garbage."

My mother yelled, "Oh, for God's sake, Fred. That's ridiculous."

"Sorry I mentioned it. And is that your word of the day?" I asked.

"What word?"

"Garbage. You've used it twice in two minutes."

"All of a sudden you're some college big shot making fun of me?"

"No Daddy. Just an observation, relax. Seriously, I think you need to get out of the house for a few hours a week. It would be good for you— and Mom."

"I got a great idea. Let me take over your job while you're at college. That would be right up my alley."

One thing I never did was to employ family members. It never worked out and you couldn't fire them if they turned out to be a disaster. I would certainly call in favors to get interviews with business contacts if a relative was looking for a job, but I made a policy of no nepotism.

"Ah, no thanks. I've got it covered. I appreciate the offer."

I owe my life to my parents, and not for the obvious reasons that children owe their lives to their parents.

Parked beside the floor-to-ceiling windows in the sleek, modern art building, I looked out over the quad that was bereft of any sign of life, be it human, flora, or fauna. January was such a lonely month. I hated its arrival and it was never welcome. It stretched before the calendar like an endless drone, dark and desolate. I did, however, find great beauty at dusk in January, taking in its quiet peace from the warmth of a cozy chair, inside a heated room. The winter sky usually compensated for the monotone color of the frozen grass and bare, skeleton-like trees, and was often ablaze with gold and orange streaks.

I notice life. And death. I do, because I almost lost my life. And my parents saved me. And that is why I am here, at this moment, resuming a life I left almost twenty years ago. Maybe it wasn't just the challenge unwittingly put forth to me by the obsequious Phillip Gunderson. Perhaps it was all a grand master plan that I would return to the one failure in my life, to right the wrongs, to settle unfinished business. The guilt I harbored from the past never left me. I compartmentalized it where it sat, locked in a box in a dark corner of my mind.

It may have been the time of day or this time of year that I realized I was cloistered inside this warm shelter to protect myself from the harsh elements. Or it could have been the fact that I was left here alone with my thoughts and memories to remind me. I guess that was why I came back here. You can only hibernate for so long until someone or something decides to wake you.

It was fall of my senior year, and I was flying high. I had managed to get the perfect schedule, with no class before ten in the morning and no classes on Friday. I could participate in guilt-free, party night Thursday, or, if I chose, head home early for the weekend after sleeping until noon on a Friday.

I was finally living off campus, no longer under the scrutiny of a resident assistant or the usual on-campus restrictions. My parents weren't thrilled with my decision and insisted on inspecting my living quarters before we signed the lease. As long as it was in a safe area and within walking distance to campus, they were fine with it. I was also looking forward to cooking the majority of my own meals, because the food in the dining hall was barely edible on a good day.

I was living in a two-bedroom apartment with three friends, sharing a bedroom with a girl named Nicki. Nicki, with an i. We had become friendly the year before, sharing a love for punk rock music and Mexican food. I was outspoken, she was quiet. We were both night owls and crammed for exams. I had parents I adored; she had a mom she despised and an absent father. We were basically the same size and often shared clothes. Nicki told me one day I would rule the world, and who wouldn't adore someone who said such great things to you? Besides, she had a couch and a kitchen table and chairs that actually matched, and I had two large dressers for our bedroom. All the stars aligned for us to be a good match to cohabitate, and we spent the summer before school started talking about how cool it would be to live together in this fabulous apartment in Philadelphia.

The first few weeks of school went fast. Now that we were seniors, we knew the drill, and things fell into place easily. It was a blistering day in August when Nicki and I moved in, and we should have staggered our arrivals because there were the four of us, three sets of parents (including Nicki's single mom), four boyfriends, and a couple of stray siblings.

Yes, I did have a boyfriend at the time. His name was Max, and we met at a frat party in April of my sophomore year. It was his mouth that drew me to him—not what came out of it, but how it looked. It was pouty, and I thought he was the best-looking guy I had ever met. The fact that he was just as attracted to me sealed the deal, and we became exclusive after a week of seeing each other. What he lacked in brains (I still wonder how he ever got in to Pennwood) he made up for in the bedroom, and in how he treated me. He was kind and generous, or so I thought. He would come and get me at night if I had a late class or meeting, I never had to pay for anything, and he liked my friends. A wrestler in high school, he was pretty jacked in the muscle department. His one physical flaw was that he had thin, blond hair and was probably bald now at forty. Also, he often used words in the wrong context, which drove me crazy. Overall, he was about an eight out of ten, and at the time, that was good enough for me. At least I wasn't some loser who was alone.

Yes, this is how I thought back then. This was the person I was a thousand years ago in another lifetime, and these are the people I spent the most time with. We went to classes, hung out in our apartment, went to parties, stayed up all night—typical college students. We were a close-knit group of friends and we got along well.

Until that cold day in October. The day that changed everything. The day it all went black.

CHAPTER THIRTEEN

"Please, Teresa. Give me some good news for a change."

I was sitting at the desk in my office, back in New York City. It was great to be home for the weekend. It felt as if I had slipped into a pair of my most comfortable shoes. All that surrounded me was familiar, logical, and I was completely in charge. This place fit me like a glass slipper. And when shoes are your bread and butter you tend to make quite a few footwear metaphors and puns.

Teresa rushed over, throwing her arms around me. Despite the casual, weekend environment, she always managed to present herself in full makeup, no matter what. Alyce was on her way, and I was happy to have a few moments alone with my assistant.

"Everything's good. Reports are on your computer, ready to review. Funny, I never thought this place could survive without you here, but I was dead wrong. I'm finding out how valuable I really am, so get ready because I will be asking for a huge raise this year. I hope you appreciate all I'm doing," Teresa said.

Pressing my lips together, I reached into my drawer and pulled out a one hundred dollar gift card and tossed it to her. "Here you go. You and your daughter can go online and order some shoes for Valentine's Day. Will that appease you?" The woman was so easily bought it was ridiculous—and shameful.

"Thanks, boss," she said, stuffing the card into her pants pocket.

"Let's wait for Alyce to get here before we go over the numbers so I don't have to repeat things twice," I said.

"Okay. How's school? Playing nice with the other kids are we?"

"Save the sarcasm. As a matter of fact, I have been hanging out with a sweet, younger graduate student named Aiden. And I have made another friend. Her name is Heidi, and we have lunch together on a regular basis. She's a few years older than I am, and she is very cool. And the faculty worship me. Oh, and I have a bunch of young female friends who think I'm the greatest, too." I loved to mess with both my mother and with my assistant. It was a hoot.

Teresa squinted her eyes, "Have you been handing out tons of gift cards at that college?"

"I don't need to buy friendship, Mrs. Jenks. I'm a magnet. People are naturally drawn to me."

"Yeah, okay."

Teresa had an audacious sense of humor—one of the many unique aspects of her personality—and she lived for any opportunity to put me in my place. I admit, over the years I had developed a bit of an ego, exactly like and equal to my male counterparts in business. It was an asset to think highly of oneself, a necessary evil and side effect of financial success and power. My assistant was also enjoying a certain level of control and power in my absence. I hoped she would be able to come back to reality when I eventually returned to MD Shoes after my graduation in June.

Teresa stopped at a coffee shop on her way in, bringing dark roast coffee and doughnut holes—my personal favorites. Alyce arrived, looking glamorous as usual, sporting a designer handbag and a full-length fur coat. I could never pull-off wearing fur because I would be crucified in the press by the animal rights groups. It wasn't an issue for me anyway. I loved animals and had no desire to drape myself in them. I enjoyed spending my wealth on houses, restaurants, vacations, and clothes. I couldn't imagine choosing to parade around like that for such an inhumane reason.

Alyce pulled the carcass off her frame and unappreciatively threw it on my sofa. I stood to give her a hug, and then the three of us attacked the doughnuts like a pack of hungry wolves. Stirring cream into my large coffee, the three of us settled around my massive, mahogany desk. I loved how well the three of us worked together. We were a great team.

"So, ladies," I said, scrolling through the reports on my computer, "everything appears status quo. Anything important, or unimportant, I should be made aware of?"

"Only that the new line of sketches are due soon. Have you gotten a chance to take a peek at them?" Alyce asked, sipping her latte.

Teresa stared at Alyce. It was the Teresa death stare. What was that about?

I had long since handed over the majority of the responsibility for the design of my shoes to other talented folks in my company. Once in a while I would have a brilliant idea for an amazing new pump. I would call my lead designer and department manager, Felix, and show him my rough sketch and let him finish or often, improve on my vision. Now that I was in college as a full-time student, I didn't have time for much of anything, let alone designing a new line of shoes for the fall preview.

"It's on my to do list this weekend. I will email you and the team with my final recommendations by start of business on Monday. Anything else?" I asked, biting into a chocolate glazed hole of heaven.

"We need to hire the new interns soon. We have doubled the amount of applications this year, thanks to the ink you got from *Wealth and Success,*" Teresa said, apparently cooled off from the shade she had just thrown Alyce's way.

Thank you, Phillip Gunderson.

"Alyce, can you and Debbie handle that for me? You know what we are looking for: sharp, creative, hungry. Any men in the pool?" It made such a difference to have a male perspective on our staff. It kept things interesting.

"A few," Teresa confirmed.

I nodded in approval. "Any other pressing matters on the agenda, ladies?"

"No," Alyce said. "You picked the perfect time to take a sabbatical. It's been drama-free, and calm. Even Ed has been behaving himself and hasn't pissed of too many of the staff. But then again, employees love when the boss is out of the office. It puts the staff in a good mood," she grinned, clasping her hands behind her head.

There was that death stare again from Teresa.

"Well, remind them that it's temporary and that the boss will be back before long. Make sure everyone pulls their weight, Alyce. No running amok through the office. Understood?"

"Got it. How's campus life? Met any cute, young things?" she asked.

"For your voyeuristic information, I have. His name is Aiden, and he's twenty-four. We are friends. I had to set him straight on our relationship. I think he harbored a few cougar fantasies about me, but I can't go there. If the dean ever got wind of any improper behavior on my part, my reputation would be destroyed. The risk is not worth it."

"You sure?" Teresa asked, shoving an entire doughnut hole in her mouth. "Might be worth it. You are getting up there. This may be your only shot."

I flipped Teresa the bird. Alyce nearly spit out her coffee.

"Teresa, as much as I would like to spend my weekend sharing caustic barbs with you, I need to get work done here. Why don't you both finish then get the hell out of here. Go enjoy your weekends."

"Sounds like a plan. I'm meeting my sister for lunch. Then, I want to shop until I drop," Teresa said.

Stretching, Alyce stood. "Well, have fun. I'm off for a mani-pedi. Can't believe I've let it go so long. Mel, keep in touch. And reconsider that young guy. I would love having someone interested in me like that. You only live once."

"Yes—living dangerously. Not my style, but I appreciate the suggestion. Thanks for holding down the fort." I smiled.

"You're welcome. Talk to you soon. Teresa, I'll see you Monday. And thanks for the coffee and calories," Alyce said, balancing her latte, purse and dead animal outerwear.

Teresa mock saluted her. "You got it. Mel, I'm out, too. Call me next week?"

"Sure thing. Enjoy." I watched as both women headed toward the elevators. I was lucky. I had employees—no they were friends—I could depend on.

After they left, I went to reheat what was left of my coffee in the microwave in my office. I grabbed two more doughnut holes and sat back at my desk to work. I was keeping pace with the deluge of daily emails pretty well, but I also had a ton of phone messages on my voicemail. I went through them as I ate. Halfway done, I listened to one call from a special friend.

Melinda, it's Steven. I hope you are doing well and enjoying college. I realize it's strange, but I thought of you today. I was reading the newspaper and saw a political cartoon I knew would make you howl with laughter. I was hoping to share it with you. Oh, well. Wanted to let you know I've been thinking about you and to say hello. Maybe we could have lunch or dinner sometime and catch up. Be well, Mel. Bye.

Closing my eyes, I sighed remembering so many great experiences with my former lover and friend. Our romantic relationship had ended rather abruptly but amicably. I harbored no ill feelings toward this man, even though he had sought the affections of another woman while dating me. Men were often strange, mercurial creatures whose appetites for more or bigger or better often got the best of them. I understood the male mentality, perhaps because my brain functioned like a man and I knew how to walk in their shoes.

Shoe puns were endless.

I contemplated calling Steven back but then became distracted by the weekend cleaning crew who were vacuuming the carpet in the hallway. I stood to close my door and saw that Alyce had left the door to her office ajar. Executives in the building were required to keep their offices locked after hours, and since Alyce served as president, I needed to secure it immediately. Maybe she thought she pulled the door shut when she left, and the lock didn't catch properly. It didn't concern me; she had a lot on her plate with me gone and was in a rush to get to her nail appointment.

She had left a small lamp lit on her desk, so I walked over to shut it off. Leaning in, I noticed an envelope sticking out from under her blotter. The return address read SHOE MIZER. Shoe Mizer was one of our biggest competitors. Based in London, they were a second-rate manufacturer of shoes who used inferior materials, often producing poor imitations of some of our top selling styles. The hair on my neck stood up. The donut holes and coffee churned in my stomach.

What the hell was this about? Why would the president of my company have an envelope on her desk from a company we had zero dealings with?

Grabbing it, I rushed back to my office and locked the door. I sat and opened the perfectly slit envelope. It contained a pay stub for a direct deposit transaction, made out to "Alyce Cumberland" in the amount of $500,000. My eyes glazed over as a million questions raced through my head. Why would Alyce have a payment from Shoe Mizer on her desk?

What was it for? What was she trying to hide? Was she trying to hide something?

Oh, God.

Had Alyce Cumberland, President of MD Shoes, betrayed me?

No, please not Alyce.

Next to Teresa, Alyce was the person I trusted most at this company. *My* company! What was going on? I slammed my fist on the desk, clenching my jaw. I was livid. My head started spinning with questions: how, what, when, but above all—why? I paid her a more-than-generous salary. She received a huge bonus each year. She had a healthy spending account and company credit card.

I collapsed in my chair, gutted, stunned. It felt like I had been electrocuted, and the current was slowly coursing through my entire body. So many questions were swimming around in my brain and emotions stomping my heart, smacking me in my trusting face. I walked over to get a bottle of water from my credenza, honestly fearing I was about to faint....

An hour later I woke up in the emergency room at the hospital. Apparently, a man from the weekend cleaning crew found me shortly after I passed out and called an ambulance. I must have hit my head on something as I fell to the floor, because I was unconscious and he told the paramedics there was a small amount of blood on the carpet. When I came to, Teresa was sitting in a chair next to the gurney I was laying on, in a darkened cubicle, a curtain pulled closed around the space to provide me with privacy to recover.

I turned my head toward Teresa and slowly opened my eyes.

"Mel—Jesus, what the hell? What happened? You were absolutely fine when we left. Oh my God, you aren't pregnant—are you?" She asked, hovering over me.

"No, Teresa. I am definitely not pregnant."

My head was pounding, and I felt nauseous. A nurse came in and pulled the curtain open making a scraping noise that intensified my excruciating headache. Teresa stepped aside as the nurse wrapped a blood pressure cuff on my arm.

"Hi, Ms. Drake. I'm going to check a couple of vitals. The doctor will be here in a minute to speak with you. How are you feeling?"

I struggled to turn my head. "Like I was hit by a midtown bus. Can I get out of here, please?" I asked. I hated hospitals and wasn't too fond of doctors, either. I wanted to go home.

"As soon as the doctor releases you," she said, unfastening the cuff from my arm. The nurse jotted the numbers on my chart and walked away.

Teresa leaned in, her eyes scrutinizing my face. "You look like crap."

"I feel like crap."

A stocky, young doctor stepped inside the curtain. "Ms. Drake? Hello, I'm Dr. Ford. Do you remember what happened to you earlier? You fainted and were brought in unconscious."

"Unfortunately, I remember why I fainted, but the actual act of passing out escapes me."

He smiled. "That's usually how this goes. Bottom line is that you probably sustained a mild concussion, and incurred a small laceration on the back of your scalp. We cleaned it and put some cream on it to prevent infection. No stitches were necessary. I would like to do an MRI to ensure there is no bleeding on your brain from the injury. If the report comes back with no issues, I will send you home with instructions to take it easy over the next few days. Take acetaminophen for the headaches and nothing strenuous for about a week. If you begin to vomit when you get home, I want you to return to the hospital immediately." He took out a small penlight and examined my pupils and tested my reflexes. "Any questions?"

"Nope, got it. Thank you, Doctor."

Nodding, he excused himself, and the nurse informed me it would take about fifteen minutes for someone to come and take me to x-ray.

"You scared the ever-livin' bejesus out of me. I was on the subway, going to meet my sister when my cell rang. The security desk called me, and I ran here as fast as I could. I couldn't believe my ears. Why, in God's name, did you faint? You are the healthiest person I know. I think this college BS has you under too much stress. Running a corporation, going to school full-time—it's more than you can handle."

I struggled to sit up. "I'm fine." My entire world had just been flipped on its head by the possible betrayal of Alyce. Because of this, I would question all those around me. Was Teresa involved too? Oh, God—the idea turned my stomach into knots. Until I had the chance to sort this out in my bruised brain, I decided to keep silent about what I had discovered. I wasn't sure if I could trust anyone at this point. I was devastated.

"Do you want me to come stay with you tonight? I can, if you need me. You shouldn't be alone," Teresa asked.

"No, I'll call my parents. I need my mommy," I joked, leaning over to pull out my phone. Luckily, I had stuck it in the pocket of my Pennwood University hoodie. I typed a quick text but didn't send it.

"There. You can go home," I tell her. "I can't stand anyone fussing over me. I'll call you later when I get home."

"Are you sure? I can wait until your parents get here."

"I'm sure. Go."

"I want a phone call the minute you get home—promise?"

"Pinky swear. And thank you for rushing over here. I appreciate it." Fighting back tears, I felt horrible, like I had lost my best friend. The uncertainty of who I could trust and the fog that invaded my brain was overwhelming. I couldn't think straight.

"All right. Please take better care of yourself—okay? This scared me," she said, squeezing my hand.

"I will. Please don't worry. I'll be fine. GO!" I laughed. "They will be taking me for an x-ray, and you can't come with me anyway."

Teresa slipped her coat on and collected her purse. "Talk to you later. Right?"

I gave a thumbs-up, and she finally left. I was alone, in every way possible. Who could stay with me? My parents would be frantic for the simple reason I was in the hospital, so I made the mature decision not to tell them what happened. They would call my siblings and all of them would appear at the hospital, causing a huge scene. I would have to explain why I fainted, and I needed to process this and think through things with a clear head. But I knew I shouldn't be alone after suffering a concussion, even a mild one. Who could I call? It had to be someone I trusted to keep quiet about this news and help me sort out the mess I was facing. Even with my judgment impaired and my ego badly bruised, I knew there was only one person who could help.

Scrolling through my contacts, I located the number just as the attendant came to take me to have my head examined.

CHAPTER FOURTEEN

He was there, waiting for me as I was wheeled back to my cubicle in the corner of the emergency room. In spite of my murky, vague vision, I could recognize he was still attractive. But I wasn't looking at him in that way, even though we shared so many intimate moments. I needed him for other things. The first thing that hit me when I laid eyes on him was that I was—safe.

"Steven," I said softly. "Thank you. Thank you for coming. I can't tell you how much I appreciate this."

He draped his coat over a chair and walked over and took my hand in his. It was warm and strong, exactly what I needed.

"Don't be silly. You know I would still do anything for you. But I must admit, I am dying of curiosity on several levels. First of all, how did this even happen and better yet—why did this happen?"

My bruised brain flew to the reminder of what I had discovered or may have discovered. I was praying it was all some strange misunderstanding or had a logical explanation, and it caused my head to throb again. I winced as I tried to sit up straight against the pillows to attempt a conversation. The nurse came back in as I was starting to relay the sordid details.

"Ms. Drake, the doctor is reviewing your test results. As soon as he's done he will be in to speak with you. If he gives the okay, you should be discharged within the hour. Any questions?"

"No, thank you. I would like to get out of here as soon as possible."

She nodded and left.

"Steven, wait until you see this doctor. I look old enough to be his mother," I complained.

His hand gently caressed my face. "I think you hit that beautiful head a little too hard."

"Now that I think of it, would you mind if I closed my eyes for a few minutes while we wait for the doctor? I'm exhausted and I'm going to need some energy before I tell you what happened to me." I was struggling to stay awake; my eyes were heavy, seeking to close and drift off into a world without Alyce Cumberland.

"Go ahead and rest. I'll sit here and scroll through some emails. I'll wake you when he comes in."

I don't think I uttered a thank you before I fell asleep. Three hours later, I was sent home with explicit instructions to rest the remainder of the weekend. The doctor informed me I sustained a concussion, but there was no evidence of bleeding on my brain. He said nothing of the damage that had been done to my heart.

After I had nestled into my plush, warm couch with a couple of blankets and a hot cup of tea (courtesy of my wonderful caregiver) Steven grabbed a beer and a dish of pretzels and sat beside me.

"All right, Melinda. What the hell happened in your office today?"

"Oh Steven—it's so ghastly. You are the only person I trust right now, and I need your help and legal advice," I sighed.

"Legal advice? This must be bad."

"It is. And I'm devastated. Long story short because I have a headache on top of my concussion."

"Stop with the jokes and get to the details, please."

"It is possible that Alyce Cumberland—yes, the woman I made president of my company—has done something to betray me to Shoe Mizer for a price—$500,000 to be exact. Can you believe it? After all I've done for her? I am beyond furious and hurt, and I have no clue what to do. How should I handle this, Steven? I've never been this unsure of myself in my entire life. I feel so…"

"Blindsided? Yeah, I can imagine. What do you think the money was for?"

"The only thing I can think of is that it must have something to do with our new line. What else would Shoe Mizer be interested in? They have been trying for years to buy me out and compete on a level with MD Shoes. But they are a third-rate company with sleazy leadership who would sell their soul to the devil for money. And they may have found a willing disciple in Alyce Cumberland."

"Jesus, who would have thought that Alyce was such a…"

"Go ahead, say it. A heel? If it wasn't so pathetic it would almost be funny."

"You have always prided your staff on their loyalty to you and the company. I wonder what made her do it," he asked.

"Money, obviously. I always thought I paid her enough—believe me Steven, she was well compensated. Guess I got that wrong, huh?" I laughed, but I wasn't laughing. This was so unexpected.

"How did you discover this?" Steven asked.

"I found an envelope from Shoe Mizer containing the direct deposit transaction receipt under her blotter. Since I'm away from the office, I guess she hadn't thought to hide it better or take it home, or maybe she forgot it was there. If it's true, she probably has been meeting with them in person, sending correspondence through her personal, home computer and phone. My leave of absence to go back to school has given her the perfect opportunity to pull this off without having me around every day. No wonder why she gave me so much encouragement to go back to get my degree. She couldn't wait to get rid of me, to stab me in the back." My entire body ached from my head injury and the mental stress of the situation.

"Mel, listen. This could all be a horrible mistake or misunderstanding. You have to begin an investigation immediately. If it's true, do you think she acted alone?"

"I have no idea. I can't trust anyone if I can't trust the president of my company."

"By any chance, did you have a patent on these new designs?"

"No, they had just been drawn up by Felix. They were not finalized because we were waiting to find out the viability of using a new, more environmentally-friendly material."

Steven chewed his bottom lip. "It's possible it may fall under a theft of trade secrets. Let me ask you this: did Alyce ever sign any type of confidentiality or non-disclosure agreement as part of her employment? If so, you could get her on breach of contract for disclosing a trade secret to a competing company."

"Yes. All my senior-level employees are required to sign a non-disclosure and a non-compete agreement. My non-compete prevents them from getting a similar position with any of my competitors for at least a year after leaving. Oh, and Teresa, of course, was required to sign a non-disclosure agreement as my personal, confidential assistant." Then a sinking feeling hit me: oh please, God Not Teresa, too!

"You don't think..." Steven asked.

"No. If Teresa was involved in this I will have to be institutionalized for a nervous breakdown or incarcerated because I will kill her!" I hissed.

"Calm down. This stress will not help your concussion."

"Please Steven, cut to the chase. What recourse do I have besides firing her?"

He frowned. "So here's the deal, Mel. In this country it is against the law to steal secret or confidential information or content without the expressed permission of the owner of said information or content."

I smiled. Feebly, but I smiled.

"Don't get too excited yet. If the trade secret is represented by a product, like your shoe designs, other competitors may be able to discover the secret and use it legally by what is called reverse engineering."

"What the hell is that?" I asked.

"Reverse engineering is the ability to discern how a product is made or created and then duplicate it a tad differently, sometimes even better than the original. Unfortunately, the law doesn't penalize what's known as "fair discovery" which means that Alyce could claim that she came up with the idea for the sketches on her own. Trade secrets don't guarantee exclusivity, so anyone can claim that it was their idea and go ahead and use it."

My eyes blazed with rage. "But Alyce Cumberland is not a shoe designer like I am! She is an overpaid pencil pusher who I've allowed into the inner circle of my corporation—my baby, for God's sake—and she repays me by stealing my ideas, my visions! I won't let her get away with this. I'll sue. I'll ruin her reputation in this industry if it takes all my energy and resources." My head pulsated in pain, like it had separated from the rest of my body. This nightmare left me physically exhausted and mentally depleted.

"Listen, Mel. You've had a traumatic event happen to you. I think you should try to get some real sleep, and we can tackle this again in the morning. We'll figure this out, I promise."

"You're right. I have nothing left in me. I need time to process this rationally, and I can't do it right now. Besides, I'm so tired."

"Things will look better in the morning; they always do. Let's get you into bed. I'm here for the entire night, and I will be checking on you periodically. I've had my share of concussions over the years, playing high school football," he said.

Steven took my arm, slowly walking me into my bedroom, a place he had spent many nights with me, wrapped around me. He pulled back the covers on my bed, flashing a nod of remembrance. I hoped those moments we shared filled his undamaged head. The laughs, the affection—it was all so wonderful while we had it. So many memories came flooding back as I felt his strong arm enfolding my waist, his firm grip comforting, not possessive. He was a good man who had entered my life and fit perfectly, in so many ways. He dropped everything to be at my side when I needed him, and I treasured loyalty from the people in my life. So why hadn't we lasted? Why had Steven sought the affections of a salesgirl with bleached blonde hair and a size 2 frame? Was it because I didn't give enough? Or was it because I wasn't enough—for him?

It was then I realized I must have hit my head pretty hard to let my mind wander off into such negative territory. I came to the concussed conclusion using my badly bruised brain and equally fractured ego and heart that my feelings for this man, my friend, were just that: Steven was my dear, cherished friend. If I didn't feel like I'd been run over by a garbage truck that had backed up and run over me a couple more times for good measure, I may have invited my friend to join me under my soft, cotton sheets and my warm comforter, where he could lay his head on this fine, fine feathery, soft pillow…

CHAPTER FIFTEEN

The smell of bacon roused me. Halfway through the night, I vaguely remembered my guardian angel waking me to take another couple of acetaminophen tablets and to make sure I was still alive. I peered at the clock on my nightstand. Through the dazed slits in my eyes I saw it was around nine, and I gently pushed myself back against the headboard. At first, I was a bit disoriented, forgetting I was home in my New York apartment. The familiar sounds of the city filled my waking mind as I listened to the blaring of horns, the singing of sirens, the buzz of businesses surrounding my privileged, urban life. Although it was another large, American city, Philly sounded and smelled differently, maybe because it was my temporary home and didn't, for me, have the permanence Manhattan possessed.

I pulled myself out of bed, glancing at the pathetic image that stared back from the mirror across the room. Not only did my head pulse with pain but I must have really hurt myself on the descent to the floor in my office because the left side of my body was killing me. Sliding my feet into slippers, I gingerly approached the kitchen.

Steven stood at the stove with a spatula in his hand, flipping pancakes. Dressed in the same clothes as the night before, he was a welcome sight. Turning, he smiled as I shuffled to the table, set for one.

"Good morning. And how are we feeling today?" he asked.

Gently easing into a chair, I sighed. "Terrible. Like I have a bad hangover. And it feels like a few things in my head came loose."

He laughed. "That's a pretty accurate assessment of how a concussion feels. But I can assure you that in a few days you'll be fine."

"I have to get on the phone with legal, security, and human resources today. An investigation has to be launched into what Alyce may have done. But I have a bad feeling this will not end well." I reached for the bottle of pain reliever on the table, carefully swallowing two tablets. "And unfortunately, I don't have a few days. I never finished everything I needed to do at the office, and now I have to deal with this horrible Alyce debacle. I have a ton of homework, and I have a search committee meeting that I have to be at tomorrow afternoon."

"Search for what?"

"New university president. The dean is counting on me being there and I owe him."

"I'm sure he would understand. Send him an email," Steven suggested.

I pointed to my coffee machine. He knew that I drank dark roast, and popped a pod in for me.

"Thank you, but I can't. I'm going to call Buddy to take me back to Philly." Buddy was my driver who had been with me for years. I had taken the train into Penn Station on Friday because it gave me the necessary quiet time to answer emails and do a bit of work.

"I'll drive you back."

"That's not necessary. I appreciate the offer, but you've done enough already."

"Please—let me do this. Besides, I'd love to see your place and make sure you get settled."

He sauntered around my kitchen like he belonged, opening cabinets, placing dishes on shelves, folding dishtowels in perfect unison. I stared at him for a moment before I realized what was happening. My brain was on a delayed reaction due to its injury, but it finally clicked. Steven was trying to atone for cheating on me with the salesgirl by going above and beyond what a former boyfriend needed to do. I was surprised at this behavior because we had discussed the entire, sordid situation and had come to an understanding. I wasn't sure where this was coming from.

Placing a cup of steaming coffee and a plate of pancakes and bacon before me, Steven sat at the table.

"Nothing for you?" I asked as I drizzled maple syrup over the stack.

"I couldn't wait. I ate earlier. Sorry."

"No apology necessary." I looked into his dark eyes, "For anything, Steven."

He leaned back in his chair, looking at the floor.

"As good as I am at reading people, I suck at reading minds. What is going on with you?" I asked.

Leaning forward, he took my hand. "When you called me yesterday and I heard your voice, it reminded me how much we meant to each other and how good we were together. And I screwed everything up. I realized it last night while watching TV, knowing you were sleeping in the next room."

"Did something—besides me having this meltdown about Alyce—happen? Because I thought we had this all worked out. We agreed to move on and maintain our friendship, which, as we also agreed upon, was much stronger than the physical side of our relationship. That's the reason you strayed. You need new, different women, and I get it. It's not a flaw. It's who you are. And as long as I can do what I did yesterday—call you out of the blue—well, that's fine with me. Friends last longer than lovers."

"It got me thinking. I'm fifty-three years old. My daughters are off living their own lives. Maybe I should finally settle down for good with one woman, and the one I always picture is you. You are beautiful and smart, and we have fun together. You will never pester me to have more children, like a younger woman might. We could have a great life, grow old together."

Steven was so sincere it made me consider his proposal for a fleeting moment until the functioning part of my noggin took over. Poor Steven. He was having a reverse mid-life crisis. A domestic existence for him might last for a year or two at most, but then he would become bored as hell. He needed the chase; one woman for the rest of his life was simply not in his overly male DNA.

I took a bite of the bacon that was swimming in a sea of syrup. After swallowing, I looked into his pleading eyes.

"While I am flattered beyond belief that you would choose me to spend your happily ever after with, I'm certain that before long your wandering eye would settle on another woman in line at the grocery store or a casino manager in Atlantic City or the new associate in your office. And as much as I love my life—the life Alyce Cumberland is trying to steal from me—I think if, and I mean IF, I ever decide to marry someone, he will have to knock my socks off and be my match in every way. I care about you, Steven. But I am not desperately in love with you. It would have to be the kind of love my parents have for each other, where the person pulls my strings for all the best and worst of reasons. One who challenges my patience yet is my reason for living; the one person in the world who gets me but hasn't quite figured me out. That is what I want, and unfortunately, I don't feel it with you. I'm sorry."

He closed his eyes and sighed. I actually think he was relieved, realizing that once the words came out of his mouth they didn't taste so good. Steven was happy I turned him down.

"Out of all the women I've ever known, you have understood me best. You accept me for who and what I am. Maybe that's why I love you, Mel. And I do love you."

"I know you do. And I love you, too. But not in that forever kind of way," I said, spooning a forkful of pancakes into my mouth. I realized I was starving and remembered I hadn't eaten since early the day before.

"As I get older, I'm starting to fear that I'll be alone in my old age. I would only say this to you, but it scares the living daylights out of me."

I swallowed, placing my fork on the table. "First of all, you will never be alone. You have your daughters and future grandchildren and your siblings. You have a ton of friends, like moi, who will never abandon you. And if someday you end up in a nursing home, you will charm the life out of all the ladies there and have plenty of company. You have nothing to worry about."

Steven rose from the table and walked over to me. He pulled me into an embrace.

"Had I been a better man, I could have convinced you. I envy the guy who will finally win your heart. He's one lucky bastard."

Pulling away, I sat back in my chair to finish the generous plate of pancakes and bacon sitting before me.

"Ah, yes—Prince Charming. For your information, the elusive glass slipper is probably not in the plan of my life. And if it was, Alyce Cumberland would probably try to steal that one, too."

Steven insisted on driving me back to Philadelphia, and I was too tired and bruised to argue with him. A light snow was falling as we drove along the Pennsylvania Turnpike, and the landscape appeared gray and frozen. A pretty sunset was unfolding before us, and the sky was streaked with an amber glow. The empty tree branches appeared emaciated, lining both sides of the highway. Living in the Northeast, I appreciated the seasons and the moods they ignited in me. Winter was quiet and reflective, a time for work and planning for the future. Spring was hopeful and a time for renewal in all things, both business and pleasure. Summer was childhood and a time of rest, filled with family and friends. Fall was always the beginning of the year, crisp and cool with a renewed desire to get back to work.

As we drove, Steven reached over and took my hand, bringing me back into focus.

"Have you decided what you are going to do about her?" he asked, turning for a brief moment to glance at me.

"You mean Benedict Cumberland? I still can't believe it. I am going to have major trust issues with people after this," I said, shaking my head.

My aching head.

"Everything as of now is conjecture. You will need concrete proof that she actually did something wrong. Your instincts aren't enough here. God only knows what else she has been doing behind your back. I would recommend you also hire a discreet private investigator to check it out. I have a great contact. When we get to your place I'll write down his name and phone number for you."

"Thank you. Last night I spoke with my team and a plan has been put in place to investigate Alyce while monitoring her every move. I guess I'm going to have to inform Teresa about what has been going on. You don't think she knew any of this—do you?" I prayed Steven would tell me what I wanted to hear.

"I can't imagine Teresa would be involved in this. The woman thinks you walk on water. As a matter of fact, she may kill Alyce with her bare hands when she discovers what she did to you. Be prepared for bloodshed."

"I hope you're right."

Teresa had called my apartment several times over the weekend, telling Steven he needed to put me on the phone so I could tell her I was all right and not dead. She offered to come over and take care of me, but

I assured her Steven was being the perfect nurse (and a less neurotic choice than my parents). I told her I would check in with her on Monday.

Steven offered to provide additional legal advice if my latest line of shoes had been compromised. Provided the investigation revealed Alyce Cumberland had stolen or sold anything related to MD Shoes, she would be terminated immediately with legal action to follow. It was a huge, complicated mess I never anticipated would happen. My focus had been getting this damned degree, and as I gazed out the side window of Steven's car, I wondered: did I make an error in judgment going back to college? Had I abandoned my life's work to chase an elusive piece of paper that only meant something to me? Have I put my company and my employees at risk because I made a decision to leave them and traipse off to Philadelphia to play coed again?

Had I made the biggest mistake of my life?

CHAPTER SIXTEEN

Monday morning I managed to pull myself out of my self-imposed pity party and get myself to class. I had spent Sunday night ensconced in my Philly apartment on the phone with my legal team, human resources, and security personnel discussing how we would handle the situation with Judas Cumberland. Her phone calls would be monitored, along with her email and computer access. Cameras would record her every move, and surveillance devices would be installed in her private office. The minute we had concrete proof of her betrayal to the company, she would be immediately terminated and possible legal action would be initiated against her. Meanwhile, my team would be compiling a dossier of information. Her phone records had already been pulled. The investigation had begun.

I texted Teresa and asked her if she could work it out with her family so she could meet me here in Philly on Friday. I told her I would send Buddy to pick her up and drive her to me. Loving any excuse to be treated like a queen to escape the duties of her home life, and to be with me would be fine with Teresa. I needed to observe her reaction, in person, when I told her about Alyce the backstabber, to gauge whether or not she had betrayed me, too. It was imperative I spoke with my assistant and assembled all the facts and a timeline.

I muddled through my three classes, forgoing lunch with Heidi because I still suffered from a bad headache. Keeping in mind the search committee meeting was scheduled at four that afternoon was already taxing the small amount of energy I had left, so when I finished that day I decided to go back home and take a short nap. My mother—the clairvoyant—called to ask if everything was all right. I lied to her, even though it was a lie of omission. But she was my mom, and I knew she didn't believe me. Thankfully, she decided to let it go.

Arriving at Dean Samuels' office, I ran into Aiden who, as usual, was rushing to be on time. I scolded him constantly that he would need to clean up his act in the tardy department when he went out into the real world to work. He smiled and nodded his youthful head, uttering back in response, "Yes, Mother."

"Where have you been? I called you a couple of times this weekend, but you never answered your cell. Everything okay?" He asked, as we walked to the meeting.

"Yeah, everything's great." I lied again. I liked Aiden, but I hadn't known him long enough nor chose to trust him with the details of my horrendous weekend. And since Aiden was basically a kid, he was oblivious to anything outside his immediate orbit, not noticing that I was visibly off my usual, jovial persona.

Jack Sweeney, however, squinted at me quizzically after I sat in the seat across from him at the long conference table. I was totally shocked when he scanned my face and mouthed, "Are you all right?"

This man had not acknowledged my existence until this point, so I was dumbfounded that Mr. Frosty was astute enough to deduce something was different about me, that I wasn't my usual self. I nodded, whispering, "Had better days, but thanks."

He let a half-smile pass his lips before he slipped back into Jack Sweeney, jackass.

All of the committee members were there, except for Gavin. The dean informed us that he was out of the country on business, but had forwarded his recommendations for us to consider. As we combed through curriculum vitae and dialogued, the committee selected a final list of five candidates to interview. They hailed from all over the United States, three from large universities, one from a small liberal arts college, and one from a mid-size community college out west. Satisfied with our choices, Dean Samuels convened the meeting after an hour, thanking us for our time.

After checking his watch several times, Jack headed out, saying goodbye to the dean. He grabbed his messenger bag and overcoat and rushed out. Surprised he had shown a tiny semblance of emotion toward me earlier in the meeting, I actually didn't hate Jack Sweeney as much today. But I still had a headache from my concussion. I was hungry, and

I needed to rest. Aiden asked if I wanted to grab something to eat, but I declined his invitation. I wanted to go home, pull on my flannel pajamas, order a pizza, and call my mom and dad. I needed the comforts of home tonight. It had been a grueling weekend, and I promised myself that tomorrow I would feel much better and be able to resume some sense of control and normalcy. I had to mentally prepare for my interrogation of Teresa later in the week, and I silently prayed that my loyal assistant would never have betrayed me like the lecherous Alyce Cumberland.

As I waited for my sausage, pepper, and onion pizza to arrive, I relaxed in my big, brown oversized chair with a can of soda. I didn't have any alcohol the entire weekend because I was still taking the pain pills. The solace I sought was in a large circle of sauce and cheese and at the end of the telephone line.

"Hello?" My mother answered. Marion always answered the phone, unless she was in the bathroom or not home. My dad hated to talk on "that dopey thing" unless it was one of his kids, proclaiming that he had nothing to say to anyone else but his offspring.

"Hi, Mommy." I sighed.

"Melly? Are you all right? I don't like how you sound."

"Oh, Mom, I am so happy to hear your voice. I had a terrible weekend. Sit so I can fill you in."

"WHAT?" She asked. I could picture her at home, in our raised ranch circa 1962, standing in the kitchen hand to her throat, mouth open wide.

"Put Daddy on the extension so I won't have to repeat everything twice, please."

"Fred! Pick up the phone. Melinda is calling us, and something happened!"

"Mom, relax. I'm fine."

"Are you sure? We don't have a whole lotta luck with you and phone calls like this, Dolly. And with you back at that university…Surely, you can understand my fear again."

My dad picked up the extension in their upstairs bedroom.

"Melly? What's wrong? Are you okay?" He asked.

"Daddy, I'm fine. I just wanted to talk to my parents," I said, rethinking that maybe I should keep this whole, sordid story to myself. I still didn't have all the facts, and I decided I should probably keep the Cumberland fiasco confidential.

"Thank God, you scared us," my mother said.

"That's right. I don't ever want a phone call like the one we got that day, in this life or the next, thank you," he added.

"That day" was code for my car accident. It was the worst day of my life, but it must have been more terrifying for my parents, whose lives had been turned inside out when a Pennsylvania State Trooper had to call, informing them their daughter was in a car crash, hospitalized in critical condition.

It had been the second week of October in 1998, and the students at Pennwood had become entrenched in their routines and classes. The campus was ablaze with colorful leaves, and there was a crisp chill in the air. I was excited to break out my sweaters and boots and transition my look from summer to fall. I brainstormed some great ideas for a presentation in one of my 300-level business courses, determined to achieve a 4.0 GPA for the semester. It was my senior year. I loved where I was living, off campus in a cute apartment with my friends. My boyfriend Max had also moved off campus, deciding to live in a gross slum house with his moronic fraternity brothers, most of whom I couldn't stand. But Max was gorgeous, and he was crazy about me.

My mother had called earlier in the week to see if I could come home for the long Columbus Day weekend because it was my godmother's birthday and my uncle was having a big surprise party for her. At first I said no because I had a paper and this presentation to work on, but Marion laid a huge guilt trip on me and, being Catholic, I caved. Agreeing to leave on Saturday morning, I told her I could be home by two at the latest.

My roommate Nicki and I decided to go out on Friday night to a bar and meet some of our design-major friends. Nicki was single and in the market to hook-up with some random dude. My one stipulation was that if she did, she had to go back to his room because I had to be up fairly early the next morning. Unfortunately for her, the bar was hosting a ladies night, and the majority of the clientele that evening was female. After two hours of drinking beer, doing shots, and dancing with desperate women, I announced I was bored and was going home to bed. I said good-bye to Nicki, informing her that I would see her on Sunday night. Giving me a sloppy kiss and a hug, she pumped her fists, returning to the dance floor.

When I got back to my apartment, I tried calling Max but he never answered. He told me at lunch that he was probably going out for a couple of beers with his brothers that night, and he would call me later. I had a fierce buzz on as I dizzily crashed on my bed, falling into a deep sleep.

If my phone rang, I never heard it. Max had been acting weird since we got back to school for our final year at Pennwood. I blamed his current fraternity crowd and the fact he was a senior and was stressed out over having to go out and get a job after graduation and act like a responsible adult. At one point in our relationship, we couldn't keep our hands off one another, needing to fool around every day, sometimes twice a day if our schedules permitted. So when he started blowing me off for his buddies, I assumed it was some kind of phase that would pass.

The following morning, I awoke to see an empty bed where my roomie slept. I deduced that Nicki had indeed gotten lucky last night. After a quick shower, I threw a few clothes in a duffle bag along with my makeup and backpack filled with homework, calling my mother to inform her I would be leaving after I stopped by to say good-bye to Max. I thought he might appreciate the fact that I checked in with him before I left. Also, I was planning on an early morning liason I was positive he would appreciate.

The morning air was cold so I cranked up the heat in my car. It would be nice to crawl into a warm bed with my boyfriend. I figured it would get Max and me back on track and make things better between us.

It was around nine when I pulled behind his frat house. There were a few cars, including Max's. Since it was a three-day weekend, a lot of kids were going home for the first time in the semester to grab their winter clothes, visit their high school friends, and get a much needed home-cooked meal.

Walking in the back door (which was never locked) the house was relatively tidy for a Saturday morning. Most Thursdays were party nights here, so someone must have gotten rid of the garbage and empty beer cans, making this dump of an abode actually presentable. As I headed through the kitchen and up the back staircase, I thought I heard the sound of someone moaning as I walked the long hallway. It was one of those gigantic, Victorian homes with plenty of small bedrooms but not enough bathrooms to accommodate all of its residents. I thought the moaning was coming from the only bathroom on the second floor, next to Max's room. Obviously, one of his fraternity brother's or their date had partied a little too hard the night before and was paying homage to the porcelain gods.

As I arrived at Max's door, I realized that the moaning wasn't coming from the bathroom after all but from inside his room. Ready to scold him for a night of drinking, I smiled as I gingerly turned the doorknob and entered the darkened room. But what I saw when I stepped in, knocked the wind from my lungs and caused me to stop dead in my tracks. There, in his bed, with my boyfriend, the guy I had been with for two years—was my roommate Nicki. Max was the one moaning in ecstasy, not in a drunken hangover. And the thing was, they didn't even see me at first they were both so into each other. It wasn't until I moaned myself, that Max turned to see me standing there, watching them. And here's the kicker: instead of jumping up, and throwing that backstabbing harlot off of him, he smiled, holding out his hand, motioning me to join them. Back then, I, Melinda Drake, was a lot of things, but a fool and kinky I was not. And that two-timing, boyfriend-stealing piece of trash Nicki, who was always jealous of me, had one-upped me with the thing she knew meant the most to me.

Gloating triumphantly, she leaned over to kiss my boyfriend. "Let her go, Max. We don't need her. You only need me. She can't satisfy you like I can, and you know it."

Her statement was meant to let me assume that this was not the first time they had been together, and I would eventually discover that they had been fooling around behind my back shortly after we had started back at school in September. I was angry, hurt, and confused. I needed to scrub my eyeballs clean from what I was witnessing and get the hell out of there. And yet, I wasn't going to walk away without some small semblance of revenge. Grabbing a jar of crimson dye that he had on his desk because he was using it for one of his design projects, I marched over to the bed and quickly poured the thick slime over Nicki's head first and then his, relishing the fact it would stain their miserable cheating scalps for about two weeks. It was my version of marking them with The Scarlet Letter, and they would spend the next month having to explain their red hair to friends, family, and faculty. It would remind them that *this* redhead would never endure their deceit.

Throwing the jar on the floor, I ran out of there, needing to escape. Anger and shock were quickly replaced by pain and panic. Betrayal was not something I had ever experienced, and I could not get the image of the two of them, engaged in such an intimate act, out of my head. It was the worst thing someone could do to another person, short of murder.

I jumped in my car and started the engine. Slumping over the steering wheel, I sobbed uncontrollably, my eyes burning with hatred. If anyone had seen or heard me, they would have told me I was in no condition to drive. But there was no one to stop me—not Max, not Nicki, not my parents. Wanting to get the hell away from there, I put the car in drive and fled. My eyes were fuzzy from crying, my brain was clouded with the thoughts of them—together in his bed. Each time I tried to push them out of my head, they seeped back in. I made a sharp left turn on to the highway ramp, headed to my safe place, away from this nightmare.

But the real nightmare was about to entangle me on a highway outside of Philadelphia. What I couldn't predict was that it would change the course and direction of my life for years to come.

CHAPTER SEVENTEEN

I consumed three slices of doughy pizza, two cans of diet root beer, and a small garden salad. Climbing into bed early, I snuggled under my new Egyptian cotton sheets with a trashy novel. First, I grabbed my laptop to check on some things in the works at MD Shoes. I missed being there every day, although I had finally settled in to a comfortable routine at school. Meeting Heidi a few times a week for lunch or coffee was my sanity, and the Baes, these crazy new friends I had made, kept inviting me to their parties. Instead, I would meet them once a week in the student center, where they would catch me up on the stories of their boyfriend/hookups/friends drama. Hearing their complaints and issues took my mind off my own stress, and I couldn't have loved them more. They truly were my Baes (translation: my significant others).

Later that week, our fierce female posse sat around the lunch table in the student center.

"Hey Melinda?"

"What is it, Courtney?"

"I have to do a résumé. Will you help me?"

"Of course I will. And I'll do you a solid, Miss Courtney," I said, as I tapped out an email to my sales director at MD Shoes. Turning to face her, I continued. "If you maintain that stellar GPA of yours, I will seriously consider you for a job in my organization after you graduate." The Baes had transformed my vocabulary into an edgier, hipper lingo.

This miraculous gaggle of women exchanged a round of fist bumps with Courtney, wondering if fortune would smile upon them as well at the hands of their new fairy godmother: me.

"That goes for the rest of you. I can offer any one here an entry-level position at MD Shoes, provided you have a decent grade point average and the desire to start at the bottom, learn the business, and work your way up. There is a misconception by your generation that you enter the workforce acquiring a higher-level position at an inflated salary. You ladies need to live in the real world. I can give you a chance to make your mark, but you will have to prove yourselves."

"Hundo P! You are so perf, I can't stand it." Courtney said.

Peeking over my glasses, I looked to Lucy for translation.

"A hundred percent, and you are perfect, Melinda. We all think so," Lucy smiled. She still thought Aiden had a crush on me, but I was secretly highlighting Lucy's many assets nonchalantly to Aiden whenever I could. She was terrific, and he needed to see it.

"Omg, this is so adulting—thinking about real jobs after we graduate. Melinda, my dad would freak if I told him I got a job with you, I can't even," Blake said.

"Can you imagine how great it would be? Our squad, living in NYC, taking the Big Apple by storm! But seriously, Mel, I would slay in a job at your company." Courtney proclaimed. "It would be fire to be where all the action happens, starting my career with you as my boss."

Sometimes I simply gave up on trying to comprehend what it was like to live in their world. "Well ladies, my offer stands. Do well academically and I will find a place for you. Some of you may even want to consider going to the new facility in London," I said.

Shrieks and whooping ensued. My Lord, I loved these young women. I loved their youth, enthusiasm, and friendship. They made me feel like a rock star. Even though I had a hard time understanding Generation Z vernacular, they made me feel like a kid again.

"How about this: I will hold a résumé writing workshop for all who are interested. We'll do it at my apartment, and I'll get pizza and wings."

"OMG that would be off the heezy, Melinda. I am dying to see your place," Lucy said.

I think she wanted to see exactly what had Aiden so enamored besides his infatuation with an older woman. "It's a date. Let's say six o'clock, next Wednesday. Does that work for all of you?" I asked.

They all took out their phones, thumbs flying over their screens.

"Okay, guys, I gotta bounce. See you later, Melinda. You're fierce," Katie said, grabbing her latte, looking fabulous with her highlighted hair and form-fitting workout ensemble.

First, the translation: fierce—I was bold, exceptional, groovy, da bomb. Not a bad word to describe me. I liked it. Second, youth was so wasted on the young. I sucked in my gut.

I happened to look over as Katie and a few of the ladies walked away, noticing Jack Sweeney standing in the cashier's line with a large cup of coffee. Here was the kicker about Jack Sweeney: he was usually in a bad mood and kind of a mess with his hair in desperate need of a cut, and yet—I'm not sure what it was about him that made me continually gawk at him or what it was about him that piqued my curiosity. I was beginning to think he was actually attractive, in a weird, nerdy sort of way. His hair hung over his blue eyes and he had an indentation in his chin that fascinated me. He was tall and lean, without being emaciated. I was used to Steven, who was big and burly, which suddenly reminded me that I hadn't been involved with anyone in an awfully long time. Not that I wanted to be with Jack Sweeney. Wait—did I?

No. Definitely no. Not with that constant stick up his rear end.

I returned to writing my email, deciding not to even acknowledge Jack's presence a few feet away. All the Baes had left, so I gathered my stuff and moved to one of the more comfortable chairs along the wall. A few minutes later, a tall figure stood directly in front of me.

"Excuse me, Ms. Drake?" The voice spoke.

Lowering my chin, I peered over my designer eyeglasses. "Yes, Professor?"

"Actually, I prefer doctor to professor, if you must know," he said.

"I don't need to know anything about you, Mr. Sweeney."

At first, I thought the joke went right over his head. But then, a wide smile spread over his face and he nodded. There may be a human being in there after all, I surmised.

"I wanted to ask you, because I left rather abruptly the other day and neglected to record the date of our next search committee meeting in my calendar."

"February 14th, Valentine's Day," I said, "At four. Hope that doesn't affect plans with your wife—or girlfriend." I decided a little fishing couldn't hurt.

Immediately, Jack Sweeney shut down, and the small smile I had gotten from him quickly disappeared from his face. In fact, he looked like he had seen a ghost.

"Ms. Drake," he said softly, "have a nice day." He walked away.

I sat there perplexed, unsure about what I did to offend the Professor, I mean Dr. Sweeney. Whatever it was, it scared him off, retreating into the sea of students clamoring for caffeine in Daniel Webster Hall.

At one o'clock, I finished my work, packed my things and headed home to my apartment. Since I was living so close to campus, I made it a point to walk to and from my classes, except for my evening class, and then I took an Uber. I noticed my jeans became a bit looser from this newfound exercise regime, and I must admit, I liked how I felt and looked. Being back in academia gave me a new perspective. I was developing my mind and body, challenging myself again. Working in my office each day, running my business, caused me to become complacent, flabby, and intellectually starved. I was actually toying with the idea of pursuing my masters in business administration back in New York City after I graduated. Learning was a kick; I felt alive again, and I hadn't felt that way in a long time.

After spending the week in constant contact with my office, my worst fears were confirmed. The internal investigation into Alyce's misconduct uncovered disturbing results. In collecting phone and expense account records, along with Alyce's appointment calendar, email correspondence and computer hard drive, my forensic team in a few days was able to determine that Alyce Cumberland sold our latest shoe designs, set to debut in fall of the following year, to Shoe Mizer. And the worst part was that she was planning to become their new CEO. I hung up the phone after speaking to my HR, legal, and security heads, dazed. There was no time to deal with this on an emotional level—that a trusted officer of my company, and a friend, betrayed me. I needed to act like the person in charge of hundreds of employees who depended on me. I told my team to investigate the appropriate legal action we could pursue, and that I would return to New York by the end of the following week to terminate the employment of Alyce Cumberland. Until then, her every move would be monitored and documented.

Teresa was due at my place at two, so when I arrived home I cranked the heat up a notch and flicked the switch next to the stone hearth, illuminating my gas fireplace. I had made a dinner reservation at a four-star restaurant in Penn's Landing, because I loved treating Teresa to the best places to eat, but if I discovered she had betrayed me too, I would cancel in a heartbeat. I missed my petite cohort, and I had been praying that she would never have been disloyal to me. One of my strengths was the ability to read people, so her demeanor would determine whether she knew about Alyce Cumberland's deception.

Teresa and I would sit in my living room for a couple of hours, and if she proved not to be a lying turncoat I would take her on a tour of the city, followed by an elegant dinner. If not, she would be on a bus headed back to Brooklyn and the unemployment line. I was on the phone with my father when my doorman called to inform me she had arrived. I found that I was actually nervous, which surprised the hell out of me. I think I just didn't want any of this to be true, and the idea that my bestie Teresa would ever go against me was unfathomable.

Hearing the elevator ding in the hallway, I walked toward the front entrance. My heart was beating through my chest. Everything was turned on its head, and I still laid the blame (and praise) at the feet of the exasperating Phillip Gunderson, who started the runaway train that was my life.

A forceful three knocks caused me to open the door, where an over-joyed, exuberant mother of three stood with a bunch of multi-colored carnations and a large box of plantain tarts she knew I constantly craved.

Teresa hugged me. Pushing through the door, she surveyed her surroundings as she entered, her gaze panoramically scanning the perimeter of the room to inspect my college digs. Nodding but not speaking, I knew this woman long enough to see that my apartment had met with her approval and that Aiden Flanagan's cousin did right by me.

"Well? Are you going to comment on my home, or just loiter in it? Nice, right?" I asked, while taking the flowers and tarts from her.

"You were right. It's nice. I like it. Although I think it's time you came home, back to New York. It's not the same without you there in the office, and I'm getting sick and tired of running the whole damn company—if you must know."

Laughing, I asked, "So you are the one head honcho there in my absence, huh? I could have sworn I put Alyce in charge." I didn't expect to start my fishing expedition the minute she walked in. Teresa had barely gotten her coat off and we were already off to the races on work-related items.

My assistant let out some sort of grunt, and had I not been aware about Alyce's backstabbing it would have thrown me a bit. The three of us had always worked so well together, and we genuinely cared for each other. I considered Teresa's attitude strange, knowing what I knew, the story I assumed Teresa didn't know.

"Give me your coat. I made some coffee we can have with those tarts. Jesus, my mouth is watering thinking about them. You still spoil me, Mrs. Jenks," I smiled.

"You knew I would bring them. And don't be shy about putting a shot of something in that coffee. It's frigging freezing outside, and my bones are pleadin' for a little somethin' stronger."

When Teresa was alone with me, she would often let her professional guard down. I loved it because it meant she had a comfort level with me that she shared with no one else. I enjoyed listening to her crazy stories of when she was a kid, living in a house full of people. Her mother was born in Italy and came to America when she was nineteen after she married Teresa's father, an older man in his early thirties who was a hotel manager. Growing up in a family of nine children was sometimes a challenge, but Teresa was a fighter who learned early that if you worked hard you could have whatever you wanted in life. In the real world, at the offices of MD Shoes, Teresa Jenks was competent, efficient, and controlled, sometimes snarky and often spunky. We all live so many lives and are so many different personalities at times. This always fascinated and surprised me.

I was happy to have one of my favorite people here in my second home. Teresa changed into her furry moccasins, coming to help me in the kitchen. After a quick tour of my residence, I was ready for the inquisition. "Let's sit in my great room so we can talk. Grab your coffee and a dish." I placed two tarts on a plate and we fixed our coffee. Mine had cream; hers had a generous shot of Irish cream whiskey. I ordered cookies from a little bakery around the corner, which I plated and placed on my coffee table. This was going to be another one of those high-calorie days, but I might need it. Either this conversation would turn out as just another work discussion between my assistant/friend and I, or it would blow up right in my face. At this point, I wanted it over with. I preferred hearing bad news before the good. I was hopeful, but less optimistic than usual.

We settled into my lovely, white sofa. Teresa stared at it, shaking her head.

"What? Do you have a comment?"

"Only you would have a white sofa in your house," she laughed.

"For your information, white is actually easier to clean than colors. You can bleach it or use my tried-and-true method which, you can't use otherwise."

"What's that?"

"Baby wipes, preferably with alcohol. Works like a charm on any and all stains. My mother taught me that trick."

Teresa crinkled her nose, surprised that it was something she didn't know but would try in the future. She seemed distracted, and I hoped it had nothing to do with the evil Alyce Cumberland. If she was an accomplice in any way, it might well destroy my faith in humanity. I realize I was being overly dramatic, but my history with people betraying me was there, and at least I acknowledged it.

Sitting back on my sofa, I crossed my legs, letting out a sigh. I thought, here I go. Please don't let it be true.

"I need to talk to you about something that's happened. Something that I discovered." I searched her face for a reaction, a clue into her psyche. Always being able to pride myself on reading people, I was struggling at the moment. "The incident in my office on Saturday wasn't because I tripped and hit my head, or passed out from fright, or from anemia or low blood sugar. Certain circumstances have come to light, and I uncovered disturbing information about a member of my team that stunned me. Actually, it has gutted me, because it was the last thing I ever expected from a person I trusted and cared about. It is a betrayal I can't seem to wrap my head around or get over. I summoned you here because I need to know if you knew anything about it, or God forbid, were complicit with this person. Because if you were, I swear I am going to crawl into a hole and never come out."

She stood, her arms flailing manically in the air, "Jesus Christ Almighty! I thought for a minute there you were going to fire me! You scared the living daylights out of me. When you asked me to travel all the way out here to this Godforsaken place on a weekday, having Buddy pick me up like I was in the witness protection program, not telling me why over the phone or emailing me, I told my husband you were giving me the boot. He said I was crazy, and I said, 'No, I'm not. Melinda trusts me with her life and something is wrong and she's not telling me.' And you actually think I would betray you? You can't be serious. I would do anything for you. You have done more for me than anyone I've ever met. You have spoiled my family and me, and been the best boss, the best friend I have ever had. Short of going to prison, I would move heaven and earth for you, and you know it. Wait a minute—does this have something to do with that little maggot, Ed Ross? I swear if he did anything, I will string him up by his…"

"No. It's Alyce, Teresa. It's Alyce." I buried my face in my hands and cried. I was weak and exposed, and I hadn't felt like that in such a long time. It made me angry, and I despised falling apart in front of her. I was always the strong one, tempering her rants and outbursts, calming her in the face of chaos.

Suddenly, like she was the victim of some weird exorcism, her expression changing from rage and disgust to amusement and giggles. Throwing herself on my navy blue designer rug, she was laughing uncontrollably.

"Um, excuse me. What the hell are you doing, Teresa?"

Sitting, she stifled another laugh, trying to regain her composure. "I need some tissues."

"For God's sake," I said, pointing toward the bathroom down the hallway.

A minute later, she walked back in, wiping her eyes, shaking her head.

"Would you care to explain yourself?" I asked.

"Oh, Mel. I thought you knew me so much better," she smiled.

"Yeah, well that makes two of us," I said, taking a slug of my lukewarm coffee.

"Would you mind starting at the beginning and tell me what the hell happened in your office on Saturday, please?" Teresa asked.

"This is not the least bit funny. This is my company! The company that gives you your paycheck, the one I have built my life on, so get serious here." I was actually getting annoyed with her cavalier attitude. MD Shoes was my whole life, and I think I realized for the first time, that this fact was in reality, sad.

"After you and Alyce left, I went in her office because she left her lamp on and the door open. I saw an envelope sticking out from under the blotter on her desk. Since anything in that office belongs to me, I decided to take a peek. The return address was marked Shoe Mizer and contained a pay stub copy for a direct deposit transaction made out to Alyce Cumberland. She must have forgotten to take it or hide it, in her haste to get out of there. I just got word from legal and security that she sold the designs for our fall shoe line to our biggest competitor, and she was planning on resigning to join them as CEO. My company president, our friend, has betrayed me in the worst way possible. I still can't get over it. So please, please, Teresa. Tell me you had nothing to do with this. Please."

She looked right into my eyes, letting out a loud sigh, her shoulders relaxing.

"You silly girl." She walked over and sat next to me on the sofa.

Tears streaked my cheeks. Teresa gently swiped her thumbs over them, cradling my face in her hands.

"Look at me. Listen to me. I realized weeks ago that Alyce was up to something. When has either one of you not let me stay in your office while you were on a phone call? Never. So right after you left in January to start school, I got suspicious when she asked me to leave when she got a phone call. And then I got a phone call—a very interesting, disturbing phone call. So I did some digging. I made a friend in London when we launched the new store, and she has a friend who works at Shoe Mizer. Long story short, there was some hoochy, involved with stealing someone's boyfriend, so the scorned woman spilled the beans. This girl sent me confidential copies of the emails and told me about the secret deal Alyce brokered with them. This girl Camie, wanted revenge on her boss and gave me all I needed to know. So I took care of things for you. As I always have, and always will. You have nothing to worry about."

"What do you mean? You knew about this? And you never told me? Are you kidding? She stole my designs and sold them to our competitor. Our fall line is gone. I talked to Steven Hill about this. Alyce can legally claim them as her own, and there is little I can do to contest it because of some loophole in the law."

She smiled. "Don't worry. As soon as that line hits stores, Shoe Mizer will be sending her to wait on the British equivalent of the unemployment line."

"What are you talking about? That was some of our best work ever. Those shoes will sell millions of pairs and make them a fortune!"

"Wrong. They will make you a fortune." Teresa grinned like a Cheshire cat.

Staring at her in disbelief, I thought she had lost her mind or had some sort of stroke, because she didn't seem to understand what this would do to MD Shoes and our revenue. "I don't think you realize, but…"

"Mel, listen to me. Alyce never got your designs—your real designs, that is."

Teresa Jenks winked and giggled an evil laugh, like some deranged clown who scared kids at birthday parties. It was amusing and yet totally frightening.

"Teresa, what did you do?" I asked.

"What do you think I did? Did you think I would let that sneak stab you in the back and betray us? Oh, no sir. I took care of things, like I said. When I found out what she was planning to do, I fixed her miserable soul but good."

"Would you please tell me what you did, for Christ's sake?"

"Okay, already. Calm down, cause you are going to love this. So remember that guy who kept trying to get a job with us in design—the dude with the pink streak in his hair?"

"Toby Horton? Yes, what about him?" I asked. He was a young kid who attempted many times to get me to hire him as a designer at MD Shoes. He had potential, but needed several years as an apprentice at a fashion house where he could learn better techniques to develop shoes women would like and would actually be able to wear. The last time he submitted a proposal, I told him that if a woman wore his shoes, they would fall apart on their feet after an hour. He walked away dejected, but he appreciated the constructive criticism.

"Remember how the new line had to be approved before we submitted them? When Alyce asked me if she could see them before they went to anyone, I put two and two together that something was amiss. And since Alyce hadn't seen your new designs yet, I switched yours for Toby Horton's and put them in the file on her desk. The minute I left her office, she was on the phone, probably to Shoe Mizer, emailing stuff, selling you up the river. Such a traitor! So like I said: I fixed her ass. And Shoe Mizer is so pathetic, they thought they had genuine Melinda Drake designs and would finally be able to compete with us. Poor Toby. He will finally get his shot at the big time. Except that anyone who buys Shoe Mizer's fall styles will end up with blisters or barefoot because they will fall apart at the seams! But, thank God, poor Toby will never get blamed. Actually, thanks to him and his horrible designs, he saved you. Maybe you should give him a job after all."

I jumped from my seat, grabbing Teresa mid-sentence, hugging her until she couldn't breathe.

"Oh, Teresa. I apologize for doubting you! I should have known you would never betray me. Please, forgive me," I pleaded, in tears once again. Suddenly, I realized I was conflicted. My assistant had way overstepped her boundaries, and I was angry. "But why the hell didn't you tell be about this immediately? I would have fired Alyce on the spot. You should have told me. I had a right to know about this as soon as you knew. This is far beyond your job responsibilities and you should have come to me. I'm not sure if I should kiss you or fire you."

"I agree, boss. And I apologize. But you have so much riding on your shoulders all the time, especially with all this college pressure. That's why I handled it for you. Obviously, I was going to reveal Alyce's deception, but I knew this plan was so much more devious and she would get what was coming to her. I knew MD Shoes was still safe and this betrayal wouldn't affect anything. I would do anything for you, like you have done for me. I could never pay you back for all you have done for me."

I knew she was referring to the fact I had established trust funds for her three kids to go to college. Since I had no children of my own, I did it because I wanted to. I insisted, over the futile objections of Teresa and her husband. I used my money as I wanted, and I wanted to ease Teresa's burden with the financial impossibility of triplets going off to college.

We sat on my sofa, hands clasped together, once again sharing the circumstances of life together, as a team of two. I loved Teresa, and I felt as if a huge weight was lifted off my chest. Although she had gone too far in making a decision on Alyce's deception without informing me the minute she discovered it, the universe was righted again, thanks to the loyalty and friendship of one woman. I was grateful for her, and for all the wonderful support I was fortunate to have.

"Go get me some tissues, will you?"

She bounded to the bathroom and back, sitting with me as I wiped my bloodshot eyes. I must have looked a wreck, but I didn't care. The worst was over, and I could move forward. One woman betrayed me. Another saved me.

"What are you going to do about Alyce? Can you sue her? Better yet, can you throw her sorry ass in jail?"

At this point, I was exhausted thinking about her. I wanted her to go away; I wanted to erase the memory of her from my business and from my life.

"The team and I are working on it, compiling the evidence against her. There must be a good reason why she did this."

"Well, whatever it is, I can't wait to hear it. You are a nicer person than I would ever be."

I gazed at my amazing, wonderful assistant. With her flawless skin, her petite, fit figure, her boundless loyalty and heart, I leaned over and kissed her on the cheek.

"Guess what, Mrs. Jenks?"

"What, boss?"

She knew what was coming. Teresa loved every minute of it.

"I have reservations tonight at a fabulous place. It'll blow your mind. But we need to get dressed in something fancy. So let's go shopping here in the City of Brotherly Love and buy you something appropriate. How does that sound?"

Beaming, Teresa stood. "If I haven't told you lately, I'm glad you did this."

"What? You mean going back to college?" I asked.

"No. Making me your right-hand woman. It was the smartest decision you ever made."

"I couldn't agree more."

CHAPTER EIGHTEEN

Teresa and I had a blast last night, because after dinner I took her to a college hangout in Philly. She flirted shamelessly with guys half her age, drinking a couple of shots of God-knows-what. My Gen Z chill (translation: cool) squad (translation: friends) had told me they were going to the bar, and they were feeling no pain when we arrived. Gyrating on a quasi-dance floor, they were trying to sing, but it came out more like a chant.

"MELINDA'S IN THE HOUSE, GONNA GET LIT!!!"

Heads turned to gape at Teresa and me—the geezers—obvy (translation: obvious) making an awk (translation: awkward) attempt at trying to turn back time. Aiden was there, and Teresa stared slack-jawed, impressed that this guy was interested in me. He bought us both a drink when we arrived, and I reciprocated the second round, sending a few pitchers of beer over to his table of cheering friends.

The previous week, I had invited Aiden over for dinner. Scheming, I summoned my best matchmaking skills, trying to get him to ask Lucy out on a date. The poor girl was beginning to get frantic.

"Don't you think you should find a nice girl, maybe start dating just one special person?"

"I will when you will. Hey—I have a great idea! Let's date each other, or at least, start hooking-up. You do know what friends with benefits are, right?"

"Oh, I know, all right. And I told you—no. You need someone your own age, and I happen to know the perfect girl."

"Who?" Aiden asked.

"Lucy."

His faced scrunched like an accordion. "Little Lucy with the blonde hair?"

"If you mean little as in young, she is a junior, and she is fantastic. You should ask her out before someone else does."

"If I ask her out, then can we have just one booty call? I think that's a reasonable request."

"That's never going to happen. Seriously, you should ask her out," I repeated.

So when Lucy strutted her stuff into the bar, I nudged Aiden to take a look and check her out. She looked great in a pair of dark jeans and smoky eye makeup. Aiden stared as she moved toward us, his gaze gliding over her tiny frame. It was as if he were seeing her for the first time.

"Hi Melinda," she said. Glancing casually at the object of her desire, she uttered, "Hey Aiden, how've you been?"

My girl was playing hard to get. Like I told her, it works every time. Some men are such pushovers and so easy to sway.

"What's going on, Luce?"

"It's my birthday—the big one. I'm finally legal. It was so crae that I could flash my real ID to the bouncer. I'm sure my friends are going to want me to get turnt tonight."

I glanced at Teresa. "Crazy and drunk."

"I have teens, remember? I'm cool."

Aiden draped his arm around Lucy. Her face flushed as she swayed into his side, wide-eyed from the sheer contact with him.

"Well, birthday girl. Twenty-one deserves your first legal shot of tequila, don't you agree?" he asked.

"Sure!"

I leaned in to whisper in his ear. "You had better take care of her tonight or else—understand? No shenanigans or I will hunt you down. She is a little naïve with this whole bar scene. No monkey business. Tread carefully."

He looked at me and grinned. "I love when you use those retro words that I don't even get. Don't worry. I'm always a true gentleman. I pinky promise."

"You better be."

"If you ladies will excuse us, we are going to start this birthday right. Catch you later," he winked.

Then he guided Lucy toward the bar through the maze of drunken college students. I nodded my head in the direction of the exit, indicating to Teresa I was ready to leave.

"Oh come on, Mel. The fun is just getting started."

"Exactly. It's time for us to get out of here. I've been promising my posse that I would stop by once to say hello and have a drink, but now we have to go. All these kids have phones and could take pictures of shoe magnate Melinda Drake and her assistant getting turnt in a seedy bar in Philadelphia. How do you think your husband would like seeing photos of his wife downing shots with young guys splashed on the cover of some tabloid?" I asked.

"I think he would say, "Damn, girl, you still got it!""

I grabbed her by the arm, dragging her out the door just as Aiden and Lucy shared their first shot at the bar.

The following morning, Buddy arrived to take Teresa back home to Brooklyn, and I decided to go for a nice walk in the park, steps away from my apartment. I needed to regroup and decide how I wanted to proceed with confronting Alyce. My team suggested we give Alyce a few days under surveillance to bury and incriminate herself. We set up a sting operation that would culminate in her termination and possible prosecution. Security was following and recording her every breath, so I was forced to lay low and let them do their job.

I showered and slipped on some warm clothes and a parka. No hat was needed, but I made sure I had gloves in my pocket. My doorman greeted me as I zipped my coat and smiled at him.

"Nice day out there, Ms. Drake. Go and enjoy it."

"Thank you. I intend to. Family all good?" A person's family is usually the most important part of their lives, so I always asked.

"Everyone is great, thank you," he said, holding the door for me.

As I stepped outside on to the sidewalk, I could have sworn I smelled spring. Something happens to the cold winter air when the next season tries to intrude on its territory. It softens and surrenders, agreeing to take a back seat for a day or two.

Slipping my sunglasses on, I turned and headed toward the walkway in the park. The trees and grass remained brown and dead, but I felt alive and hopeful. I picked up my pace and started to think about my personal future and the future of my business. MD Shoes was in great shape financially but I would need to consider who would replace Alyce as president. There were a couple of possible candidates from within, or I could go outside and recruit someone new, oftentimes a necessary option to inject a fresh perspective. I would take my time on this, still reeling from the betrayal of a person I once trusted with my life.

The London store was going well, and we were thinking about expanding operations out to Los Angeles, San Francisco, and possibly Paris. I felt so proud of the company I founded and built into a business with a name that was desired and respected. MD Shoes was my whole existence wrapped in a lovely mint green and magenta (our signature colors) shoebox. As I changed the direction of my walk, I had a revelation. The strange thing was sometimes you choose your path and sometimes your path is chosen for you. If it weren't for the painful experiences I endured in my life, I probably wouldn't have built my shoe empire.

Pumps and circumstances.

This was the story of Melinda Drake. I stopped and smiled. These two things defined me, and it felt like an epiphany. All the heartache that spawned my vision made sense to me now, because at the time I was at my lowest point, I never thought I would ascend from the depths of that deep, dark place.

I lived a great life, I must admit. I wanted for nothing. Material things, family that loved me, a fulfilling career—all were mine. But what did I feel I was missing? Did I have the right to have all of this and still want more? Was I being greedy in my desire to have everything?

These were the heavy questions I was contemplating on such a lovely day in Philadelphia. With my head down, not paying attention, I collided with a semi-sweaty, rather broad-shouldered, solid piece of human flesh.

It was none other than Jack Sweeney, bane of my existence, ass extraordinaire, dressed in shorts, running shoes, and a threadbare, Pennwood University T-shirt, all sweaty and messy hair.

As I felt myself in slow motion, heading toward the ground, thinking *I can't hit my head again, I can't hit my head again,* a pair of strong arms grabbed me, righting my center of gravity. In all the confusion, I was smashed up against a lean, muscular, male body. Despite the sweat factor, he smelled fantastic.

Dear Lord, I am in big trouble when I can't think of any other words to describe someone I don't care all that much—despise actually—about except in terms of the following adjectives: appealing, striking...

"Melinda? I can't believe I almost ran you over. I apologize. I wasn't paying attention. I have a lot on my mind. I'm sorry," he said, pushing his hair back from his forehead.

"No, listen, it's my fault. I was the one looking at the ground, not watching where I was going, thinking about a million things, too. I apologize."

He smiled. That smile I loved the last time he used it, the one that made him almost human rather than the Scrooge-like scowl he usually wore. He looked boyish, innocent, and so damn attractive.

"We're even. I guess we both think too much, and it almost got us killed," he laughed.

I snickered along with him, and our eyes caught for a brief moment before I attempted to fill the silence between us.

"It's brave of you to be out running in shorts in February," I said, looking at his lean, well defined, hairy legs while I attempted to put my mane of auburn hair back into something presentable.

"When I quit smoking back in my undergrad days, I replaced it with running. I never had a cigarette again, and I've run in several marathons. It keeps me sane," he said, scraping a few pieces of gravel and dirt from his left leg.

"Well then, that's impressive. I struggle with exercise, so I make sure to walk whenever I can. It's such a beautiful day, I didn't want to waste it by staying inside."

I realized he was watching my mouth intently as I spoke, his eyes following my every word. It made me a tad self-conscious, as he scrutinized each thing I said. I never had someone notice (for lack of a better term) me like this mercurial professor. I wondered if this was unique to the manner in which he dealt with me, or if this was how he behaved with everyone he encountered.

"Well, as long as you are all right, I'll leave you to your walk. Sorry, again."

I did not want him to leave just yet, so I decided in a split second to finally crack the nut that was Jack Sweeney.

"Would you like to grab a coffee? We seem to always be rushing from one thing to the next on campus. It might be nice to get to know each other a bit, don't you think?"

He answered with a typical reply. "Well, I don't normally socialize with students. It complicates things, and it has always been a policy of mine. I don't mean to offend you, but it's worked well for me as long as I have been teaching."

Raising my chin defiantly, I said, "I admire your professionalism, Dr. Sweeney, but I am not one of your students. Actually, I consider us more colleagues and equals than anything else, as you hold no power over a grade for me. Although, I must admit I hear from my younger friends here at Pennwood that your classes are quite good and that I should have registered for one instead of my rather dry political science course."

He welcomed the compliment, but continued to hold firm.

"It really doesn't matter whether you are in my class or not. I make it a practice not to socialize in public with students. And you are an undergraduate student here at Pennwood. I'm sorry, it's my policy, and I don't intend to change it.

Feeling defeated, and a little annoyed, I put my hands up in a gesture of surrender. I didn't need a brick wall to fall on me to realize that although I may have been, this man was definitely not interested in me.

"Very well, Dr. Sweeney. I'll be on my way then."

"Please, you can call me Jack."

"Oh, no. I'm sure you aren't on a first name basis with your students. I love to bend the rules sometimes, but I also realize the need to follow them. It has been a pleasure running into you. Enjoy this beautiful day. I'll see you at our next committee meeting. Meanwhile, I'm going to plop my tush in the nearest cafe and relax. See you soon."

I turned walked away, mortified that I had asked this tool to go for coffee and he shot me down like a plastic clown in an arcade game. Jack Sweeney was a pompous, stuck-up Neanderthal who thought he was better than everyone else. Needing caffeine, and definitely a drink later, I headed out of the park. Turning briefly, I saw that Jack Sweeney was standing still where I had left him, apparently lost in thought once again. He was probably going to crash into another unsuspecting bystander who would be smart enough not to ask him out on a coffee date.

What was I thinking?

Although it was an unusually mild, winter day, it felt good to tug open the coffee shop door and feel a burst of heat. I stood on the long line to order a cappuccino. From behind, I felt a hand tap me on the shoulder. Turning, I encountered the charming Gavin Beck.

"Hello there, Melinda. What a surprise."

"Gavin! What brings you into the city today?"

"I'm going to see my nephew play basketball later at a high school around the corner. He's a freshman who starts varsity, and since I'm his godfather, I'm really proud of him. Sorry to brag."

"Don't apologize. I have three nephews I'd kill for. I get it."

"What's going on with you? Taking a break from studying? It's such a great day out there," he said, as he looked at the menu board.

"Yes. Not the kind of day to waste. I've been putting the finishing touches on a presentation in one of my classes in my major and decided some fresh air would do me good."

I was next in line, so I pulled Gavin next to me, much to the annoyed stares of folks standing on line before him.

"Cappuccino, with cream, please. Listen—this is my treat."

"Hell no, Drake. I've got this." He flashed that toothy grin again.

As we waited for the barista to make our drinks, Gavin and I grabbed a highboy table vacated by two men in Pennwood University sweatshirts. We draped our coats over the chairs to reserve them as our names were called out. Ever the gentleman, he pulled out my chair for me and went to grab a few napkins.

As we settled with our coffee in the crowded café, I noticed several women, mostly young coeds, staring at Gavin. He was devastatingly handsome, impeccably dressed even in casual attire, emanating an air of wealth and sophistication. This man probably had women falling at his feet at all times. I enjoyed the fact that although it was a kick to have these females envy me, I couldn't care less about it.

Gavin and I lived in the same world. It was so great to sit there with him, discussing finance and markets instead of schoolwork and search committee minutiae. After all, I was back at Pennwood University on a whim, eager to attain my college degree, but MD Shoes was the thing that fueled my fire. Business was the thing that drove me, excited me. I assumed it was the same for him.

"So Mel, what's after graduation?"

Sipping my cappuccino, I paused, placing my cup on the table. "Back to New York to resume my rightful position as leader of my company. It's been difficult being away."

"Everything all right?"

"It is now. Let me ask you something, if I may?"

"Of course."

"Have you ever had a colleague turn on you—betray you? As in give away company secrets to a competitor?"

"No. But Beck Industries is not that type of business. Why? Has that happened to you?"

"Yes. Someone I trusted with my business and my life."

"See that was your biggest mistake. You have to keep your professional and personal relationships separate. It's easier and safer that way. No drama, no problems."

It was the second time in an hour a man had declared that philosophy to me. Perhaps it was advice I needed to take.

"I don't agree. I think you need to have trusted people around you at work. I always thought I did." I gave him the bare bones of what Alyce had done and how I intended to handle it. He agreed with my strategy, providing me with a few helpful suggestions.

At one point, we both pulled out our phones to check messages. Gavin informed me he had to run, but he was staying at a local hotel for the weekend and asked if I would like to join him tonight for dinner.

"That would be lovely." The idea of dinner with an attractive man was the perfect antidote to lift me from the funk of a cold winter and a dating slump.

"Perfect. I'm looking forward to it. I'll pick you up around eight o'clock."

"Not necessary. I'll call an Uber. Let's meet in the lobby bar at seven-thirty for a drink, okay?"

"Seven-thirty, it is."

We both stood, slipping on our coats. As I was zipping my parka, he leaned over, placing a kiss on my cheek.

"Can't wait for our date. Dress your best. I aim to impress you," he smirked with the utmost confidence.

"Don't worry. I'll impress, too."

As we turned to walk out, standing at the window watching us, was none other than Jack Sweeney. And he did not seem happy.

Was it my imagination, or had he had a change of heart on that no fraternization policy after all?

CHAPTER NINETEEN

Rolling over, I turned to admire a sleeping Gavin beside me. It was a wonderful evening, filled with great food and fine wine, stimulating conversation and a rousing night of desperately needed physical release. It was a long time since I had been with anyone, and he made me feel alive again. I was a woman with many appetites, and I was starving in the intimacy department. Gavin was a thoughtful, enthusiastic partner. I understood, aside from his looks, why he was never without female companionship.

"Good morning," he yawned, pushing his thick, wheat-colored hair out of his eyes.

"Back at you," I said, leaning over and placing a kiss on his mouth. "Last night was lovely. Thank you."

He laughed. "You were very, um, energetic. I'm not complaining, but I was pleasantly surprised."

"So you could tell it's been a while?"

"Like I said, I was surprised. You are gorgeous and generous in a lot of ways. You really have it all."

"Well, thank you." I scooted over to snuggle against him as he opened his arm in invitation.

The opulent suite was lit from the sun peeking through the slit in the heavy drapes. Our clothes were scattered all around the room. He had worn a tailored suit, while I dressed in a midnight blue cocktail sheath that left little to the imagination. Barely making it to the room after dinner, we lunged on each other immediately.

"Have you ever been in a serious relationship?" I asked, as I lay comfortably in the tangled mess of sheets.

"Yes. I was engaged a few years ago, but I broke her heart after I cheated on her with a cocktail waitress at a bachelor party. She couldn't get past it."

"Can you blame her?"

"I know I was a complete idiot. But it was a bad, drunken mistake. I was hoping she cared enough to overlook it. My parents were extremely pissed off at me. They loved her. I loved her."

"Newsflash, Gavin. Worst thing you can do to a woman, or a man, for that matter, is cheat. Because once trust is gone, you can never rely on that person again. You can't build a life with someone without trust."

"Is that why you've never settled down, Melinda? You've never found a guy you really trusted?"

I thought back to when I found Max and Nicki together. I thought about Alyce's betrayal. I thought about Steven and the salesgirl. Lack of trust played a focal point in my decisions as well as for the direction my life had taken. It hindered and helped me, yet maybe I never truly came to terms with it. But here, in this hotel room where I had fulfilled my physical needs, I realized I had no desire to share my deepest fears and concerns. So I gave my standard answer.

"I've been told by more than one family member and my friends that it would take a unique type of man to be able to handle the real me. I haven't found him. And to tell you the truth, I don't care. Because if I can live the wonderful life that I do and have great people around me— not to mention passion like you and I shared last night—then that's all I need."

"What about kids? No desire there either?" he asked.

"No. Besides, I'm almost forty. What about you?"

"Some day. Maybe."

This conversation was getting too serious. It was time to shift gears. So once again, I made him stop talking.

Hours later, I walked back into my apartment realizing the one image that continued to invade my brain since yesterday had nothing to do with work or classes or fantastic sex with an attractive man. It was the odd look on Jack Sweeney's face as he watched me through the coffee shop window.

I opened my front door to retrieve copies of the Sunday *Philadelphia Inquirer* and *The New York Times*. Always a voracious reader of newspapers, I eschewed digital sources on my computer and phone. Nothing was as satisfying on a Sunday as a big, fat, newspaper, a pot of strong, hot coffee, and a fresh bagel with cream cheese. Include being wrapped in a set of flannel pajamas and I have the perfect day.

After I showered, I decided to call my parents to see if they wanted to drive in and have dinner. My mother declined because my father's bursitis was acting up, and they couldn't make the drive. I decided to go to the library for a couple of hours and then head out to a department store for a few needed items. Maybe I would see if Aiden was around later, and I could make him a nice meal and watch a movie or have him teach me how to play one of his video games.

Frost covered the ground overnight. Today the temperature had plummeted to freezing, so out came the boots, scarf, and gloves again. I looked like a Nordic goddess as I bid my doorman farewell and ventured over to the library. The sky was gray and dismal as I walked along the winding concrete path en route to the library. Saturday had been a reminder of hope, that the long winter would soon be over, making way for life again: trees, flowers, and birds. Almost a year ago, I began my journey back to Pennwood University. So much happened in that short span of time. I made new friends, and lost one. I would soon have the precious degree that came at the expense of a friendship. I wondered if I had never left New York would Alyce have made the decision to stab me in the back like she did. We were accumulating enough evidence to bury her professionally, but I still wanted her to tell me to my face why she chose to throw it all away.

The winter air was frigid as I blew a decent white cloud with my breath. It was so damn cold, and my nose was running. I walked quickly to my destination, eager to enter the warm recesses of the building and get some work done. I saw three of my young friends studying in the library with a couple of guys wearing Pennwood football jerseys. The team had a great season, or so they told me. I had about as much interest in sports as I had in going to the moon. Sports bored me to death, and when I attended a few football and basketball games last year with Steven, I sat glued to my phone, engaged with my email and social media sites.

After putting in a couple of hours in a cozy alcove I discovered on the third floor, I decided to pack it in and head off to the store. I stopped back at my place, dumped my messenger bag of textbooks and notes, and brushed my teeth. I obsessively used my toothbrush a few times a day. That minty taste was a trick that kept me from overeating.

My doorman arranged for a driver to take me to the nearest retail store, about ten minutes outside of the city in a modest suburb. The thing about Philly is that you can be out of the city in a few short miles, and be in an average, middle-class town. Go even further down the Main Line, and you will encounter stone mansions and wealthy upper class neighborhoods. I felt at home in both worlds. Row houses, comprised of tall, brown buildings, stood like wooden soldiers outside the city limits. Further out from the city were the blue-blooded, old Philadelphia-moneyed rich who made their family fortunes in steel, coal, and finance. It was a melting pot of amazing history and different social classes dotting the landscape.

The driver, a young man trying to put himself through community college (as I learned during the ride over) dropped me off in front while I retrieved a shopping cart, swiveling around the store. I hit the personal hygiene aisles first, then cleaning products, and snacks. I really loved shopping in a department store. All the things you need under one roof. I slowly strolled the store, enjoying myself immensely.

I was observing the most fascinating sociological study within one hundred thousand square feet of space. In the dairy aisle, a toddler was throwing a tantrum because he wanted chocolate milk and the mother refused to buy it. Teenage girls were huddled together in the cosmetics section comparing brands of mascara. A young couple was loading up on diapers and formula, while arguing whether or not they could afford a new vacuum cleaner. As I approached the clothing section, I turned my cart down the aisle that displayed women's panties and bras.

While digging through the display of thongs, I overheard a father and daughter arguing, an apparent disagreement regarding bra choices. And I definitely recognized that voice.

"Dad, I don't need a bra. Would you please leave me alone? You are so extra!"

"Spencer, you need to wear a bra. Your, *things*, are popping out for everyone to see."

I deduced he meant nipples. Educated guess.

"You know how I feel about this, Daddy. It's enslavement. Just because society says I should wear one, doesn't mean I have to. Didn't you teach me to be my own person?"

Score one for the kid. She made a good point.

"Yes, but I can't get another phone call from your guidance counselor. Now *that* is embarrassing. Come on, Spence. Work with me here. Please?"

"What if I wear a big sweatshirt every day instead? Then no one will notice."

That will only work while it's cold outside. Come on kid, you need a better comeback.

"That's fine for the winter months. And what about when you have gym? You can't wear a sweatshirt while you are running around, getting sweaty. My God, you'll look like you're in a wet T-shirt contest. The boys must already notice your, um, curves."

He had to have been beet red. I decided to intercede and put him out of his misery.

This was about to become a whole lot of fun.

Rounding the aisle, I came face to face with Jack Sweeney and his teenage daughter. "Oh my gosh, hello Jack, I mean Dr. Sweeney. Imagine running into you here, of all places. Long time no see."

His face contorted with embarrassment, looking like he wanted to crawl in a hole and be swallowed up. Here he was, seeing me, a student, while holding a pale pink bra in his hand. It was poetic justice, and in that moment, proved there indeed was a God and she loved some good old-fashioned karma payback.

"Um, Melinda, I mean Ms. Drake. Ah..."

The poor guy was speechless. I decided to be the better person and rescue him from his humiliation. Jack Sweeney didn't deserve my pity, but this was so parentally pathetic. I imagined my own brother in this situation and how he would have died. I love my brother, and I would have swooped in to save him, too. Not that I love Jack Sweeney, by any means. I just felt sorry for him.

Eyeing me suspiciously, Jack's daughter grabbed the bra out of his hand and threw it on the shelf.

"Dad, please. This is so lame and awk."

"Hey, don't worry about it. I work with your dad on a committee at the university. And I don't blame you: I think bras are the worst. I swear, if I wasn't a grown-up, I wouldn't wear one either."

"Thank you. See Daddy? I told you."

"But—and here's the big but. It's a bigger deal if you don't wear one than if you do, so if you don't want hormonal boys creeping on you, I would definitely go with one."

She looked at me like I made a good argument in support of the bra (no pun intended).

"But they are so extra and uncomfortable. And it never fits me right," she said.

Jack Sweeney stood there, watching me navigate his daughter's latest crisis as though I was negotiating a major business deal. He looked damned impressed.

"I hear you, and I agree. They can be pretty uncomfortable. Frankly, I can't wait to take mine off the minute I get home at night."

Jack Sweeney's face flushed with uneasiness. Was that a hint of interest on his face as he imagined me slipping off my bra at the end of the day?

"So—I'm sorry, what is your name?" I asked.

"It's Spencer."

"Nice to meet you, Spencer. I'm Melinda. So, you know what you can do?"

"What?"

The kid was hooked. I would have her strapped in before you could say boobies.

"Come here," I motioned, leading her over to the active apparel section across the aisle. Jack Sweeney followed like an obedient puppy, intrigued. "Here we are. Take a look at this, Spencer."

I guided her to a rack of sports bras, intended to serve the purpose of both support and fashion, made by a designer who specialized in understanding the needs of today's women. I had met her at a fashion show in New York, because she was a big fan of my shoes.

"Listen, Spencer. I am friends with the lady who designs these. She hates traditional bras just like we do. She found a way to make this whole thing of keeping *our girls* in check, without constricting us. Know what I mean?"

Spencer loved that I was addressing her in such an adult manner, and she became instantly mature.

"Yup. Def."

"I knew you would. You seem, I don't know, really mature for your age."

"For sure!" She said.

"What are you—fifteen, sixteen?" I asked, inflating the stats.

"Fifteen, a sophomore this year. My school sucks."

"Spencer, your mouth," Jack scolded.

"I hear you," I said.

"So how do you know the lady that makes these?" she asked, as she examined and touched the display of colorful undergarments.

"Well, Spencer. I design and sell shoes for working women— comfortable, super pretty heels and boots that won't kill your feet when you are in them all day. It's like these bras. Sophia, the bra lady, and I bonded because we have the same philosophy that what a woman wears should be pretty and functional. Don't you so agree?"

"Oh, yeah. It's so awesome that you make shoes. I'd love to make, clothes and stuff."

I'm certain Jack was almost at his saturation point in hearing about bras, shoes, and fashion.

"Well, maybe someday, if you are in New York City, you can come and visit. I'll show you my factory and show you how MD Shoes are made. Would you like that?"

"Def!"

And in a nanosecond, her teenage mind registered that she was hungry and asked if she could get a popcorn from the snack bar in the store. I couldn't blame her, because the heavenly scent of freshly popped, buttered corn was beginning to permeate through the entire space.

Jack robotically reached into his jeans and pulled out a five-dollar bill. I knew from my siblings that kids were a money pit of revolving cash, where asking for money came as easy as breathing.

"I want change, and for you to come right back."

The snack bar was within our sights, as Spencer sauntered off clutching her cash. Jack Sweeney turned to me, stuffing both hands in his coat pockets in capitulation.

"You win, Melinda. After that mortifying scene, I give up. Can we please be friends instead of my faculty/student charade?"

"Yes we can. And your little girl is amazing. What a spitfire. She reminds me of myself at that age. I drove my parents crazy."

"She's great, but sometimes a handful. Spencer loves to buck the system. She is a rebel who I think would have fit in perfectly in the sixties, attending protests and, naturally…"

"Burning her bra?"

"Def," Jack said, imitating his offspring.

We walked toward the front of the store to join Spencer, ordering her snack at the counter. I hadn't been sure Jack was a father, so I asked the inevitable question.

"If you don't mind me asking, why didn't Spencer's mom handle this female landmine? It's rough territory for a dad."

His expression dulled.

"Spencer's mother is not in her life. I'm all she has."

Jack Sweeney's face betrayed the wall of privacy he fought so hard to maintain. Etched in the lines on his weary brow were shades of sadness, resentment, and love. I wanted to reach out and embrace him. Obviously, the subject of his either former wife or girlfriend or partner, whatever she was to him, was an extremely difficult subject, and I didn't want to press him on the issue.

I nodded, and he looked in to my eyes.

"Thanks for your help. You were great with her. Do you have any kids? You're a natural."

We all have our baggage and skeletons, myself included. Like him, I relayed as little as possible.

"No, no kids of my own. Nephews; I adore and spoil them. My work fills the majority of my time." After it emerged from my lips, I realized how truly sad, even pathetic, that statement sounded. I think Jack did too.

Spencer returned with a paper bag of popcorn, offering a sampling but no change for her father.

"Looks good, but no thank you," I said.

"No thanks, sweetheart."

Shrugging her shoulders, she waltzed over to a display of nail polish, toying with a piece of her hair, fascinated and disgusted by the array of neon colors. I looked to Jack for clarification.

"Don't even ask. It would take a dissertation to explain the mind of my daughter at this stage."

"I won't ask. Maybe sometime you'll want to tell me. I'm a fabulous listener. It happens to be one of my best qualities."

Jack looked at me, flustered, replaced quickly by relief. I got the impression he was a man who had no one to trust or confide in, and he seemed surprised at my offer of friendship.

"I'm sure I'd be a fool to question your ability to do anything at this point."

"Well, she seems like a great kid; kudos to you, Dad."

"Thank you. Since my cover has been blown, what do you say we start over, Ms. Drake?"

"Sounds like a great idea, Professor."

Jack offered an outstretched hand, and I took it. When our skin connected, I actually felt a slight chemical reaction between us. I realized he did too, when a sexy grin passed for acknowledgment.

Spencer ambled back. She was dressed in baggy jeans, work boots, and an oversized shirt. Her brown hair was cropped short. Licking the salt and butter from her long fingers, she put her arm around her father's waist.

"Dad, I'm starving."

"You just ate popcorn."

"That was an appetizer. Excuse me, Miss Drake, would you like to get a burger and fries with us? There's a great place next door.

"I'm sure fast food is not Ms. Drake's restaurant of choice," Jack murmured.

"Who says? I love a quick burger every once in a while. But I'm more partial to the chicken nuggets and fries. If I'm still invited, that is."

Jack smiled. "Of course you are. It's a date."

"All right, let's go," Spencer said.

"Let me pay for my things first. I'll meet you over there," I pointed.

As we moved to the exit, Jack turned to me. "Are you sure? You must be busy or maybe we are intruding on your plans for the night?"

"I meant what I said. I would love to join you and Spencer. It'll be fun," I said, grabbing him by the arm. Once again, feeling a tingle when we touched surprised and delighted me.

An hour later, we sat, satisfied thanks to great American fast food. I observed Jack Sweeney eat his cheeseburgers and came to the realization that some people are simply interesting to watch. He ate methodically, consuming the burgers first, then the entire large container of fries. He ate with gusto, but he was obviously taught nice table manners by his mother or whoever had raised him. Consequently, I observed that Spencer had similar mannerisms to her father, not mixing a bite of meat with her potatoes. The human species was an anthropological study in amazement, I concluded. I wondered what the deal was with Spencer's mother. What mother wasn't a part of her child's life? For my mother, her children were her whole life; I couldn't imagine my world without that woman at the center of our family. And I had an entirely new picture of Jack Sweeney—one I was eager to learn about. He was more than a cartoon character I conjured in my head, because I didn't like him. Here, with his daughter, I was looking at him through a different lens, viewing him in a whole new light.

Spencer talked freely while we ate, about her school and how boring tenth grade was.

"I bet you have a ton of friends," I said.

"Um, no. More guy friends than girls. The girls are prissy and pissy..."

"Spencer Sweeney. Watch your language," Jack said.

"Sorry. But they are, Ms. Drake."

"Call me Melinda. We are friends, right?"

"Def."

"Well, sometimes you have to give prissy and pissy girls a chance. They may turn out to be okay."

"I doubt it. But anyway, Ms.—I mean, Melinda—can I ask you a question?"

"Sure."

"Do you actually make the shoes where you work? Like, are they made right there?"

"Yes. I have a top-notch factory in the heart of New York City. All of our shoes and boots are made right here in the USA."

Jack leaned in to whisper in my ear. "Best advice: don't reveal your political affiliation. She is very civic-minded for a 15-year-old, thanks to me. She may start to lecture you."

Nodding, I whispered, "Relax. I'm an independent."

He made a sign of the cross. I laughed.

Jack Sweeney had a sense of humor. Who knew?

"Nice. I want to take shop next year. My grandpa has been teaching me how to use some sweet power tools. I'd love to see a real factory." Spencer sighed, sipping her soda through a plastic straw.

"Well, maybe you and your father could come to New York sometime and I'll give you the grand tour. How does that sound?" I offered. I won't lie: the idea of Jack Sweeney seeing me in my element, more than pleased me.

"Daddy, could we please go?"

"You have school, Spencer."

"How about over spring break? That's soon. My lame high school is off the same time as the college. We could go to all the places in New York you promised we could see. And Melinda could take us. Right?"

My spring break was going to be the week from hell. I had planned to confront Alyce Cumberland, visit with all the friends and family I neglected because of school, reconnect with my staff at the office, and squeeze in some crucial me time.

"Absolutely. I will be back in Manhattan for the entire week. It would be fun." I turned toward Jack. "And a promise from a parent should never be broken. Isn't that right, Professor?"

Jack gently stepped on my foot under the table, which I thought was hilarious. He knew I had him. In reality, that thought appealed to me. But I needed to get my mind out of the gutter. There was a child present in the room.

"Of course, Ms. Drake. We can plan a date after our meeting this week."

We were having our final committee meeting before the break to discuss our top two finalists for the position of president of the university and tie up the loose ends of committee business.

"Wonderful! I promise you, Spencer. You'll love my factory, and some awesome folks work there. We'll roll out the red carpet for you and your dad."

"I'm p pumped." Spencer said.

Jack looked at her.

"P means pretty, Jack. Your daughter is pretty pumped to see my pumps!"

Spencer rolled her eyes and giggled. Jack shrugged. He was outnumbered.

"Hey Melinda, I'll give you the 411: my dad has, like zero sense of humor."

"Don't be so salty, Dr. Sweeney," I smiled. My lingo impressed my new friend. Jack stared at me.

"Grumpy, Professor. Salty is grumpy in this context."

His forehead creased in confusion. "Spencer, are you ready to head home? I have some grades to finish and post by tomorrow."

Mid-term grades would be out soon. The semester was flying by.

Spencer turned to me. "You won't forget, right Melinda? I want to come to New York and see your stuff. Please don't forget about me." Her eyes widened with panic.

My heart sunk. What happened in her life that made her act so tough, yet insecure?

Embarrassed, Jack buttoned his coat collar and pulled a pair of wool gloves from his pocket. "Time to go, Spencer. Thanks again, Melinda. For...everything."

"No problem. I'll be in touch, Spencer."

"Wait, Melinda. I want to give you my cell number so we can set a day soon."

This kid was determined. I reached into my purse and pulled out my phone. "Okay, give me your digits." I tapped her name and number into my contacts. I looked up. "Jack, why don't I take your number, too."

Reluctantly, he recited his number, and I added it also. I had singlehandedly blown Dr. Jack Sweeney's entire stand on student/faculty fraternization policy in one fell swoop.

CHAPTER TWENTY

Heidi was leaning against the wall outside our political science class, studying her phone, waiting for me. Her calming presence every Monday, Wednesday, and Friday was a welcome gift. If we had met in high school or at orientation back in the '90s, we probably would have been roommates. I was convinced Heidi and I would be friends for life. Her friendship would be one of the best prizes I would take away from Pennwood University aside from my diploma.

Sitting in class, I leaned forward scribbling notes, attempting to absorb what the normally interesting Dr. Kramer was teaching. Dr. K wasn't at his dazzling best at the moment; my brain floated off into another world. I surveyed the sea of young, fresh faces surrounding Heidi, myself, and two senior citizens who were auditing the class. I wondered how different our reasons were for being here on a cold morning.

I came for the acquisition of a degree, screaming to be completed (thank you, annoying Philip Gunderson). My priorities had taken a dramatic shift since I had attended all those years ago, when the only goal I sought was a cool dorm room, new friends, good parties, interesting classes, and guys. Flash forward twenty years, and those reasons passed me by in a time warp. Studying the fresh-faced students in the room, I came to the conclusion that I was old enough to be the mother of most of them. Where did the years go? I didn't look like my fellow undergrads, but I identified with them. I still worried about grades and time management, my personal life and relationships, my family left behind back home. We both were concerned about money, but in a different way. I didn't need to become a potential employee a company would seek to hire. My concern was ensuring my business flourished and succeeded so that my employees could work, earn a paycheck, and take care of their families. I had a huge responsibility to thousands of employees who depended on me for their livelihood. A student like Heidi needed to go to school, hold down a full-time job, take care of her kids, a husband, and a house. If I went around the room and questioned each person regarding their reason for being here, I would get a different response from each one.

I harbored the arrogance to assume I could teach the class better than the instructors, particularly the courses in my major. There were several times I wanted to interject or correct my professors on simple things such as the use of this material over that, this management technique over one that appeared good on paper but failed miserably in reality. I held my tongue, reminding myself of the ultimate goal. I didn't need to ruffle any feathers.

I discovered that one of the most profound things mature students learn either in returning to the classroom or in beginning their college educations later in life is that as we get older, our cognitive abilities are at their sharpest levels. As a result, college faculty members find us to be a welcome addition to the educational population. The reason for attending college, which most eighteen to twenty-two-year-olds fail to realize, is that as students, we learn to become critical thinkers, not simply degree holders. Adult learners tend to be more open and aware of the process of developing higher level learning skills. We understand what we are learning and, more importantly, why.

I never understood this fact when I was twenty. At almost forty, I found school to be exciting and stimulating, exercising a part of my brain that laid dormant for a long time. All the things I didn't appreciate in my academic life back then had become center stage and vital. I turned to gaze out the window. Why had I never made the decision to complete my degree years ago? Aside from the guilt of my past actions, I realized my greatest challenge in going back was fear. Not fear of tests, or grades, or fitting in with students younger or smarter than me. I was finally able to admit the simple truth: embarrassment prevented me from going back. The shame I would feel from my colleagues in the business world, my peers in the industry, and frankly my employees who looked up to me that I didn't have my college degree. I felt they would see my deficit and not my strength and, thus, think less of me. It took a random reporter to point out the one circumstance of my life that didn't go my way because of another circumstance. My parents taught me that God moves in mysterious ways, and sometimes the road of life leads us in different directions towards our destiny. I sat there in a political science class, surrounded by students who were either dozing or rapt, contemplating the mysteries of life and the universe, realizing the purpose of acquiring higher-level thinking had been rightfully achieved. Mission accomplished. Thank you, Pennwood University.

After Dr. Kramer's less-than-stellar diatribe on the practices and function of state government, I insisted on taking Heidi to a nice lunch off campus. I was so done (Gen Z speak) with the repetitive dining hall fare. My next class was cancelled, and she was free until two-thirty. We were both dressed more formally today. I was tired of the usual jeans and Heidi had to attend the wake of a co-worker's spouse. I called to make a quick reservation at the upscale Belle's Bistro, popular with Pennwood faculty and the local business crowd.

As we settled in the warm restaurant and ordered hot cups of tea and turkey club sandwiches, I noticed a bit of sadness in her eyes.

"What's up? Was it Kramer's snore-fest today?" I asked.

"I wish that was it. I'm just going to come out and tell you because I've been hiding this news from my family and friends, and I need to tell someone."

Oh, Jesus. Please don't let it be that her husband is having an affair. I braced myself, ready to hear the worst.

"It's Billy," she said, lowering her head.

That piece of …

"He lost his job. They told him on Friday. Just told him to pack his things and go." Tears welled in her eyes.

"Oh, Heidi, I'm so sorry. What was their reason?"

"Apparently, they had a lousy year and had to cut a couple of upper-management positions. Billy's department has been underperforming, and he became a target. He is so humiliated and afraid of what everyone will think, especially our kids. I feel so bad for him."

I reached across the table and took her hand. "Unfortunately, this happens every day. Does he have any options?" I asked.

"They gave him a severance package, but it's not going to get us very far. Thank God I have a job, but I may have to drop out at the end of the semester. In fact, I am positive I will have to drop out. College was a luxury at this point, and we're going to have to cut back. My girls may have to give up their dance classes, and they are not going to be able to understand any of this."

The waitress arrived with our sandwiches. Heidi pushed hers away.

"Listen—you have to eat. We'll figure this out, don't worry," I said, trying to comfort her.

Heidi looked at me. "With all due respect, Mel. You are a millionaire, many times over. You have financial security for the rest of your life. You can't understand what this is like. You've never been in this position—when you are unsure of what the future holds, when your whole life gets turned upside down."

I did know. I knew all too well. But this wasn't about me. I needed to help a friend.

"First of all, I do understand. Secondly, I'm going to help. I know a hell of a lot of people."

I signaled our waiter. "Please bring us two mimosas."

"Mel! I just told you my husband lost his job and you want to celebrate? I thought you were my friend. That's pretty insensitive, if you ask me," she said, crossing her arms over her chest.

"Well, I didn't ask you, did I? And you must learn to trust me. I always take care of my friends."

She opened her mouth to speak, and I held up a finger to silence her. "Observe and listen, please." Pulling my cell phone from my purse, I scrolled through my contacts and tapped on a name.

Heidi watched with a puzzled expression as someone answered on the other end and said something that made me blush. And I won't say what it was because I'm a lady, but it was pretty damn sexy.

"Same here. You bet. Hey—I need a favor. A friend's husband was just laid off on Friday. He has years of experience, and I can vouch for his character and work ethic. Would you take a look at his résumé for me?"

The look on Heidi's face was priceless. She pressed her hand to her heart, bowing her head. I was some sort of fairy godmother sent to answer her prayers. Her tears flowed as the mimosas arrived.

"Listen, Gavin. This is a guy with a wife in college and they have two kids. I want you to move fast on this before someone else grabs him."

I blushed again after he said something quite inappropriate, seductive, and naughty.

"Okay, sounds good. Will I see you later? Great. How about a thank-you-for-this-favor dinner at my place this week? I can do that. Thanks again. Good bye."

I disconnected the call and slipped the phone back in my purse.

"He's as good as hired at Beck Industries. Have Billy email me his résumé ASAP. And no more talk of dropping out, okay?" I raised my glass. "Here's to moving on to bigger and better things."

"Beck Industries? Oh my God, Melinda! You are the most amazing CL I've ever met!"

"What is that?"

"You know, baseball…"

My face was blank.

"A CL is a closing pitcher in baseball who steps in at the end of a game to win it for the team."

"I have no clue who or what that is. I just have a lot of contacts. And I always help my friends, like you have helped me."

"How have I helped you? You have taken me out to lunch and bought me coffee countless times. I could never repay you after this."

"People don't realize. I do because I can, and therefore I will. I don't keep a scorecard. We found each other here on campus for a reason, and I'm grateful for your friendship. Some people tell me I'm a lot to handle, so I'm grateful you choose to hang out with me," I chuckled, taking a sip of my drink. Aside from my high school buds, Teresa, and my family, I hadn't made any new friends in a long time. Since I returned to Pennwood, I had Heidi, Aiden, my gal-pal young friends, and Gavin. I was a lucky woman.

"Well, I think you are the best friend I have right now. And you are so wonderful to be with. Not many people would do what you just did. Thank you, from Billy and me. He is going to die when I tell him! Beck Industries is fifteen minutes from our house. Billy was commuting an hour to that hell-hole that fired him."

"See, then? It was a blessing in disguise. So let's eat, drink, and enjoy our lunch," I said, picking up a piece of my sandwich.

"Who would have guessed this day would have turned around like this? I love you, Melinda," Heidi was emotional again.

"I love you, too. Let's change the subject. What are your plans for spring break?" I took a big bite of the turkey club that was generously stuffed, including a layer of maple bacon, my favorite.

"Well, I was going with my husband to the unemployment office. With this happy turn of events, I think we'll go and get him a new suit to interview in."

"Please take the kids somewhere fun and enjoy your family."

"I will. But I still have to go to work. What are your plans?" she asked.

"Back in New York for the entire week. I have a lot on my plate that needs to be addressed." Having a week off from classes would enable me to focus on work.

The only person I told here at school about Alyce was Gavin. Heidi didn't need to know about the mess with one of my employees. I also realized that my new relationship with Jack Sweeney was something I wasn't ready to share. For some reason, it felt personal, and I didn't want it to be tainted by petty gossip between two girlfriends.

As if the gods had read my mind, I glanced over my shoulder because I heard one of the wait staff drop a tray of dirty dishes he was carrying. Across the room, seated by the windows was none other than Jack Sweeney, and he was deep in conversation with an attractive blonde whose hand possessively gripped his arm.

I must have been staring, because Heidi asked, "Mel, are you okay? You look like you've seen a ghost."

It wasn't a ghost, but a green-eyed jealous monster that had overtaken me.

"Wait. Isn't that your Jack Sweeney over there with that attractive woman?" Heidi asked, straining to stare at the couple huddled together, deep in conversation.

"Yes, it's him. But he's not my anything. We sit on a committee together."

"Um, that's all I meant. Did I just hit some sort of nerve? Is there anything you want or need to tell me?"

"Of course not. I barely know the man. And he's a pain in the ass. I have no use for someone who is in a perpetual bad mood. And he's rude and ..."

"You know, seeing him away from campus—he's actually kind of cute." In a singsong voice, she taunted me: "Somebody's got a crush!"

"Oh, shut up, I do not. I hate that man. He is exasperating. And annoying. And he has no clue about how to interview and hire the right candidate." I was irritated by the feelings I was trying unsuccessfully to squelch.

"I don't think so. What's going on with you two?"

"Absolutely nothing," I said, picking apart my sandwich.

"Something, I think. Because he just saw that you were here and his eyes are laser focused on you and not the blonde bombshell he's with."

"Stop. I don't care what Jack Sweeney is doing. Wait—he's staring at me? Are you sure?"

"Sure as a heart attack," she said, sipping her mimosa.

Heidi was facing Jack's table, while my back was toward him and his lunch companion.

"Care to tell me why he is gawking at you like he just got caught doing something he shouldn't be doing and you are flustered more than a prepubescent girl who just got asked out on her first date?"

"I swear there is nothing to tell. I ran into Jack and his teenage daughter in a store the other day. I helped her with a rather delicate purchase, and she and I hit it off, and Jack Sweeney acted halfway human. That's all."

"And you obviously like the daughter and the daddy. This is great!"

Heidi was pleased with herself, and all I wanted to do was smack that grin off her face. She was right, and she knew it.

"Don't act so smug. There is nothing going on between us. I connected with his daughter and helped her out, and Jack was appreciative. End of story."

"Is he divorced, or widowed, or what?"

"I'm not sure. When I asked, he said Spencer's mother wasn't in her life. That's his daughter's name. Spencer."

"What the hell does that mean, not in her life? What kind of mother is not in her kid's life? What if she's in an insane asylum or a drug rehab place or in a state penitentiary? Poor kid, I wonder what the deal is there. Do you think he'll tell you?"

"Probably not. He despises me as much as I hate him."

Heidi nodded toward his table. "Um, I don't think so."

"Oh for God's sake. Can we change the subject, please? Let's talk about Dr. Kramer's midterm and how we need to study for it. It's on Friday, and then I'm out of here for a week. Do you want to meet on Wednesday after class and cram with me?"

Talking and thinking about the potentially sordid details of Dr. Jack Sweeney's personal life was beginning to wear on my psyche. He didn't offer any details, and I didn't ask. It was none of my business. But as I deliberately dropped my spoon and leaned over to retrieve it from the floor, I turned to catch a glimpse of the professor and his dining companion. Still deep in conversation, I realized that even when you assume someone is too annoying, reclusive, and unlikeable, you can be wrong.

I may have misread Jack Sweeney on several fronts.

CHAPTER TWENTY-ONE

I was sitting in Dean Samuels' conference room on Thursday afternoon, scrolling through my emails, when Gavin waltzed in. Since it was just the two of us, he walked by and gave my shoulder a squeeze.

"Good afternoon, Ms. Drake." Leaning over, he whispered something delicious in my ear that made me smile. Having been so annoyed by the whole Jack thing at lunch on Monday, I appreciated Gavin's attention. Why did I care anything about Dr. Sweeney? How did he manage to get under my skin? All I wanted was to get back to New York for a week and sit in my office overlooking Times Square. Don't get me wrong: I loved college and everything about it. But I sought my work world where I felt most like myself. Here at Pennwood University, I was a small fish in a big pond. I thrived on complete control and being the final decision maker. I was happy to finish my degree and accomplish this goal, but I was equally anxious to resume my old, normal life at MD Shoes. Before that happened, our committee was going to decide on the two final candidates to bring to campus for interviews. I had my opinions and suggestions, and I was confident in what we should be looking for in our next president.

As was customary, Rose set out refreshments for us, and I stood to take a cup of coffee and a couple of cookies that the dining hall had sent over. Don't ever let anyone tell you that all college food is deplorable. I ate it regularly and although it tended to be repetitive, I found it to be more than adequate, particularly the cookies. The chocolate chips were soft, even a bit gooey, and the snickerdoodles were to die for. Teresa would love to get her hands on a few of these. I couldn't wait to see her.

I had been mulling around in my brain how to repay Teresa Jenks for her evil, yet brilliant plan to fix that phony, backstabbing snake, aka Alyce Cumberland. I still couldn't believe Alyce chose to throw away her career and our friendship, but at this point I didn't care. I was going to do all I could to bring her down and ruin her in the industry. She would never work at another fashion house, and I was planning to bring legal action against her. It was first thing on my calendar upon returning, and security would be called to escort her out, hopefully in handcuffs, in front of all my employees. I was dreading and looking forward to it at the same time. My mother would yell at me if she knew I was wishing the plague and imprisonment on a fellow human being, but it couldn't be helped. Revenge is a dish best served cold, and Alyce Cumberland was about to be sent packing to Siberia.

I took a seat with my afternoon caffeine and treat while Gavin grabbed a bottle of water and parked next to me. The other committee members arrived, followed by an almost tardy Aiden Flanagan. I had spoken to him about this, explaining that serious work required serious habits. He assured me that once he had a "legit gig" he would toe the line and be there on time. Aiden figured that for the short time he had left to be a student, he was going to continue, "living his best life." Jack Sweeney was also late, probably sucking face with his girlfriend when he was supposed to be here at this meeting. Attempting to banish that image, I watched as the dean took his seat at the head of the conference table. As Dean Samuels cleared his throat, Jack finally graced us with his presence.

"Happy you could join us."

Jack took a seat across from me, eyes narrowing at the sight of Gavin positioned next to me. He stared at me in that way he always did, like he wanted to say something but chose not to. It infuriated and intrigued me—such was my limited relationship with him. I tried to concentrate on the task at hand and the fact that I was having dinner later in the evening with a man who actually wanted to spend time with me and who made his intentions clear. Gavin made me feel like a woman; Jack catapulted me back to a time in my life when boys sent unreadable signals and vague cues.

"Welcome folks. So here we are, almost at the end of our quest to find the next president of Pennwood University. I appreciate all the time and effort this committee has devoted to this process, and I'm certain that our final selection will enrich our campus with fresh ideas and new perspective."

Dean Walter Samuels was a former English department chair at Pennwood, and there was talk among the ranks he was in line to become provost after the current chief academic officer retired next year. I had a great deal of respect and admiration for him, and I knew he would hold me to the promises I had made him the first time I barged into his office. He enjoyed picking my business and design brain often, as I would stop in between classes simply to say hello.

Shuffling the résumés before him, he passed out copies to all seated at the table. I retrieved my glasses from my purse and looked to find Jack studying me. He smiled, the corner of his mouth curling up, as if to say, *yes, Melinda. The two of us share a secret, revealed in the underwear aisle.* I nodded in response, jotting a few notes on the curriculum vitae of my preferred candidate. I decided to push back; what I had witnessed in the restaurant demonstrated the sobering fact that Jack Sweeney did have someone in his life, and although it wasn't Spencer's mother, it was someone who was obviously in Jack's.

"I would like to invite our two final candidates to campus the week after spring break, to be interviewed by our current faculty, the provost, the other deans, and myself. The members of this committee will be invited to a lunch for each candidate's interview day to meet and ask any questions they wish. All final comments, recommendations, and observations should be submitted to my office by the end of that week. A formal offer will be extended after we have decided. Are there any questions?"

The dean stood to fix a cup of coffee as Ruth Forrester spoke. She was mid-fifties, with salt and pepper short hair, smart, and friendly. In addition to teaching psychology, she headed the women's studies initiative at the university. We were similar in our approaches to the world—strong females with much to say.

"What is the plan moving forward if neither candidate is selected or decides not to accept the position?"

"I don't anticipate that happening. My phone interviews indicated we have two serious applicants who both desire the position and come with impeccable references. I believe we will be able to select from either one of these and be satisfied with our final decision."

"What I think Ruth is wondering is: will this be the last time we see each other or should we pencil in a possible return engagement to this wonderfully efficient search committee should things not work out as we assume they will?"

We all laughed, and Gavin reached over and placed his hand over mine in a gesture of friendship and agreement. Jack's eyes zeroed in on this action, which confused me. Didn't he just have lunch with some gorgeous woman who couldn't keep her hands off him? What did he care if Gavin Beck flirted with me?

"As much as I've enjoyed working with all of you, I realize how valuable your time is. I want to thank all of you for participating in this most important effort to find our next leader here at Pennwood. Search committees are time consuming but a necessary part of filling the vacancies that arise at this institution. But I think we have completed our task in record time, thanks to the people sitting here at this table. I have appreciated your input and respected your opinions. Each member has brought something unique to the discussion, and I hope all of you will consider another appointment in the future to sit and serve the university."

Aiden, looking a bit frazzled from what I assumed was a rough mid-term schedule of exams, spoke up. "Anytime you need me, I'm in, Dean S. You can always count on me."

"I appreciate that, Aiden. If there are no further concerns or questions, we can convene and look forward to spring break. Anyone going anywhere interesting or doing anything out of the ordinary?"

He knew most of the faculty would be grading tests and papers, with a little relaxation time thrown in. This juncture in the spring semester was hectic, both for students and professors, and it was a welcome time away from the classroom. Traditional students returned home to reacquaint with family and friends, eager for a little of mom's home cooking and the comfort of the much missed bed in their childhood room. Typically, coeds were getting on each other's nerves, and many of their partying bodies required detoxing. Levi Stone from residence life would be staying in his on-campus apartment because the university's international students still had to be fed and housed for the week. Margaret Garren from admissions was going with her family to Florida, and Jack Sweeney's daughter would be pestering him to take her to New York to hang with me. Gavin and I would be in our offices, performing our duties as CEO's, business as usual.

Although I had been hard at work with my studies, I longed to be back at MD Shoes. I missed all of it: the staff, the smell of the factory, the stores, restaurants, and shows in New York City. I loved working, and I was anxious to address the whole Alyce Cumberland fiasco and put it to rest.

Teresa and my team had been keeping close tabs on Benedict Arnold since I uncovered her scheme. She couldn't do any further damage because she had already passed on the fake sketches to whomever, and her every move was being monitored. The truth of the matter was that she was a huge asset to my company before her indiscretion. Alyce was a fabulous find and talent, and I mourned the loss of her and her friendship.

"I'm heading back to New York for the week and back to work, Dean Samuels." I referred to him by his title when in the presence of his peers and students. In private, chatting his office or in the halls or academic buildings, he was Walt.

"And I never get a break," Gavin said.

"No? Weren't you in Mexico six months ago?"

"Yes. And I'm planning on Turks and Caicos in a few weeks," he answered, looking over at me as if an invitation would be forthcoming.

Jack watched my reaction as he was gathering his things. There was a look on his face I couldn't make out, and it infuriated me because he was the one person I could not read. I was always so good at people, but this man continued to confound me at every turn. Wondering why it was, I decided to not waste any more energy on the complicated subject of Dr. Sweeney. I needed to focus on finishing all this so I could go home.

Home.

My last class on Friday was cancelled, so I was able to leave earlier.

155

Buddy had driven in from Manhattan to collect me. And I don't use those words in jest. I needed to be gathered up and returned to my comfort zone.

Welcoming me with a wide-open car door and a warm smile, he said, "Come, Ms. Drake. I'll take you home."

As I slid into the toasty town car, Buddy shut the world of Pennwood University behind and we sped out of Philadelphia. Burrowing into the fine leather seat, I took out my phone and texted Teresa: *On my way. Stopping at my apartment to change and should be in by three. Have everything ready. Tks.*

I planned to spend Friday dealing with Alyce and the following week reconnecting with my management team and department heads. Needing to be briefed on where we stood in every facet of the operation, my calendar was packed with back-to-back meetings. Giddy with excitement, I realized I would probably never stop working, and they would one day find me dead at my desk at a ripe old age. I would instruct Teresa to emblazon the following on my headstone:

Here lies Melinda Drake. Her body finally gave out after giving her soul to MD Shoes. Too pooped from her pumps, she kicked. ☺

Sometimes, I crack myself up. Shoe puns were endless.

CHAPTER TWENTY-TWO

Teresa, in an act of absolute devotion, arranged a "Welcome Back Boss" extravaganza that was nothing short of embarrassing. But I must admit: I loved every minute of it. Some people hate attention; I thrive on it. My theory was simple: successful people had to possess large egos so they could take on the bull and glory simultaneously. The ability to accumulate extreme wealth and success, because the average person on the street could not, was something out of the ordinary. I earned every wrinkle on my middle-aged face, each scar on my soul. I welcomed the accolades that were awarded to MD Shoes and to me, personally. I considered myself the quintessential career woman, and I never wanted to be anything else or be anywhere else.

Walking through the glass front doors, I spotted Teresa who arranged for the staff to fill the lobby. They applauded as I entered past security. Stopping, I pulled my sunglasses from my face and gazed over the sea of faces. Smiling, I saw my management team who had maintained the status quo and order in my absence. I glanced at my secretaries and administrative assistants who kept the wheels in motion every day. I saw my custodial staff and tech team, my customer service, designers, and factory personnel. Overwhelmed and grateful, I tried to touch each and every one of their hands as I passed through the throng while thanking them for holding down the fort in my absence. Mama Bear Drake was back in the den for a week, and all was well with the world.

Front and center, of course, was my company president, Alyce Cumberland. Smiling and applauding with the crowd, she scampered forward to greet me.

"Welcome home, Mel. We're thrilled to have our chief back for an entire week. Listen, go get settled in your office. I believe I'm on your calendar at four-thirty."

You bet your soon-to-be unemployed, criminally charged ass, you are.

"I have so many issues to discuss with you, and I was hoping our meeting could carry-over into dinner—business, followed by a little pleasure, right? I want to hear more about your college escapades. I could use some excitement in my life."

Oh, you're going to have some surprises. Alyce. At four-thirty, in the form of security guards and the police taking you away in handcuffs.

"Let me check my schedule with Teresa first. We'll go over everything when I see you later." Alyce searched my expression, attempting to gauge my mood. But I had no time for her right now; there was a huge situation looming before me, and I needed to escape to the fortress of my office.

Trailing behind me was Teresa, notes in hand, barking out instructions to my staff to get back to work, that the party was over (except for the welcome back sheet cake that would be available at four o'clock in the second floor conference room). It still amazed me after all these years that a little flour, water, and sugar could reduce a bunch of adults into a gaggle of children, chomping at the bit for any form of celebration.

Even though I had been in my office not that long ago, entering today was different. The work environment had a specific personality on a weekday than it did on say, a Saturday. Weekends at work were for completing unfinished loose ends; weekdays were the meat on the bones when business was decided on and carried out. I was ready for action.

I told Teresa to give me some private time to go through the mountain of emails she flagged that required my immediate attention. Mrs. Jenks, my illustrious, industrious assistant had been going through these daily, deleting the garbage and saving the vital correspondence that only I could handle. Teresa was extremely bright, well versed in the business of MD Shoes, and could most likely run the whole damn show if I needed her to. I was lucky and I knew it—and Teresa knew it also. I'm not entirely certain that was a good or a bad thing.

Teresa followed me into my large office. My desk was ready, with a sheet of paper that spelled out my schedule in organized splendor.

"Okay. After I get your coffee..."

"Please do that ASAP. Then we can go over this," I said. Nodding, she left and closed the door. Taking off my long, white overcoat, I went in my private bathroom to check my hair and makeup. Teresa returned with a large mug, my favorite. It read, *Those Who Can, Just Do Everything!* in black script on the perimeter, a gift from my parents on my thirtieth birthday. My assistant had also gotten me a bagel with cream cheese because I hadn't eaten any lunch in my haste to get back to the office.

I was ready for battle.

"So as I was saying before: you have about a half- hour to go through some of your emails and voice messages. Then you have Sheila from marketing at four for a brief meeting and Armageddon at four-thirty."

Leaning forward in my chair, I groaned. "I'm dreading and looking forward to this—does that sound crazy?"

"No. Let her have it. Hey—can I hide in the bathroom so I can listen to you fire her sorry butt?"

Teresa was pure evil.

"No, you can't. I'll fill you in after. I want this entire sordid matter to be over and for her to be gone. Please leave so I can be productive before this hits the fan. By the way, thank you for the welcome back and for getting a cake. You're the best."

"I'm well aware, boss. And you're welcome. It's so good to have you back. I'm going to enjoy every day of this week because we need to have things back to normal. I still say this whole stupid college thing was a waste..."

"Good-bye. You are now cutting into my precious time."

Humming, she walked out and shut my door. I had officially left Pennwood University behind, delving into my rightful place as CEO, slipping effortlessly back as I powered up my computer and went to work.

The time flew by in a whirlwind of planning, listening, and decision-making. As I finished making a few notes, I noticed Teresa standing in the doorway.

"Heads up. She's on her way. You need anything before that sack-of-dung gets here?"

Teresa's humor escaped me, because this was no laughing matter. I was about to confront an executive in my company with fraud and deception. Worst of all, I was about to end a long friendship with a woman I had trusted with my business and my life.

After retreating to the restroom, I stood at my desk, staring at the file compiled by my legal team. Sitting in my chair, I hesitated touching the damn thing, like it was radioactive. My thoughts were interrupted by a gentle knock on the door.

"Come in," I said.

I decided to be seated when I confronted her, needing a large symbolic barrier between us. Also, I was afraid that once I started speaking, I would feel the need to lunge over my desk and wring her miserable neck.

Alyce breezed in, her ash blonde, shoulder-length bob swinging as she walked. In a designer outfit and MD heels, she was one of the faces of our brand. A sudden sadness washed over me. I forced myself to ignore the melancholy and focus on the anger. I wanted this over. I pictured Teresa, ear glued to the door, trying to hear what was about to happen.

She sat in front of my desk, crossing her long legs. "So—how's the day been going so far? Happy to be back in the driver's seat where you belong?"

"Very happy," I said, fingering the file as I searched her face for any trace of regret.

"Um, the strangest thing just happened to me. I tried to get into my email and all of a sudden it said I am blocked. Are you experiencing the same thing? Maybe the system is down or there is a glitch going on in technology. I'll call them if you want…"

"That won't be necessary. There are no problems with the system. However, we do have a big issue here, don't we Alyce?" My voice was colder than the frigid weather embracing New York City.

The blood drained from her face.

"What do you mean, Mel? What's going on?" she asked, turning ghostly white.

"Why don't you tell me, Alyce? Explain what's been going on in my absence."

I wanted her to feel trapped so she had no choice but to confess. The walls were closing in fast.

"I…I don't know what you are talking about. Nothing's going on. What's this all about?"

Bright red splotches appeared on Alyce's neck, and I could see a thin layer of perspiration spreading across her forehead. She knew. She knew she had been found out. The game was over. Alyce Cumberland was in a panicked state.

"Well, let's review, shall we?" I glared at her.

She stared back, like she was hoping I would say something, anything but the truth. Alyce swallowed, closing her eyes as she did.

Opening the file, I looked down with pursed lips as Alyce watched me read over the information before me. "It would seem that the president of MD Shoes—the company I have spent my life building—has decided to go rogue, betray me and this firm, steal our fall designs and sell them to our biggest competitor, Shoe Mizer. Isn't that the story, Alyce? Don't try to deny it. I have copies of everything right here: the cancelled checks, the emails, phone records—all of it. So please. Spare me the indecency of denying this. Your deception has been verified by our lawyers, security, and human resource personnel, and the police will be notified as soon as I am ready to do so."

Alyce whimpered pathetically, sinking into the depths of my richly upholstered chair and her own despair. She looked like a caged animal that had been cornered, unable to escape. My anger welled inside me, as I continued my interrogation.

"How could you? How could you do this to me? I thought you cared about this company! I thought you cared about…me." The tears formed behind my eyes, but I pushed them aside. I wanted answers, and I was going to get them before Alyce Cumberland was escorted out by the police. She would be treated like a criminal, but this was the path she had chosen.

Her face became pale and suddenly, she appeared much older than her forty-five years. The wrinkles around her eyes and mouth were more pronounced, like a balloon that was slowly losing air. Alyce's chin was practically buried in her chest, as she tried to process having been unexpectedly exposed, and now she had to come clean.

I slammed my fist on the desk. "Answer me, dammit! Tell me why you did this. Why did you decide to throw away your career and our friendship? Have I read you wrong all these years?" My voice was inching up an octave with each pointed question.

"Have I mistaken a close relationship for petty jealousy and revenge? Were my instincts about you always wrong, or did my going back to college enable you to carry out your deceit when I trusted I had left this company in the best of hands? Jesus Christ, Alyce. Tell me. Look me in the face, you coward! I want to know. Do you hate me that much that you would stoop so low as to sell our designs to a competitor? Tell me!"

"Oh my God, no! I don't hate you. I am so sorry, Mel. I'm so damn sorry."

She sobbed—gut wrenching, regret-filled weeping that served to make me more incensed at her actions. The sight of her, lamenting this betrayal, was making me sick.

"Save it. You made a choice, and you can't undo it. You will have to live with the legal and moral consequences of your greedy decision. I hope the money was worth it. Because now it will all be going to pay your legal bills when I sue you."

I wasn't enjoying this; I felt physically ill having to confront her.

Covering her face with her hands in shame, Alyce kept repeating over and over, "I'm sorry, I'm so sorry."

"And one last thing, Ms. Cumberland. Teresa—my loyal assistant—overheard one of your early conversations with Shoe Mizer. In order to protect MD Shoes, our employees, and her boss, she had the brilliant idea to switch out my confidential, actual design sketches with a portfolio of rejected designs by some third-rate amateur. If Shoe Mizer chooses to produce those shoe designs, they will literally disintegrate off the feet of the women who wear them and their company will go down the toilet along with their reputation and yours. So you see, Alyce what goes around comes back around, every time."

Alyce slumped even further into the chair at my revelation.

"Oh my God," she whispered, "our life is over."

Staring at her, I asked, "What do you mean our life?"

Defeated, she sat back in her seat. "My kids, Mel. My kids."

"What are you talking about?"

"You said I chose this. I didn't choose to do this. In fact, I had no choice at all."

I was confused. "What do you mean? You need to explain yourself."

Standing, Alyce walked over to my credenza, pulling several tissues from a black lacquered box. Wiping her eyes and nose, she sat on the nearby sofa.

"About a year ago, my husband became involved with a group of investors who made some bad business decisions. And, I discovered Doug had a gambling addiction, and had been siphoning off our savings, retirement, and our kid's college funds to pay off some very dangerous people he was in trouble with. When I confronted him, he confessed to it all but we still were left with a mountain of debt and threats to him and our family. I wanted to kill him or at the least, divorce him. But we were trapped. These are some nasty people. And I told you that my Jessie had dreams of going to medical school. We were stuck, buried in a hole so deep I couldn't see a way out. We were going to lose everything."

"Why didn't you come to me? I would have found some way to help you."

"I don't think you have ever been so desperate that you have had to make a life-altering decision to save your family. When you are forced and at a fork in the road where you have no choice but to survive however you can, even if it means choosing the wrong way to move forward. I was not in the right frame of mind to make a rational decision. All I could see were the faces of my children who were the innocent victims of a deeply flawed father they still adored. I knew I was doing the wrong thing by you, but the only choice for my family. I had to choose between you and this company, and my kids. I'm sorry. I chose them. I chose my kids."

She hung her head and softly cried.

I was speechless. It rarely happens, but I was. Not expecting this at all, I sat on the sofa next to Alyce. Not sure if it was a latent, maternal instinct that had never reared its head or simply pure, human compassion, my infuriated heart quelled, my anger subsided. All I could picture was Alyce's kids and a family in turmoil. I was so lucky: I had a wonderful support system in my life that Alyce lacked. She was right about my never having to make the choices she was forced to make, yet wrong about never having been at a crossroads. I had my own mountains to climb, but fortunately, they hadn't been insurmountable.

Alyce turned to look at me. With utter emotional surrender, she realized the inevitable: her situation had become even more dire under these new revelations.

"So now, I have no job and huge legal issues from MD Shoes and Shoe Mizer on top of all the other crap. My career is over, my family's lives are in danger and I want to die. But I am trying to hold it all together. And I'm barely hanging on by a thread."

Reaching over, I took her in my arms and held her as she sobbed. She was the child now, and I allowed her to be. I realized that her desperate circumstances superseded my pain over her betrayal. It was an irremediable, no-win situation for both of us. Alyce had made a grave decision to save her loved ones. I was collateral damage.

Clinging to me, I softly spoke to her. "All right. Sit back and let's talk."

Embarrassed and ashamed, she once again expressed regret.

Shaking my head, I gathered my thoughts, choosing my words carefully.

"What's done is done. I don't agree with how you handled your predicament, but I understand why you did it. Obviously, I cannot let you continue in your role as president, and your job will be terminated. I would never be able to trust you again and you have violated every tenant of our mission statement here at MD Shoes. However, I have decided I will not press any charges against you. You have also forfeited any severance you would have received under normal circumstances, but I will agree to write you a letter of recommendation so that you may secure employment to support your family. No one but my legal team and Teresa will know about this sordid affair, and I will announce you have decided to pursue other opportunities outside this company. You can walk out of here with your head held high, with one less thing to worry about. And a letter of support from Melinda Drake carries a whole lot of weight. But I need your word that you will never let things sink so low again that you will jeopardize everything because of it."

With a weak smile, Alyce nodded. "Thank you. I don't deserve your kindness or your generosity, but from the bottom of my heart, I appreciate it. You have been more than fair and I will never forget it."

I stood and walked over to my desk. I scribbled a name and phone number on a piece of paper and handed it to her.

"Here is the name of an excellent debt counselor. I strongly suggest you and your husband contact him for professional advice on how to manage your financial situation. I'm sure he's seen and heard it all. You have to crawl out from under this mess. I hope you can."

Taking the paper and the advice, Alyce stood, anxious to leave.

"I—thank you, Mel. I hope one day you will find it in your heart to forgive me. I loathe the person I was forced to become because of Doug, and I need to make some hard decisions regarding our marriage. Thank you, on behalf of my children, for granting me amnesty when I don't deserve it. You are one hell of a woman, boss, and friend. I'll never forget you, and will regret that of all the things I lost, your friendship was the most precious. I'm truly, truly sorry. I'm going to go quietly and clean out my desk. You can have Teresa and security watch, as I'm sure you have no faith left in me that I won't take anything more from you. Until the day I die, my greatest regret will be that I lost you."

"Just find yourself. And take care of your kids. That's all that matters. I'll have Teresa email you my letter of recommendation by the end of next week. Good luck, and be well, Alyce."

Collapsing into bed that night, I turned on my side, burying my face into the pillow. This had been the day from hell. When I finally allowed myself to remove the armour and feel something besides anger and betrayal, the emotion of the day overtook me. It took a hell of a lot to make me cry, but I was gutted.

My phone buzzed on the nightstand with an incoming text. Straining to read it through tear filled eyes, I smiled.

Hi Melinda, it's me your new friend SPENCER ;) HAHA LOL ☺ Can I come visit next week? I am soooo bored!!! My dad is being so extra ☹ How about tomorrow!!!!!!!!!!!!! :D

And just like that, God sent me a new friend when I needed one the most.

CHAPTER TWENTY-THREE

"Sorry, Mel. But you look like the angel of death. What a debacle that was. I sure wouldn't have been so nice. I would've thrown her, along with that lousy, gamblin' husband's tush in the pokey." Teresa's tirade began first thing Monday morning.

Rubbing my throbbing temples (even after a feeble attempt at swallowing several doses of ibuprofen) I checked my reflection in the large, ornate mirror that hung in my office. From a distance, I didn't look too worn out. All I kept seeing when I finally closed my eyes Friday night was Alyce and the look of utter desperation on her face. Having never married nor committed fully to someone else to the point where I put complete faith in them to always do the right thing—especially with joint finances—made me appreciate that I had ultimate control of all aspects of my life. Love was a gamble, in so many ways, and perhaps I had never wanted to have another person who would require that level of corroboration. This was one of the reasons I assumed no man could handle me. I needed to be in control—total control of it all. This was who I was, and I had no desire to change.

When Alyce left my office, I called Teresa in and told her to make sure Alyce cleaned out her desk, and took only her personal items. Explaining I would fill her in later, I told her not to have any discussion with Alyce. I called my security manager and asked him to come up and discretely observe her and then escort her from the building. He searched her bag downstairs to insure that no company files or property had been taken. I informed Alyce that she would be contacted by human resources. However much I may have pitied her situation, I was no saint in how I let her off the hook so easily. In the end, I had lost nothing, except a friendship. Alyce, on the other hand, had lost everything except the love of her children. I wanted her gone; out of my business and out of my life. This chapter of my life was closed, and we all needed to move on.

I have a high functioning reset button. I get over things fast, tend not to hold too many grudges, and look for the silver lining. If I harbor negative thoughts and live in the past I can never enjoy today and have hope for the future. There is always a second chance, a glass half full, an opportunity to start again. I don't dwell on what did happen; I make something better happen instead.

One of my first actions on Tuesday was to have Teresa arrange a meeting with Toby Horton, the young designer whose drawings my deceptive assistant swapped out to Shoe Mizer to save our butts. If anything good was to come out of the whole Alyce Cumberland fiasco, I was going to ensure that this kid got his shot. I knew he had potential; he needed mentoring, and I was going to pay it forward like Pierre Roussel had done for me all those years ago in Paris. This is what I meant by the silver lining of disaster, of making lemonade...

I need to stop thinking in clichés.

By midmorning, I remembered I needed to respond to Spencer Sweeney. Checking my calendar for the week, I saw my only available day was Thursday, where I would be able to free myself for the afternoon. Initially, I had planned on filling that slot with a long lunch with Steven or my parents or my age-appropriate girlfriends. On the other hand, I was looking forward to showing off my assets here at MD Shoes to Spencer and perhaps a few of my personal assets to Dr. Jack Sweeney. It was a curiosity to me that each time I thought of him lately, I felt a kinship, a warm glow flowing over me. That, or perhaps it was some kind of indigestion—or early menopause.

Hey Spencer! It's Melinda Drake. Hope you are enjoying your break. I am free on Thursday afternoon if you would like to come to the Big Apple. Please check with your father and get back to me by tonight so I can schedule it on my busy calendar. Hope to see you soon! ☺

A nanosecond later, my phone pinged with a response. I don't think Spencer could have possibly checked with Jack before she responded with an enthusiastic YES! But I'm guessing she prepped him that when my invitation came through, they would be going.

On Thursday, I bounded out of bed and performed my regular routine of coffee, a forty-five minute workout on the treadmill, and a shower. I embraced the day with a positive attitude in anticipation of touring the city with my guests from Philadelphia. The weather was beginning to soften again, so I still needed a warm coat but without the hat and scarf to ward off hypothermia. I donned a pair of jeans, a sweater, and knee-high boots with a modest heel from last year's MD line.

My schedule for the early part of the day was light. I told Teresa I wanted to catch up on all necessary correspondence via phone and email and that I was not to be interrupted. Tomorrow would be my last full day in the office, and I would be in back-to-back meetings all day. Until I finished with classes in June, I would be dropping in periodically in the New York office, and after my graduation, I would finally be back full-time. I suddenly realized how much I was going to miss my brief tenure at Pennwood University, but I knew this was where I belonged. This was my real life. I chuckled as I thought of the enigmatic Phillip Gunderson and his role in all this. I made a mental note to call him when I returned in June, to either thank him or murder him for planting the seed that had brought so much upheaval to my life.

"Ms. Drake? This is Eve Ellery from security. Your guests have arrived and are here in the lobby. Shall I send them up?"

"No, Eve. I'll come to get them, thank you."

"Very good."

Logging off my computer, I let Teresa know they were here and that I was meeting them in the lobby to take them on a tour of the factory and offices. She had made a lunch reservation for us at a place I thought Spencer would enjoy, and I put together an itinerary of tourist traps and secret places around Times Square I knew they both would get excited about. I was looking forward to a little relaxing time of my own. Hell—it was my spring break, too.

Walking through the turnstile, I observed Jack Sweeney, leaning against the wall. I must admit, my heart warmed or flipped or something at the sight of him. Not used to dealing with him out of an academic setting—or the underwear section of a store—he appeared to be already bored, as if it were the last thing he felt like doing on a precious day off from work.

Spencer, however, was animated and mobile, moving around the lobby, mesmerized by the operations and frenetic pace of corporate American capitalism. I had hoped this would be an enjoyable day for all of us, and if Jack was bored, then to hell with him. I remembered what it was like to have Spencer's enthusiasm for something you felt passionate about. Not sure what this kid's talents and interests were, I would try to expose her to all that MD Shoes had to offer, watching to spot the fire that comes with discovering the thing in this life that fits you like the perfect pair of shoes.

"Good morning, Sweeney family. Welcome to MD Shoes. I'll be your tour guide for today," I smiled, giving my best cruise director spiel. My attempt at levity sailed right over Spencer's head; Jack seemed oblivious, too. The business bustle, combined with my shoe factory held little fascination for the likes of Jack Sweeney. I knew he was a history buff, but ladies shoes? Probably not so much. But this day wasn't about him. Today was for Spencer and her desire to learn about my company. But damn—Jack was beginning to invade my thoughts at the most random of moments, and I couldn't figure out why.

"Hey, Melinda. I can't believe I'm finally here. I told my friends I was coming, and they didn't believe me. This place is so chill." She fidgeted with excitement, wrapping her arms tightly around her torso.

As my employees entered or exited the building, they waved or greeted me, while Jack's eyes followed my every response. Even though we sat on a committee together, I served in a secondary role to Dean Samuels and the other faculty and administrators. In this place, I was the center of it all, the reason it existed. Jack seemed to grasp this fact. I hoped he was impressed.

"Well, Spencer. I will have to send you home with a pair of my shoes or boots, along with a few friends and family gift cards for you to impress them with. Don't worry—they will be well aware you were here, complete with selfies, to prove we're friends." Turning in his direction, I said, "Hello, Jack. Enjoying your break?"

"Um, yes, thank you. Even more, now that my daughter will stop haunting me. Thank you again, for hosting us today. Spencer is beside-herself-excited to be here."

"I am so happy you, um she, um—let's get started, shall we?" I feared I was blushing.

"OMG, Melinda. This place is bomb. Is it all yours?" Spencer asked, running her hand along the beige, marbled wall of the elevator.

"All mine, kiddo."

Jack stared at me as I spoke. I couldn't get a handle on what he was thinking. He was guarded and cautious. Wishing I knew what the story of their family was (and the identity of the mysterious lunch companion), I decided to try and live in the moment and focus on this young woman and her eagerness to be here in New York City.

"I have a wonderful afternoon planned for us," I said, pressing the button on the wall. We entered the elevator, along with several of my employees who continued to greet me, their boss.

The doors of the elevator opened on the third floor, exposing the guts and glory of the MD Shoes operations. As we stepped out, the scent of leather and machine oil, combined with the sounds of heavy-gauged sewing machines and small hammers tapping on tables, produced a natural high for me that almost nothing else could. Creating a product that women chose to adorn their feet with every day was exquisitely satisfying, like creating a painting, a sculpture, a best-selling book, or a piece of music. These shoes were physical forms that I put out in to the world, eager to please and satisfy. I imagined this was what parenting felt like—pride, awe, fear of the public liking your creation, hoping for love and acceptance. Each season brought a new crop of styles to the market and a chance to further please or disappoint the women who purchased them. I felt a duty to deliver a quality product year after year to my loyal customers, and it all began here in this factory.

Spencer's eyes widened in wonder at the expansive room filled with massive machines and skilled workers. The factory encompassed the best innovations in technology side-by-side with craftspeople performing hand-sewn artistry. I loved entering this place, marveling at my fabricators and technicians working together with our automated robots. Both Jack and his daughter gazed around the room at the tables piled high with scraps of leather and foam. Guiding Spencer and Jack over to my lead artisan, I pointed.

"Watch, Spencer. See how he takes that pattern and uses a razor to cut around the form of what will become a gorgeous piece of footwear. Ravi, these are my friends, Spencer and Jack."

Ravi, with me since the inception of MD Shoes, smiled broadly. He loved to show off whenever I brought someone to his workroom, taking special care to demonstrate a skill gleaned long ago in a country far from the United States of America. An immigrant like so many of my employees, he worked hard to make his mark in the industry. There have been a couple of times other shoe manufacturers have tried to lure him away, but he remained loyal. For all MD Shoes had provided for him, his family, and his career, it cannot match the way he has stood by my side as well.

"Wow, this is so unreal! I wish I could do that," Spencer said, her eyes laser focused as Ravi continued to slice through the pattern, with a vision of what the final product would look like.

Grabbing the stool next to him, as it scraped against the gray, concrete floor, he beckoned Spencer. "Sit, young lady. I will teach you."

Looking to her father for permission, Jack nodded his head. Spencer shed her black coat and sat at the table to watch the process of shoe construction from its basic elements.

"Watch, Miss Spencer. I'll show you how. And then I'll show you why."

With a twinkle in his exceptionally talented eyes, he explained the process of how each shoe is put through the paces of construction, and how it passed from one artisan to another. Spencer was fascinated while Ravi explained that there are multiple operations involved in producing a pair of shoes, including designing—where sketches are created—stamping or cutting of the leather, assembling, molding the shoe into its intended shape, sewing the pieces together, and finishing and polishing the shoe. Then it is tested for the necessary quality controls so that it may be distributed and sold to the public.

"Come, Miss Spencer. I will take you to the different departments so you can see each step. Shoemaking is a long tradition that has not changed too much over the years, except for some of the improved technology of our machines. Would you like to see?" Ravi asked, looking over to her and her father for permission.

"Are you kidding me? Yes! It's okay, right Dad, Melinda?"

Jack glanced at me.

"I assure you, she will be more than fine and in capable hands," I said.

"Very well, then. Tour away."

"OMG, this is so awesome. Can I leave my coat here?" Spencer asked.

"Tell you what. I'll take it with me to my office. How much time will you need, Ravi? We have a noon lunch reservation."

"No problem, Miss Drake. I'll have her back to your office in plenty of time for lunch."

Turning to Jack, I asked, "Would you like to take the tour also? If not, we could wait for them back in my office and perhaps grab a cup of coffee."

"Coffee sounds good. Spencer, mind your manners and don't drive these poor people crazy with a million questions."

"Dad you're embarrassing me," she whispered through gritted teeth while Ravi and I smiled. I'm sure his five children probably were "embarrassed" a time or two as well.

"Let's be off," Ravi instructed as Spencer handed me her coat and trailed behind her tour guide to the back of the room.

"Shall we?" I asked, leading Jack back to the elevator.

"I'm all yours, Melinda," Jack said, suddenly realizing what he said and how it could be interpreted. "I mean, yes, lead the way."

As we walked down the hallway, I could feel his eyes on me. I felt smug, enjoying the fact that he was here in my world and that I felt good about how it looked.

When we arrived at my office, Teresa was sitting at her desk, typing on her keyboard. She looked up when she saw us approaching. I knew she was waiting to meet the mysterious man and his daughter she had made the lunch reservations for at a nearby sushi restaurant. I provided her minimal information on Jack Sweeney because there wasn't anything to say. I explained he was a colleague at the university and that his daughter had taken a liking to me. I spared poor Jack the humiliation of the shopping confrontation and how Spencer and I bonded over bras.

"Jack Sweeney, this is my assistant, Teresa Jenks."

"Pleasure to meet you, Ms. Jenks," Jack said with a polite nod of his head.

With her eyes scanning every inch of him, she stood and reached out her hand to shake his. I knew all her little devious tricks: checking to see the status of his ring finger (was he single), determine if it was sweaty (would indicate being nervous and therefore smitten), strength of grip (wuss or stud), feel skin texture (hardworking or lazy ass). Teresa would have an opinion on Jack whether I wanted to hear it or not.

"Likewise. Melinda, can I bring you and your guest anything?" she asked.

"Could you get us coffee, please? We are going to wait in my office while Ravi takes Jack's daughter on the grand tour, then we will head out for lunch. Are we good with the reservation?"

"All set. Let me exit out of this report I'm working on and I'll be right in."

I knew she thought Jack was a looker. He was in fact, quite a handsome, educated, articulate man. I led the professor into my office, leaving the door open for Teresa. Jack strode over to the wall of windows in my office, peering at the activity on the street far below him. Deciding not to sit at my desk so as not to appear like it was a normal workday for me, I took a seat on the sofa and relaxed for the first time that morning. Watching this man who was a bit of an enigma, I was hoping that today would allow me to get to know him and better understand the mystery of his personality.

"Are you a fan of city life, Jack?"

He turned and smiled. "Sometimes. I appreciate it, if nothing else. But in answer to your question, no. I am a country boy at heart. I prefer the rolling hills of Pennsylvania to the roll of trucks and taxi cabs on asphalt."

"How lyrical of you, Dr. Sweeney,"

Jack walked over and sat on the opposite side of the sofa, his long legs stretched out in front of him. His clothes were clean and pressed, yet his shoes told the story of a man who probably struggled to make ends meet on the salary of an employee of a private college trying to raise a child in an era of excess and expensive necessary items like smart phones and laptops.

"I have my moments. I'm actually working on a new book that is tapping into my romantic side." He laughed.

"Really? You have a romantic side, do you? I would have never guessed." Once again, I wondered about the woman he was with in the restaurant.

"Oh yes. Actually, this book is all about the letters that Civil War soldiers wrote to their loved ones from the battlefield: letters to wives and girlfriends, parents and siblings. I am finding it fascinating, and, I must admit, emotional, too."

"What a wonderful project that must be—sad but hopeful, I'm sure."

"It is. The idea came to me while..."

Teresa entered with a tray of coffee, cream, sugar and a small plate of cookies we kept stashed in our break room. Although lunch was fast approaching, my assistant was well aware that my mid morning hunger alarm had probably gone off. Do you see why I love this woman? Coffee and cookies at the exact minute I desire them.

"Sorry to interrupt. I didn't ask if you preferred tea, Dr. Sweeney?" she asked.

"No thank you, Ms. Jenks. Coffee is perfect."

"Teresa, please. Only my kid's teachers call me Mrs. Jenks, and only if they are in trouble," she laughed, placing the tray on the glass table in front of the sofa.

"Don't let her fool you, Jack. She has the best kids on the planet—smart, polite, hard-working like their mother. And dad."

"Thanks Mel. Best kids and best husband, and a pretty good boss," Teresa confirmed.

"Well, perhaps you could pass along a few tips for this confused and often flustered dad. Sometimes I feel as if I'm doing and saying all the wrong things," Jack uttered, reaching for a mug of black coffee. "I seem to embarrass Spencer all the time."

As she walked toward the doorway, Teresa turned. "I always told my kids: don't ever embarrass me and I will never embarrass you. It works both ways, Doc."

"I'll try to remember that," he said, dunking a mint cookie into his cup.

"Close the door, Teresa. Thank you."

She nodded, leaving us to continue our conversation.

"So Jack, go on about the book. I'd love to hear more about it." And in typical male fashion, Jack Sweeney waxed poetic on his passionate manuscript and how his publisher was so enthusiastic about it and believed it could possibly be turned into a documentary or film and perhaps his friend Thomas Clark would be interested in producing it...

I sat listening to him, yet at the same time I was making a list in my head about all the things I had to get done before I headed back to campus on Sunday. Several issues here in the office required my immediate attention, plus I needed a haircut and my eyebrows done and I wanted to have dinner with my parents on Saturday. I made a mental note for Teresa to have a car service bring them into the city because it would be more convenient than me going to them. I also wanted to touch base by phone with my girlfriends—my old girlfriends and I mean old as in age and timeline—not my new Gen Z girlfriends back at Pennwood. I realized as I was doing these mental gymnastics in my brain that my life was like a hamster wheel and it would probably never stop spinning in a continuous loop of movement.

Meanwhile, Jack finally stopped talking and was waiting for a reply to the question he had apparently asked me while I was off on a tangent.

"Melinda? What do you think?" Jack asked, puzzled.

Thank God, my phone rang and I went to my desk and answered it. It was Ravi asking if Spencer could stay and have lunch with the staff because they were ordering sandwiches and after, requested to take her to the design studio to see how the artists created their sketches. Would that be all right with Spencer's father?

As I relayed this change in plans to Jack, he agreed. I hung up and sat on the edge of my desk.

"So I guess it's just you and me for lunch, Dr. Sweeney. Are you okay with that?" I asked.

He stood, placing his cup on the tray. "Ms. Drake, I can't think of a nicer way to spend an afternoon in New York City. I'll follow wherever you lead me."

CHAPTER TWENTY-FOUR

My favorite Japanese restaurant was three blocks from the office, so we decided to walk. I must admit I was a little bit thrilled and excited that I was about to have Jack all to myself at lunch. This felt like a date. In my wildest dreams, I never expected to be alone with this man, on my turf, walking around New York City. I told Teresa to text me as soon as she heard from Ravi and Spencer. But I knew my crew; they would keep their new protégé through most of the afternoon, showing off and enjoying their enthusiasm for MD Shoes.

Before I would allow myself to make a mistake, I decided to come right out and ask Jack about the mysterious woman he was with in the restaurant that day. They obviously had a relationship that was emotionally intimate. I wasn't going to invest my time and energy in a person who was involved with someone else.

"I need to ask you something, Jack."

He turned to look at me. "What is it?"

"Last week I happened to see you at Belle's Bistro."

Jack cocked his head, thinking. "Oh, yes. I remember seeing you there."

"I was there with my friend. You were tucked away in the corner. You were also with a woman, engrossed in what looked to be a serious conversation. Is she someone special in your life?" I asked.

His eyes lit up. "Yes, very special. And to Spencer."

Crap. I knew it. Was it Spencer's mother? A girlfriend? I tried to look nonchalant. "I see."

With a slow and sexy smile, he continued. "Yes, I try to meet my sister Cara once a month. You know, stay connected with the family. She lives in Ardmore with her husband and tries to give me parenting advice even though she doesn't have any kids—yet. They are trying, but are having fertility issues. No one has it easy. We vent to each other, always have."

I nodded in agreement, lowering my head so he couldn't see my satisfaction with his answer to my nosy inquiry. Moving on...

Jack strolled leisurely down the street, noticing every detail of the architecture of the buildings we passed.

"Do you see that, Melinda?" he pointed. "The stone used here probably dates back to the turn of the nineteenth century. So many of the older structures here in Manhattan are intermingled with modern skyscrapers. It's fascinating to see."

I realized how important it is to view the world through another's eyes. In all the rushing and chaos of my life, I never noticed such details. I paid attention to other things, and maybe they were less important. Perhaps I needed to listen more closely to those around me.

"Jack, you are a man of many mysteries. In addition to American history, I assume you have a passion for architecture?"

He stared at me. "I have a passion for many things."

It takes quite a bit to stop me in my tracks, but that did. This man was a mystery. On the surface he presented himself as a bit of the typical, boring professor. Then he would blurt out these obscure statements that made me wonder about how deep he actually was. Jack Sweeney was a challenge. Who doesn't love that?

"Okay, then." We arrived in front of the restaurant. "Here we are— the best sushi in New York City."

"Terrific—I'm starved," Jack said, holding open the door.

After greeting the hostess, she led us over to my standard reserved table. We both asked for water, and Jack deferred to me to order our dishes saying he ate anything, correctly assuming I would pick their best. I selected a wide variety of sashimi, sushi, and nigiri so we could share.

As I took chopsticks out from the rolled napkin that I then placed on my lap, I saw that Jack was looking around the room with an odd look.

"Is something wrong?" I asked.

"Not at all. I imagined you lunching in a far more elegant place."

"When Spencer told me you both liked sushi, I thought she would enjoy something casual. My nephews hate fancy places so I bring them here. If I had known it was going to be just the two of us, I might have chosen differently. But you will see—this food is off the charts good."

"I am already impressed with you Melinda, and it has nothing at all to do with your choice of eating establishments."

"How do you do that?" I asked.

"Do what?"

"Render me speechless. Believe me, it's a talent you possess because it doesn't happen often."

"I say what I feel and what I see," he said, looking right into my eyes.

"You're doing it again. Your eyes disarm me." I must have been turning three shades of red, and he smiled.

"All right, I will stop. And I admit—I'm happy Spencer stayed behind."

"Why would that be?"

I needed to hear him say it. Because I didn't believe he even liked me all that much. Because I admit I was developing feelings for him, and I had no clue how he felt about me. Because I wouldn't believe anything unless I heard the words come directly from his mouth.

But of course our food arrived, and Jack was starving, and I deduced that a man's stomach superseded his heart because his focus raced from my face to his plate, and the moment was lost.

"Wow, this is unbelievable," he said, as the waiter filled our entire table with the best tuna, shrimp, crab, and vegetable delights on the menu.

"Dig in, Jack," I mumbled, realizing I was just as famished and that any conversation about feelings would simply have to wait.

As we ate, our conversation diverted to our childhoods. I told him about my siblings and my parents and my totally idyllic life in a town where no one locked their doors and everyone respected and looked out for one another. Jack hailed from Wisconsin, the fourth child in a brood of five born to a mom who was a nurse and a dad who was a mail carrier. He grew up in a normal Methodist household where the most trouble he ever got into was hitting a baseball through a neighbor's window. He never smoked marijuana or tried drugs of any kind and didn't go to his senior prom because he was too shy to ask anyone. His first girlfriend was in his sophomore year of college, but it only lasted a few months before he met Spencer's mother later that same year. That was when he fell deeply in love, he confessed.

Our waiter cleared away our empty plates, and we ordered coffee, but no dessert. My skinny jeans required a new description after this feast. I leaned back in my seat, seeing that Jack had drifted off into a sad place in telling the story of his life.

"I would like to hear about Spencer's mother, if you feel comfortable telling me. If not, it's okay," I said.

He forced a tepid smile. "I don't speak of her often, especially to Spencer. I'm not sure if it's right or wrong. I get angry, and I don't like to be angry at the mother of my child because Spencer is the best thing in my life, and I thank my ex-wife for the gift of giving birth to her."

I melted. I had no idea what happened to Spencer's mother, assuming at first she was deceased. Apparently, there was a story behind her not being around that was far worse than I had imagined.

Jack sat quietly, lightly tapping his spoon on the table. His eyes simmered with a combination of flight and fright as his jaw moved sideways in a great effort to stop from clenching his teeth. There was a bluish vein in his temple that instantly became enlarged.

It is odd to see when someone who is normally composed turn into someone unfamiliar and on the verge of erupting when it is so out of character for them. Only once did I see my father, the soul of patience, lose his mind and rail (with expletives) against my brother, Kyle. He mouthed off to my mother when she wouldn't let him have the car to take out some girl he was trying to impress. Believe me, Kyle never crossed my parents again.

Breaking this spell, the waiter arrived with two mugs of coffee and a small bowl of creamers. I reached over for two, stirring them into my cup, while Jack seemed to struggle for an appropriate way to explain the apparent debacle that was his wife and their marriage.

"Jack, if this is too hard, you don't have to…"

"It's only hard for my daughter, who deserved better than what she got. Which, by the way, was nothing. I mean, what kind of mother turns her back on her child?"

Oh. My. God.

"What?" I was stunned.

"That's right. My wife, my ex-wife, Spencer's mother, abandoned her own flesh and blood."

My eyes widened in disbelief. I thought of my own mother and how she forfeited her teaching career to stay home and raise us. How she had been there for everything in our lives. I simply could not envision my life without my mom—and my dad. They have been there for the best, and worst. But I couldn't dwell on myself. This was all about Spencer—and Jack.

"But why?" I asked.

Jack grappled with controlling himself and his feelings about his ex-wife. He lowered his head. He was trying to choose his words carefully.

"I want you to know I haven't spoken about this in a long time. My family tried to help at first, but it did no good. I took Spencer to a therapist because she couldn't eat or sleep. She had nightmares for months. I finally had to seek counseling to deal with my anger against what she did to both of us, especially our child."

"Oh, Jack—how awful. What happened to make a mother do such a thing? I don't understand."

With steely, gray-blue eyes, Jack looked at the ceiling, probably to avoid having tears roll out of them. He forced himself to sip his hot coffee, and after placing his mug on the table, sat straight in his chair.

"When I married Molly, we had just finished college and she was having a hard time finding a job. There wasn't much of a call for philosophy majors back then, and she had no direction. The only job offered to her was being a receptionist in a non-profit homeless shelter in Center City. I advised her to accept it, suggesting she had to start somewhere and build her résumé since she had no experience except as a waitress in high school and college. In hindsight, I guess I'm probably responsible for what came later because, in essence, I pressured her to take the job. We were living on my grad school stipend, and I was working an extra job in the campus cafeteria to cover the cost of food. And then Molly got pregnant."

Although I was trying not to react, I think my left eyebrow shot up when Jack said this. I mean, they had no money and she gets pregnant? Hello? What about birth control?

"I can guess what you must be thinking. How stupid can two people be?"

Busted. "I'm not here to judge. I'm here to listen. Please, go on."

"She worked until the day she went into labor. We couldn't possibly afford day care, and our families lived too far away to help, so Molly quit her job to stay home with Spencer. Luckily, she was able to take in a couple of kids to babysit, and we managed to squeak by every month. Once I finished my master's degree, I was offered an assistant professor position. We could finally breathe a little."

Jack took a sip of his coffee, while I sat there, trying to imagine the life he led with his young wife and infant daughter. My childhood was so easy. I lived a comfortable life, and now, could buy anything I desired without even glancing at the price tag.

"In the first few years of our marriage and Spencer's toddler years, we were happy. We were a normal family. I loved the small liberal arts college I was teaching at, and we made a lot of friends in the area. We took turns hosting parties, getting each other's mail when someone was away, pooling resources to fix broken pipes and cars and household appliances. It was a good life. When Spencer started kindergarten, a girlfriend of Molly's invited her to go to her church. They were looking for volunteers to help collect clothing for a mission overseas. Molly was hoping it would lead to an eventual paying opportunity, because this friend of hers was hired by the church to keep their books. After two years of being a volunteer, they offered Molly a position as lead summer camp counselor. It wasn't much money, but she was thrilled to have a job again and be contributing to our family's finances."

Our waiter appeared, asking if we wanted anything else. I shook my head, requesting the check but explained that we were not in a rush. He nodded and left while Jack continued.

"I noticed that something was changing with my wife, my ex-wife. She had become a member of this church she worked for, but one of the congregants was talking about creating an alternate branch. He and several members disagreed with some of their tenants such as having female clergy, divorce, and their acceptance of gay people into the congregation. Molly and I started to have arguments every single day, and it was beginning to have a negative effect on Spencer. She reverted back to sucking her thumb and acting out at home and school.

Molly was changing her beliefs about everything, including how she felt about our marriage. She wanted to stop taking birth control pills because she was told by this religious nut-job Josiah that it was a sin to interfere with God's plan. We could barely afford one kid and all our other loans and expenses, let alone have any more kids. She stopped taking the pill and so we stopped..." Jack lowered his head in embarrassment. "I can't believe I'm telling you this," he whispered.

"You don't have to if it makes you uncomfortable. But sometimes we need to talk about things. I'm here to listen; I'll keep listening to you, Jack. We all go through stuff—that's life." I reached across and gently put my hand over his. He grabbed my hand in return and squeezed it. "Please, go on."

Nodding, he continued.

"Although I was confused and upset about the changing relationship between my wife and me, the worst part of this whole thing was Molly's attitude and behavior toward Spencer. You see, my daughter hated wearing dresses, liked to play in the dirt, liked to wear her hair short, preferred the company of boys over girls. I am aware this is common for some females, especially at the tender age of seven. I tried to explain this to Molly, but this asshole Josiah and the other members of the church who had defected to follow him kept putting these distorted and untrue ideas in her head. She was always trying to get Spencer to play with dolls and paint her nails. She forced her to wear clothes that were feminine and frilly and told her she could only play with other girls. Spencer would rush into my arms when I came home from the college, complaining that her mother was making her do things she didn't want to do. When I demanded Molly stop, she accused both Spencer and me of being possessed by the devil and that we were doomed for hell. It became a daily barrage of fire and brimstone. I could see how much damage was being done to our family. One Saturday afternoon, I went to see Josiah

Crawford—that was the asshole's name—to tell him to leave us alone and stop filling my wife's head with lies and wild accusations. But when I arrived…"

Jack stopped talking. He took a slow breath as he remembered. Tears welled in his eyes.

"It's okay, Jack," I said, this time reaching for his hand to hold.

"My wife was a very affectionate, physical person," he said, struggling to use the appropriate terms to describe her. "I should have known. We hadn't been intimate in months."

Oh, God.

"When I arrived at his house, I went back to the small barn on his property that had become a makeshift meeting place for what he was now calling the Church of the Good News. I assumed he would be in his office, and when I opened the door and entered, there was no one in the chapel. I walked down the hall and found him sitting at his desk, with his back to the door. He turned around when he realized he had a visitor, staring like he had never seen me before when we had been introduced several times."

"I can't stand that kind of arrogance," I said.

"I reminded him who I was and insisted he leave my wife alone and stop poisoning her against me and her child. I told him he was a fraud and that Molly would not be returning to his so called flock. Turning around in his chair, he smirked. I wanted to punch him in the face. He was this scrawny, dirty piece of garbage and I had nearly a foot of height over him. It was then that he succeeded in knocking the wind out of me."

"What, Jack?"

The anger rose in his face. But there was so much more. It was disgust, even horror, in realizing that the person he thought he knew was not that person at all and may never have been.

"He proceeded to tell me that Molly had seen the light of righteousness and she had given herself over to the Church of the Good News. I was powerless to control her. When I asked what he meant by "giving herself over," Crawford leaned over and clicked a button on his computer to open a file. There, on the screen, was my wife—the mother of my child—doing things to him and other members of this so called "church" that made my skin crawl. It was beyond pornographic."

"Jack—I'm…so sorry." What could I say? I didn't expect this revelation and didn't quite know how to respond.

His face had gone pale, and he was biting the inside of his bottom lip, struggling to maintain his composure.

"How did you react? What did you do?" I asked, almost afraid to hear his answer.

"He had a bag of golf clubs in the corner, so I grabbed one and smashed it into the computer screen, yanked the monitor from the desk and threw it out the window. Then I grabbed him and beat the living daylights out of him. I broke his nose, dislocated his jaw, and fractured a couple of his ribs. I haven't fought like that since I was a teenager. My hand was pretty swollen, but I didn't care."

"Did he try to retaliate against you?" I asked. "Did he press charges?"

"No. I told him if he tried to, I would expose his secret, sordid lifestyle to his followers and the entire town. I left there and went home to confront Molly. She wasn't the least bit remorseful. I demanded she pack her things and get out and never come back, and I forbid her to have any contact with Spencer."

I swallowed. "And how did she respond to that?"

"Like she didn't even care, like I had somehow set her free from the responsibilities of being a mother so she could freely whore it up with any man she wanted. The sad part was that she ranted that I had made Spencer into a demon and that atheism was a sin and that we were overtaken by evil spirits, and yet she was the one who was possessed and consumed by a contemptuously fake, snake-oil salesman. I threw her out that day, and we never heard from her again. Weeks later when I finished out the semester, I resigned my faculty position and Spencer and I moved to Philadelphia."

Reeling, my eyes flooded with tears. I was blessed with such an amazing life and a wonderful, loving mother—I couldn't imagine the scars this type of situation would leave on a child. Jack bore his own pain from the betrayal of his wife. That was something I could and did understand.

There were no words I could say to respond to such a story. I reached over the small table and ran the back of my hand over his cheek. Closing his eyes, he leaned into my touch. When he opened his eyes sadness clouded his features.

"I've never shared that with anyone Melinda. But for some strange reason, I wanted you to know. I'm a private person, and, as you can imagine, both Spencer and I have trust issues."

Leaning forward, I took his hand once again. "Your heart has been smashed into a thousand pieces. It takes a long time to put it back together. Believe me—I get it."

A quizzical expression appeared on his handsome, strong face.

"Mine is a tale for another time. All I can say is that you are a terrific father, and your ex-wife is a complete imbecile who didn't deserve you or that amazing young girl."

"Thank you. I appreciate that," he said, squeezing my hand before settling his own back on his lap.

Our waiter appeared with the check. When he placed it on the table, Jack reached for it. I grabbed it before he had a chance.

"Melinda, please. You have been so generous already. Please let me get this."

"No sir. You are my guest while here in New York. I insist," I informed him.

Sitting back, he raised his hands in surrender. "Very well, then. After all, you are the boss."

"That I am. And I appreciate the fact that you acquiesced so easily, Dr. Sweeney. I feared a fight with you," I quipped, reaching into my purse to retrieve my wallet.

He peered at me through his dark tortoise shell eyeglasses and sighed. "Melinda, if nothing else, I am a realist. As I have just elucidated, my male ego has already been bashed and bruised beyond its limits. I am a tenured American history professor who lives in a modest house with a teenage daughter who will head off to college in a few short years, undoubtedly not choosing where her father works, where she could attend for free. No, I'm sure she will select some private school in a large city that will plunge me into debt until I die. You, however, are a deservedly wealthy woman. I accept and admire that. I hope one day Spencer aspires to the same level of success that you have achieved. I am certain the fact that you can place this lunch on your expense account gives you great pleasure and satisfaction. I am duly impressed. It is my hope that in the near future, you will allow me to show you my world and the things that are important to me. But I'm warning you: lunch will probably be served on paper plates and require several napkins."

I smiled back at the charming face looking directly into my eyes, this person who seemed to have touched something in me that I didn't know was there. Never had I met a man who simply accepted my success and stature without being threatened by it. "For your information, sir, I never put personal dates on my business expense accounts. This was pleasure, not business. That would be the equivalent of cheating my employees which I would never do," I explained as I signed both copies in the folder.

Jack looked at me and shook his head in what I hoped was admiration.

"No Melinda. Of course you wouldn't. And that is exactly what I like about you."

Be still, my heart.

CHAPTER TWENTY-FIVE

When Jack and I finished lunch, we walked back to my office so we could retrieve Spencer and tour the city. I was pleasantly surprised when Jack reached for my hand (which remarkably did not sweat) and held it as we strolled the few blocks to MD Shoes. He shared such personal, private pain with me that afternoon, and it was his way of saying *I'm taking your hand because I trust you now. I've given you a glimpse into who I am and why I am this way. Please tread carefully with my broken heart.* I stroked his thumb over our clasped hands, hoping it would reassure him that I knew the place he had been in the disastrous relationship with his wife, and that I had been similarly caught off-guard by people I had loved too.

Spencer went home that day with three of pairs of shoes, a gaggle of new friends who thought she was wonderful ("like a sponge" as Ravi described her), and a dream for her future.

"Oh, Melinda. The factory, the machines, and how fast you guys make shoes—it was so cool. I had no idea how it all worked. I want to do this stuff some day. Ravi told me to come back in a few years. He said I have real potential to work somewhere in production because I have a good eye for detail. It was so rad when I noticed something in the stitching process that no one else did. I feel bad though—I hope I didn't get one of your workers in trouble with Ravi."

"Don't worry, Spencer. I'm sure it's fine. We allow for the occasional mistake—as long as it doesn't happen on a regular basis. I appreciate your catch on that. Thank you."

"No probs. And Ravi took me to the showroom and told me to pick out a couple of pairs from last year's line. Look Dad."

Spencer held up two pairs of our funkier ankle boots and one pair of dressier shoes.

"That's great. I'm glad you had so much fun."

"It was THE best day ever. What did you guys do?" she asked.

Jack and I exchanged a look that I can only describe as intimate.

"Melinda and I had a nice lunch and got to know each other better," he gazed at me, with eyes I hoped had seen me differently. It dawned on me while standing there, by the windows in my office with the backdrop of my world surrounding me: I was falling for this man. The stodgy professor who once confounded and infuriated me, now elicited a warmth and calmness when I was in his company. I liked it. I liked him.

Some of my fellow college classmates enjoyed their spring break in Florida, Cancun, or wherever they went to blow off steam for a week. My Bae Watch crew ventured home to chillax (chill and relax) with their high school friends and fam (family). Everyone seemed to recharge their batteries, prepared to finish out the remainder of the semester.

After a week of so-called vacation, I returned to campus, ready to be in the homestretch and get this thing done. It was great to get back to the office in New York for a consistent seven days, assuring myself that everything was running satisfactorily in my absence. Teresa was doing an excellent job of holding down the fort, but I needed to start the process of searching for a new president for my company. My assistant only held enough authority to make minor decisions, and I needed an executive with experience to hand things off to. Making a note in my phone, I would ask Teresa to direct human resources to contact a few of our executive recruiters. I found myself wondering how Alyce was doing and what would become of her and her marriage. She was my friend first before she betrayed me, and as more time passed, I was learning to accept that sometimes life dealt us a horrible hand—Jack, for example. I thought of Alyce with great sadness, replacing most of the anger and hurt that consumed me.

On Monday, after a full day of classes and catching up at lunch with the Baes (who told me stories about their spring break, making even me blush) I returned to my apartment and threw myself spread eagle on my king-size bed. Across the room on the dresser, my phone rang, forcing me to drag my middle-aged butt off the bed to retrieve the damn thing. I contemplated ignoring it, but when I have a father with heart disease and a mother who could break her hip because she still insisted on climbing on kitchen counters and into spaces she shouldn't, I answer the damned phone.

"Hello?"

"Mel—you're back. I have to see you. Let's get a pizza—my treat."

"Aiden," I groaned. "I'm not sure I even have the energy to eat. I'm exhausted."

"Stop. You gotta eat, I gotta eat. I wanna tell you about my off-the-heezy break, I want to hear about yours, and I *sooooo* want to see you. Maybe you'll let me stay the night." He laughed, hysterically.

"Until the day you either die or fall hopelessly in love with someone, you will never quit, will you?" I asked.

"Nope. Never. So can I come up?"

"You're here?"

"Yup. I'm standing in your lobby."

"Come on, then. Jesus, Aiden."

He whistled as he strolled down the hallway. I opened my door, and he grabbed me in a bear hug. "I missed you. But wait until I tell you what happened last week. Got any beer?" he asked, peering into my refrigerator.

I gave my housekeeper a list before I left for break, asking her to shop for me so I could return and not have to run out for food. I left her a gift card as a thank you. She was terrific.

"Give me a minute. I just got in and need a second to regroup. Grab me a glass of wine and let's sit on my couch." I plopped on the cushions and kicked my shoes off.

Aiden handed me a full glass of pinot noir, and I sipped it, feeling myself relax as the red warmth slid down my throat. He sat next to me, always too close for comfort.

"Aiden—get out of my personal space. I want to hear about this wonderful thing of yours, and you'll annoy me if you are in my face," I scolded.

"It's so hot when you yell at me."

"Yeah, I know. So what happened that has you so excited?"

"Well, aside from seeing you, I got a call on Tuesday from—now hold onto your fancy, over-priced sofa, woman—Lexor Studios! Yes, mam—I said Lexor—*The* Lexor Animation Studios. I sent them my résumé a month ago and hadn't heard anything and figured it was either lost or thrown into some huge slush pile never to see the light of day. On the phone was some lady from HR who said they would be interested in talking to me. Can you believe it?"

"Oh my God, Aiden, that's so great. I am so happy for you." I leaned over and gave him a big hug.

"This is the biggest thing that's ever happened to me. If I got a job there, I would friggin' pass out. You do realize that's my absolute dream, right?"

Oh, I knew. I knew a whole lot more than Aiden did because I had called my dear friend Damon at Lexor and told him to pull Aiden's résumé. Let me clarify something: I never refer or recommend someone for a job unless I think they are qualified. All I can do is get them the interview. It is ultimately up to the candidate to dazzle the interviewer. And I knew Aiden would sparkle and shine because he had the right stuff. And he was charming as hell. Remember I said I always take care of my friends?

"I know it's your dream and I'm sure they will see how talented you are. You would be a great addition to their team. This is great news."

"I'm so stoked. Hey Mel?"

"Yes, my darling boy?"

"Um, will you practice interviewing me? Go tough on me?"

"I can do that."

"And Mel?"

"Yes?"

"Will you take me shopping for a new suit?"

"Yes. I may even buy it for you as a graduation gift. I'll even throw in a tie, socks, shirt—the whole works."

Aiden threw himself on top of me. "I love you, I love you, Melinda Drake. You are like my fairy godmother in a goddess' body."

We were giggling like two best friends in middle school. I pushed him away, and we caught our breath. I looked at his youthful face, so filled with excitement and hope at the prospect of being able to live out a dream he had since he was a little boy.

Aiden stared at me. "You did this, didn't you? You got me the interview."

I couldn't gauge how he would react, so I simply told the truth.

"The ball is in your court. Make me—make yourself proud. Just be yourself and show them how wonderful you are and how much you have to give. They'd be lucky to get you."

He gently held me, resting his head on my shoulder.

"You... I...how can I ever thank you?" Aiden whispered.

"I only ask one thing."

"Anything. What is it?"

"Will you order the damn pizza? And make sure you get it with pepperoni."

The following week, Heidi and I were having coffee in the student center when I saw I had an email from Dean Samuels. He scheduled a meeting for our search committee, informing us that a decision was reached. The final two candidates for president of the university had been interviewed by our committee, the faculty chairs, and the board of trustees. The offer was made, and we were waiting to see if Dr. Susan Laverty accepted the position. Five minutes later, my phone pinged.

Jack: *Did u get the email from Walter?*

Me: *Yes. Do u think she accepted?*

Jack: *Hope so. I despise sitting on searches*

Me: *It was fun. Got to know u so it wasn't so bad*

Jack: *U were best part. Thanks again for NY*

I was tired of waiting. So I asked.

Me: *Dinner tonight at my house? I promise not to poison u*

Jack: *I thought you'd never ask. Time?*

I smiled so big, Heidi asked, "What?"

I typed: *7*

Jack: *Address? Red or white?*

Me: *Making pasta. Red. See you at 7*

I texted him my address. Then I told Heidi about New York, minus the details about Jack's ex-wife. I would never repeat his story to anyone.

"So, you have a date with the professor. I better get a phone call tomorrow or you're dead—do you hear me?"

I just hope I have something to tell.

Back at my place by three, I went into the kitchen, pulling things off shelves: a box of penne pasta, dishes, and two wine glasses. From the refrigerator I retrieved a plastic tub of field greens, tomatoes, a cucumber, a pint of ripe, first of the season strawberries. In a deep wooden bowl, I mixed a salad and placed it in the fridge. Grabbing my phone, I searched for an Alfredo recipe, hoping to find one with the fewest ingredients. I took a screen shot of one from a trusted source. The one item missing was dessert, and Jack had already offered to bring wine. Pulling a box of brownie mix from the pantry, I was ready to host a dinner guest. I didn't want to fuss so much it would appear I was trying too hard, so I decided to shower and throw on one of my comfy outfits (a nice fitted ensemble, not the ones reserved for my everyday workouts).

Stepping into the steamy shower, I languished under the hot water. Wetting my hair, I reached for the amber bottle of shampoo. Believe it or not, my brand of choice was baby shampoo, not some overpriced, salon concoction containing too many perfumes and chemicals for my sensitive scalp. And I never used conditioner. I have a ton of hair piled on top of my head, and I found using it weighed my locks down and made it less fluffy. Note: I am a product of the 80s and I still like my big hair.

What did I expect to happen with Jack Sweeney tonight? What did I want to happen? I wasn't sure. I knew I wanted to get to know him on a more personal level, yet I still had no clue what he thought of me. How would he react when I reveal I own three homes? Would he be threatened by my net worth? Worst of all: would he only want to be with me because of my bank account balance? Not every man could fit in my world or even want to be in it—believe me, I was well aware. Steven and I were a great match in terms of temperament and physical attraction. But I had to be able to trust the person I'm with when it comes to monogamy, and Steven failed that test. Gavin Beck was another man who is the male version of myself. I started giggling as I applied my makeup imagining the two of us competing for mirror space in the mornings. No, Gavin was a friend—one with benefits—but just a friend.

I found my mind wandering to strange places as I pulled on a pair of navy blue, snug, tapered velour pants and a matching crew neck top. As I was hunting for the right pair of shoes (perhaps my gold moccasin slippers would work?) my phone buzzed on the nightstand. It was Lucy, who I hadn't seen since we got back from break. Jack wasn't due for another forty-five minutes, so I sprawled out on the chaise in my bedroom.

"Hello, darling Lucy. Where have you been?" I asked.

"OMG Melinda. Dr. Werewolf has me going crazy over some project in physics, and I spent spring break at home working on the lame thing and even in the library if you can believe it."

"Imagine that."

"No you can't. It was a nightmare."

"Well, I'm sure Greta Wolfe (I had met her several times and she was a lovely woman) wants to make sure you leave her class knowing all there is to know about the gravitational pull of the earth, friction, and such things." I laughed.

"It's so extra. I can't wait to be done with school."

"Relax, girlfriend. You have to finish this year plus one more. Pace yourself. Besides, the real world is actually real, and you will miss all this some day. Trust me."

"Whatever. Guess what, Mel? Let me finish my stuff and then you can tell me all about your vacay. So get this: I'm home and your lame friend there..."

"And who would that be?" I asked as I picked several long hairs from my shirt.

"Aiden-I-don't-know-how-to-have-a-serious-girlfriend-annoying Flanagan." Lucy practically spit out his last name in disgust.

"Never calls—completely ghosts me. No call, no text, no email—nada. Didn't even like my pics. I talked with my high school BFFs and they told me to give him the boot, so Thursday night of break we went to a bar in Georgetown."

Lucy made a shoe pun without realizing it. Nice job, girlfriend.

"And I'm giving off this kind of unavailable vibe because I have a so-called boyfriend, and I guess, some kind of new confidence, which I guess is like a magnet because in the first fifteen minutes I have this cute guy offering to by me a beer. And he had nice manners and didn't try to get in my pants at all."

"There you go—an officer and a gentleman."

Complete silence. Obviously the reference went right over her head.

"Never mind—continue."

"I gotta tell you. Once I saw that another hot guy thought I was actually hot, it got me thinking that maybe Aiden wasn't the only one out there and I could do better. I mean, I realize you're friends with him but jeez Mel—Aiden is—I can't even. And this guy Nick is totally hot." She sighed.

At this point I ceased trying to understand Lucy's logic and started thinking about getting off the phone to get ready for Jack. I needed to exit this conversation. I was too tired, and the last thing I needed was a headache.

"That sounds awesome, Luce. Listen, can I call you tomorrow or better yet, I'll have you ladies over one night next week. I have to finish a paper tonight, and I've barely started it."

"Oh, sure. No probs. And I'll send you a pic of Nick—LOL, that rhymes." She giggled.

"Save it and show me when we get together. I'm glad we could catch up," I said.

"But you didn't tell me about your…"

I had an incoming text from Jack. Maybe he was early and was waiting in the lobby.

"Someone's texting me, Lucy. I'll be in touch."

"Kisses, Mel. Can't wait to see you and show you Nick. You know what? I'm still sending you a pic."

"All right, talk to you later." I clicked on my message from Jack.

Jack: *So sorry Mel, but I have to cancel tonight. Spencer threw-up all over the kitchen floor as I was getting ready to leave, and she has a fever. I apologize. I hope you didn't go to any trouble making dinner.*

I was disappointed, but I knew this was one of the realities of being a parent. Kids came first—as they should.

Me: *No worries. I was going to order in pizza. Go take care of your daughter. Another time!*

Jack: *Thank you for understanding. And I'm holding you to that rain check*

Me: ☺

Guess who ate a pan of brownies and a half-gallon of cold milk for dinner?

CHAPTER TWENTY-SIX

I walked into the conference room in Dean Samuels' office to find Gavin tapping furiously on a small tablet. No one else arrived yet, so it was only the two of us. As I passed behind him, I gave his shoulder a firm squeeze in an attempt to rouse him from his trance.

"Problem in your world? You look possessed," I said, placing my coat and bag on a chair.

Not able to tear his gaze away from his screen, he murmured, "Big issue with a new contractor. I'm trying to pacify a disgruntled client, and he's having none of it. I can't lose this account."

He was biting his bottom lip as he concentrated on composing a letter of contrition in an attempt to quell a major fire that was burning at his company. I understood this level of frustration as a CEO who had to step in and clean up someone else's mess, so I decided to leave him to it. I went over and poured a mug of coffee for Gavin, placing it next to him on the table.

"Thanks, Mel."

"You need this. And eat a cookie, too," I suggested, placing it in his line of sight as the other faculty members on the committee filtered in, all seemingly refreshed from the recent week off from work. We made small talk while speculating whether or not our top candidate from a small liberal arts college in Ohio had accepted the position. I realized I would miss this group, and I was grateful I was able to contribute to such an important decision.

Aiden arrived, entering the room with his youthful swagger. He put his stuff next to mine at the table, his eyes widening in delight when he saw the tray of cookies. No matter what, college students appreciated free food, particularly in the form of chocolate chip cookies.

After consuming half of a pan of fudgy brownies last night, I passed on the cookies. I completely understood that Spencer had suddenly become ill with some kind of nasty bug and that Jack had to cancel our dinner date, but I honestly had no idea where I stood with him. In two months, I would graduate from Pennwood University, leave Philadelphia and resume my life back in New York. I wondered if anything would come of my relationship with him, and I was beginning to think that maybe, based on his past history, the last thing he was interested in was a relationship with a woman like me. Whatever transpired, I knew I would be fine and simply carry on as usual.

Always last, Jack arrived at the meeting giving me the impression he had taken an interest in his appearance today. His brown hair was styled with some sort of gel and he was wearing a tweed jacket and dress pants. Catching my eye, he grinned, while giving the others in the room a cursory nod. He positioned himself across the table, and unlike Gavin, who finally put his work away, focused all of his attention in my direction while Aiden fawned all over me.

Dean Samuels was huddled together with Rose and two of his other staff members outside the conference room. They were smiling and joking, so I assumed we had, in fact, gotten ourselves a new president of the university. I could tell he was ecstatic and bursting to share the good news. He came in and sat at the head of the conference table.

"Good afternoon. I hope you all had a restful and enjoyable spring break. I called the committee together today to share some good and rather surprising news."

"Walter, I'm assuming Dr. Laverty has chosen to accept the position?" Ruth asked.

Folding his hands and leaning forward, Dean Samuels grinned. "No, actually. In fact, she turned down the offer to accept a provost appointment at a large university in Michigan."

We looked around in disbelief.

"So did you offer it to the alternate candidate?" Jack asked.

"No. He withdrew his application to accept an endowed chair at his alma mater."

Puzzled, along with the rest of the committee, I inquired, "So we have to go back to the drawing board and select additional candidates?"

"Not exactly. When I reported to the board of trustees that Dr.

Laverty declined our offer, they told me they would take a few days to get back to me on how we would proceed. Yesterday, I was called to meet with them and assumed—like all of you—that we would have to re-open the search. But they decided to go in a very surprising direction." He smiled.

"What did they say?" Margaret asked.

"The board has decided to offer me the job as president of Pennwood University, effective immediately, and I happily accepted."

The room broke out in applause, and Aiden let out a whistle in approval.

"Well deserved." Jack leaned over to shake his hand.

"Finally, the board made a great decision and picked someone from our ranks who should be our new president. Congratulations, Walt." Levi Stone reached to shake the dean's hand.

"Dude, you'll be so awesome!" Aiden proclaimed.

"Walter Samuels, President. I like the sound of that," I said.

"I certainly did not expect this turn of events, but my wife and I are thrilled. I'm looking forward to taking the university in a new direction."

"How did they arrive at this decision?" Jack asked.

"Well, like Levi said, they came to the conclusion that I was already doing the job for months and felt it was unnecessary to reopen the search."

"Such great news. I'm so happy for you and for this college. You will be a terrific president," I smiled.

"I would like to thank all of you for your work on this committee. I believe that something of value is never wasted, and I enjoyed getting to know each one of you better as a result. I promise I will do my best to further serve this wonderful institution as your president and may be calling on you in the future to help me in achieving our goals. You are all busy people, so I won't detain you any further. Once again, my deepest thanks and appreciation for your service and support."

He stood, and his portly frame took on a new confidence and stature. It was so great to see that the place he devoted his life's work to had rewarded him with a job he never thought he would be considered for.

After expressing further congratulations to Dean Samuels, Aiden ducked out quickly because he had class, and Margaret, Ruth, and Levi grabbed a coffee and a few cookies to take back to their offices. Gavin pulled on his coat, asking if I could join him for a late lunch or early dinner. Jack overheard the offer; he was scowling at the prospect of me with the nefarious playboy businessman.

"Thank you, but I can't. I have a project due, and I'll be tucked away in my apartment all evening. Rain check?"

"Of course, beautiful. I'll be in touch," he said, saying good-bye to Jack and going over to bid farewell to the dean. Jack shook his hand limply, dismissing him.

"You're so subtle, Jack," I laughed.

"Yeah, well that guy is a player. Stay away from him."

"Maybe you haven't realized it yet, but I can take care of myself. Besides, Gavin is a good guy. He just likes women."

"Too many women. A good guy is one who doesn't need to prove himself constantly."

I studied his face to try and figure him out. He was obviously jealous of Gavin. So did that mean he had feelings for me?

Just as I was going to address it, Dean Samuels appeared at my side.

"So, Melinda. Now that I've been appointed president of this university, we should entertain the proposal you made to me when we first met. I've been trying to assess the college's needs for the future, and we could certainly use a new residence hall to accommodate our growing enrollment."

"Dean—wait a minute. I guess I will have to start calling you, what, Mr. President?" I laughed.

He chuckled in delight.

"Perhaps we can meet one day soon and discuss potential construction projects here at the university. Let me get through finals. I am so happy for you. You deserve this for all you have done for Pennwood."

"Thank you, Melinda. One of the members of the board spoke to me afterwards and told me that sometimes the best person for the job is right under your nose. You just have to recognize it."

A light went off in my head. These were words of wisdom from a very smart man.

"How is Spencer feeling?" I asked, as Jack and I left the dean's office and headed out, he to his next class and me to my apartment.

"Better, thanks. She stayed home today, and my neighbor is checking on her. I'm cutting my next class short so I can get home.

"Don't forget ginger ale—always helps a stomach virus."

He nodded. "I know. I've been playing this role for a long time."

"Sorry. I didn't mean to imply…"

"I didn't take it that way. Most people think dads are clueless. I've discovered that fathers also get the intuitive gene when it comes to their children. Women seem to get all the credit."

"You are a great parent, Jack. Spencer is amazing, and if she were my daughter I would be proud of her, too."

Keeping his gaze focused on the ground, I saw the pain still etched on his face.

"I'm glad I told you—about Molly. It felt good to talk, which I promised myself I would never do. Maybe I'm finally moving on," he said.

I stopped and turned to him. "We all have a past. It doesn't make us weak, and it shouldn't make you vulnerable."

"All of us except you. You have lived the best life with parents who loved and cared for you and you have a thriving shoe empire and millions of women who worship the ground you walk on. I'd say that's a person with no skeletons in her closet. You are blessed."

I looked at the semi-thawing lawn beneath my feet. This man had revealed his most painful secrets, trusting me above all others. It was time for me to do the same.

"So about that rain check…"

"Wait—I have a much better idea. I thought about it last night."

He thought about us last night. I felt like a teenager again.

"Since you hosted Spencer and me in New York and showed us your world, I would like the opportunity to show you mine."

"I would love it. And where would that be?" I asked, thrilled that we were finally, getting somewhere.

"It's a surprise. Dress warm and comfortable—and none of those high-heeled shoes you sell. Walking shoes will be best. I'll be at your place by nine in the morning on Saturday, so be ready."

He looked at me differently today. Not sure if it was jealousy over Gavin or the revelations about his ex-wife or the fact I would be gone in a couple of months—it was hard to guess.

"Don't worry, I'll be ready. An adventure sounds like fun," I said, not confessing that surprises were the thing I despised more than anything. But since he was trying to be more open for me, the right thing to do was to reciprocate. And then it happened, taking me completely off-guard: Jack Sweeney gathered me in his arms and kissed me. It was a slow and sweet kiss right in the middle of the busy quad, where throngs of students passed. Someone yelled, "Get a room, Doc!"

He pulled away and checked his wristwatch. Only Jack would check his watch rather than his phone.

"Wow, gotta go. See you Saturday. And, in case you were wondering, I promise I won't cancel this time."

I gave him a thumbs-up as he dashed away. I had a real, official date to God knows where, along with a kiss from the professor. Wonders never cease.

Beginning my trek across the bustling center of campus, I noticed there were still a few small piles of snow in places tucked under shrubbery, now dirty and unwanted in the anticipation of spring. I found myself beginning the process of starting my good-byes to Pennwood by noticing all the things I would miss when I graduated. Funny, but I didn't have these longings back when I was here years ago. This whole experience was different, perhaps because I was a grown woman and could appreciate life so much more. So grateful for the opportunity to return and complete this unfinished part of my life, I thought about all the friends I made here and the fact we would have never crossed paths had I not matriculated back to Pennwood University: Aiden, my buddy and food partner who never said no when I needed or wanted him to come over; Heidi, the one friend who knew all my '80s references and jokes; the Bae Watch crew who kept me young and confounded me constantly with their vocabulary; Dean Samuels who did everything to make my dream a reality; and the faculty and teaching assistants who were never too busy to answer a dumb question from a non-traditional student. Then there were the groundskeepers who maintained the beauty of this two-hundred-year university and cleared paths in snowstorms so we could safely get from place to place, the food service workers who prepared meals for us with a smile every day, and the dedicated staff who ran the offices that we depended on for information to get from point A to point B. This was one of the best experiences of my life, and I laughed as I remembered the one person who set this whole quest in motion: the once infuriating, now my forever-hero Philip Gunderson. I vowed to pay him a visit after I graduated and returned to Manhattan to thank him for a gift he never meant to give me. One day I hoped to repay him for that.

CHAPTER TWENTY-SEVEN

Jack arrived on time for our mysterious road adventure. I had no idea where we were going or what we were doing so I followed his instructions and prepared for a casual day. It was refreshing for someone else to take the lead, allowing me to sit back, relax, and be entertained. Ensuring I slipped my sunglasses and a bottle of water for each of us in my bag, I was ready when he texted me, waiting in my allotted visitor parking space downstairs.

Jack: *I'm here*

Me: *On my way*

I emerged from the building and enjoyed the warm sunshine on my face. The morning air was cool but comfortable, a great start to what hopefully would be an enjoyable day. When he spotted me, Jack jumped out of the driver's seat, beaming with excitement. This was Jack Sweeney about to share an important part of his life. I was thrilled he was opening up to me in a way I feared he never would.

"You look beautiful, as usual. I am so anxious to take you to a place that means so much to me."

"All right, Professor—where am I being hijacked to on this lovely Saturday?"

Jack clicked his seatbelt into place, adjusting a few controls on the dashboard of his automobile. He handed me a colorful brochure.

My eyes widened in surprise. "Gettysburg? As in the town or battlefield?"

"Both. The town has its own museum and shops and we can have lunch there. But it's the battlefield that holds all the excitement. That's the real surprise for today."

Opening the brochure, I examined the glossy pictures and map winding through the vast historical site. "I don't mean to sound rude or ignorant, but isn't Gettysburg just a bunch of monuments and empty fields?"

Jack was glowing and sported a devastating smile. This trip meant so much to him, and I wasn't about to spoil it because it was not my thing.

"You'll see. It's a long ride—about two and a half hours. I hope that's okay."

"Fine by me."

"Let's stop and grab a coffee and a little something to hold us over until lunch," he said.

We pulled into a drive-through right outside the city, fortifying ourselves with caffeine and a blueberry muffin for me, and two egg sandwiches for Jack. Spreading my breakfast in my lap and finding the cup holder for my coffee, we merged on to the Pennsylvania Turnpike heading west.

The restorative powers of caffeine and sugar are a miracle. After a few sips of the caramel colored liquid and soft muffin dusted with crunchy, sugar crystals, I felt like myself again. Jack too, seemed suddenly awakened, and we chatted a storm of conversation.

Road trips are underrated. If you want to get to know someone, take a long ride in a car where your captive audience is right beside you. Jack and I talked about everything. He outlined his odyssey to obtaining tenure at Pennwood, and how he was the youngest associate to ever secure full professor status so quickly. Because he had written so many scholarly papers and books early in his career, Jack caught the eye of several well-known historians. He collaborated with them to create a treasure trove of material related to the Civil War, which was housed at Pennwood University. His research was referenced by universities and colleges across the nation and abroad. The culmination of his expertise happened after he was approached by a famous documentary filmmaker to work as head consultant on his *History of the American Civil War* project a few years back. It solidified his status as one of the premier experts in his field.

We discussed our childhoods and told our best and worst sibling stories. Jack described how his brother Michael shoved his head in a toilet when they were in grade school, yet defended him when a bully teased him for being a bookworm by knocking out the bully's front tooth in front of the entire school. I told him how my sister stole all my boyfriends in middle school but gave me all her Halloween candy one year because I had to stay in bed due to strep throat.

"So you grew up in a nice, normal family like I did," he laughed. It wasn't a question. It was a statement of fact.

"I did. And they are wonderful."

He glanced over at me. "I'm sure they are, if they are anything like you."

It was a different look this time. Jack Sweeney was peeling my soul back, one layer at a time, revealing my true self.

Sadness overtook his expression.

"What is it, Jack?"

Staring straight ahead, he paused. "It makes me think of Spencer— how she is being robbed of the kind of childhood we were lucky enough to experience. I get angry and sad at the same time."

"Kids are resilient. She has you and your family, which is more than most kids get. Besides, she is strong-willed, which will take her far. Better to learn hardship early in life and develop good coping skills. No need to worry about that fabulous young woman."

"I hope you're right. You never stop worrying about them. It's a blessing and a curse."

I gazed out my side window. "I wouldn't know."

The car felt like a confessional box when Jack asked me the million-dollar question.

"Did you ever want children?"

No other man I dated (with the exception of Gavin and only because I inquired of him) asked me that because they were always older and had either divorced and were happily done procreating or were confirmed bachelors who ran from the idea of parental responsibilities. I wasn't sure if Jack was asking out of genuine curiosity or if he was trying to ascertain whether or not I possessed any maternal qualities.

Placing my hands in my lap, I paused before answering his question. "I probably did want children when I was a young girl. I played with dolls and had fantasies about raising my future kids with my siblings and having them all grow up together, but when I think back on it, I realize I was more interested in what my Barbie dolls had in their closets and on their feet than in them getting married and starting families. My parents have always told me that I was unique, but they never made me feel like I was different from my siblings and friends who wanted domesticity."

Jack reached across the console for my hand. "I find your life fascinating. I love the fact you had a vision and were able to achieve all the things you dreamed of. You must have sideswiped so many obstacles along the way. The path to success is often fraught with roadblocks—right?"

Sipping my coffee through the tiny opening, I answered, "You have no idea, Professor." I never let anyone discover how much.

Deciding to shift the conversation, I told Jack about the Alyce Cumberland fiasco. He listened intently, remarking, "You don't expect that from someone you trusted and believed cared about you. She obviously had her reasons, but it was done at the expense of her job, and more importantly, at the expense of a friendship."

Peering at this amazing, refreshing man beside me, I let out a hearty laugh.

"What?' he asked with that grin. "What?"

"I'm amused."

"Because?"

"Because I couldn't stand you when I first met you."

"A charming guy like me? Are you kidding?"

"Insufferable was more like it. You were a real pain in the ass, if you must know."

"I hate those damn search committees—waste of valuable time. And they put people on them who have no business being there."

The old Jack reappeared.

"Like who, for example?" I asked.

"That kid—the grad assistant, and that pretentious pretty boy. Just because he has lots of money, he suddenly is qualified to select a university president. A load of bull if you ask me."

"Come on. Both Aiden and Gavin brought valuable insight to the group. You're an academic elitist."

"The one bright spot in that whole debacle was you. I was in awe of your experience and, to be completely honest, your beauty and presence. You have the gift of commanding attention—in a good way, of course. Not many people can do that."

"Why thank you. I will take that as a profound compliment coming from you."

He turned briefly, his eyes twinkling. "You're welcome."

Before long, we saw signs for Gettysburg. Jack suggested we stop in town at the museum first and then have lunch. We would tour the battlefield after we ate because he said we would be doing a great deal of walking and would need energy in the form of food. Since I was starving after an almost three-hour drive, I wasn't about to argue with his logic.

Gettysburg was a charming college town that held an important place in American history books. Jack prefaced our tour by giving me a mini lesson on the significance of the town. As we pulled into the city limits and before we exited the car, Dr. Sweeney came alive and animatedly chattered on with a flurry of facts.

"The Battle of Gettysburg was fought over a three-day period in July of 1863 and resulted in a victory for the Union army. More than fifty thousand soldiers on both sides were killed, making it the largest and bloodiest battle waged during the Civil War. The Union and Confederate armies chose this site due to the road system. Ten roads led into town, making it a prime site and easily accessible for both sides. Of the one hundred twenty combined generals present on the field, nine were killed at Gettysburg—the most of any other battle in the war. General Robert E. Lee led the Confederate army, while General George Meade led the Union forces. Fresh off a major victory in Chancellorsville, Virginia, Lee had a goal of successfully invading the North, thus persuading the government to allow the South to secede and have its independence. But when the Southern forces were defeated at Gettysburg, it was seen as a turning point in the war, and all Lee's hopes for the Confederacy were lost forever."

"Fascinating," I said, as I watched this brilliant historian paint a picture of a time I had never thought much about. Jack's face became mired in pain, his brow furrowed, as he described how the townspeople complained about the shallow graves dug to bury the Union soldiers to the then governor of Pennsylvania, demanding they deserved better for their courageous service to the country.

"Gettysburg National Military Park was created to honor those lost, and a new cemetery was dedicated in November 1863. That day, President Abraham Lincoln delivered his famous Gettysburg Address. Although it remains one of the most important speeches in American history, it was also one of the shortest at fewer than three hundred words."

I turned to him and smiled. "It's so cool that I'm sitting next to someone who actually knows the word count of the Gettysburg Address. If we were in high school, I would brag that I was on a date with the smartest guy in the class. I love that you can rattle off all this information." I leaned over and kissed him.

"I look at it this way. I'll never be rich like Gavin Beck or be a youthful stud again like that Flanagan kid, but I will always have a plethora of information in my brain. I've heard it impresses—I hope it resonates with you. I don't have alot money, but I have a deep love of this country and my family, and I'm loyal as hell."

Squinting my eyes at him, I wasn't quite sure how to take his remark. "You'd be surprised at what impresses me. I'm not as shallow as you think."

"That's the best thing about you. You aren't shallow. There is so much more inside you than I originally thought. I hope we continue getting to learn about each other. I haven't felt this alive in years, and it's all because of you."

Jack slid his hand under my hair to hold the back of my neck, pulled me forward and kissed me deeply for several minutes.

"Jack." I sighed.

"I agree. But if we don't get out of this damn car, I'm going to go insane. Plus I'm starving. I changed my mind. Let's eat lunch first. Okay?"

"Def, Professor," I laughed.

We left it there—the unspoken promise between us. Jack was ignited, and I was excited. It was going to be a great day.

After devouring cheeseburgers and French fries, we were ready to explore. Jack took my hand as we walked the few blocks to the

Gettysburg Museum of History and Visitor's Center. Strolling through the displays of Union and Confederate soldier uniforms and guns, we examined personal items like books and letters to wives and sweethearts, parents, and friends. We sat through a film of Pickett's charge and examined more artifacts and interactive exhibits throughout the museum.

After exploring all the rooms, we walked out to the parking lot. Jack opened my car door for me, and we drove a short distance to Gettysburg National Military Park.

"The entire park encompasses over six thousand acres of land with twenty-six miles of roads and approximately fourteen hundred monuments and memorials. This is hallowed ground, Melinda. Many have said, if you listen carefully, you can hear the cries of deceased soldiers from the battlefield."

I shivered. Jack was providing me with the kind of perspective one could only get from an expert. In my own thoughts about war and death, any images conjured in my brain were those I saw in textbooks. Seeing all this through Jack's eyes made it pop like a three-dimensional diorama.

We left the car in a lot adjacent to where several monuments and markers stood proudly. Jack slid his aviator sunglasses on and wiggled into his black fleece jacket. He looked dashing. I was...smitten.

"Look there," he pointed.

Several soldiers were immortalized in bronze, perched high upon stone pedestals, riding majestic horses, overlooking vast acres of battlefields. Jack took my hand and led me to stand before one of the more note-worthy monuments.

"This," he whispered, "was a seminal moment for me as a child."

"Why is that?"

"My father brought us here when I was five years old. Times were different then—no staff patrolling the grounds. He lifted me up, and I stood on this exact statue. I walked around the entire thing, waving my arms like an eagle, yelling to my mother, "Look at me!" She snapped a picture of me using one of those disposable cameras. I still have it in a frame in my bedroom. That day, something changed me. I'm not sure if it was because I was standing so high and could see for miles or if the ghosts of Gettysburg were calling out to me."

I reached over and caressed the side of his face. He leaned into my hand and kissed my palm.

"That week, I asked my father to take me to the library. It began an obsession and my life's work with American history, especially the Civil War and Abraham Lincoln, my hero. Pretty corny, huh?"

"Not at all. Let's walk—I want to see more."

We took a tour through the fields, past artillery cannons and low markers detailing unknown graves, boundaries, and names of infantry regiments from several states. One of my favorite parts of the day was observing the collection of wooden crisscross fences, crudely constructed yet still standing over one hundred and fifty years later.

After an hour, Jack led me to a bench that overlooked a clearing surrounded by small, rolling hills. The trees were beginning to sprout spring buds and the grass was turning green, and off in the distance was a field of wildflowers. We sat, and Jack pulled me close to his side. I rested my head on his shoulder. We were silent for several minutes, listening to nothing but the sound of birds chirping overhead and cars driving by in the distance.

"Thank you for sharing this with me, for bringing me here. It's so much more than I imagined," I whispered.

"When you showed me your business and life in New York, I wanted then to share this with you. I think we understand each other better. We are more alike than I thought."

"Different worlds, same dreams."

"I think so. I want you to know something about me. I don't love easily, nor do I trust completely. But I would like to try—with you." He turned to face me, pieces of his brown hair blowing in the light breeze. "I realize you have a big life in Manhattan, and it's one of the many aspects about you that draw me in. You are everything a woman should be—can be, and my daughter adores you. I am a humble man, and what you see is what I am. I realize you are so much more successful in terms of wealth than I could ever be. As evidenced by my lifestyle, money is not high on my priority list, so I don't want you to think I want yours because I have very little. I've never needed much. I have saved most of my money for Spencer's education, because she of course claims she would rather die than attend Pennwood University where she could go for free."

We laughed at the utter ridiculousness of this fact.

"I've held back for so long in telling you how I feel. I fought my feelings for you at every turn. The first day I laid eyes on you, I was floored by your beauty and confidence and sheer ability to command the room. I can only hope you share any similar feelings toward me, because when I'm with you, I feel like I'm alive again."

He lowered his head, petrified and yet anxious for my response to his declaration. The symbolism was not lost on me that he chose to lay out his feelings here, on this battlefield, where I would decide whether he won or lost, where I would embrace his heart or shoot directly through it.

Searching his eyes, I gazed at his handsome, yet vulnerable face. Today was a turning point—for both of us.

"Oh, Jack," I said softly. Leaning in, I ran my hand through the hair that had grown over his jacket collar and pulled him towards me. We kissed, a kiss full of emotion and, I hoped, promise. But first, before I could say anything about my feelings for him and the possibility of a future together, I had to tell him the truth about my past. Because I wasn't so sure he would feel the same way after he knew.

CHAPTER TWENTY-EIGHT

Pulling away from him, I rose and walked over to a nearby oak tree. Leaning against its weathered bark, I wondered if any of the ghosts of Gettysburg stood under this tree, having to reveal a terrible secret about something they did. But it was time, and I knew it.

"Melinda, what is it?"

No one except my parents, siblings, Chelsea, and Gina knew what I was about to share with Jack, the one person I was ready to trust with the darkest day of my life.

"I need to tell you something first, before I talk about my feelings for you because I am terrified that your feelings about me may change when you hear what I have to say."

"Nothing you could say will change that. I hope that makes it easier for you to tell me."

"I fear you think I'm perfect and have an image of me that I can't be broken or that I'm so tough that nothing gets to me. I have fallen more times than you can imagine, and I guess one of my strengths is that I always managed to get back up and go on. But I assure you, it didn't come easy, and if it weren't for a few vital people in my life—mainly my parents—I would never have gotten to this point."

Jack gently cupped my chin in his hand. "I'm going to sit here and listen to what you need to tell me. I promise you: if the result is that it makes you appear more human, I will feel even closer to you. So take your time. We have the rest of the day in this field of spirits, all ready to hear what you have to say."

I prefaced my comments by telling Jack about finding Max and Nicki in bed together back when I was a student at Pennwood in 1998. I took a deep breath and continued.

"I had to get as far away from the scene of discovering my two-timing boyfriend Max and my back-stabbing roommate together. It was October, and the road was slick from rain. I kept visualizing them in the act and wondered how long it had been going on. Feeling like a fool, I reached into my glove box to grab a wad of napkins to wipe my eyes because I could barely see. I was racing down the highway at a high speed, way over the limit. All I wanted to do was get as far away from them and the campus as I could. I needed my mother, and I wasn't thinking clearly nor was I paying enough attention to the fact that I was operating a car under the worst of circumstances. In a slow motion moment, my car swerved from the right lane to the left, smashing into the concrete divider. The sounds of glass breaking and steel bending like a pretzel overwhelmed me in that single minute of impact. My car rolled over several times toward the shoulder before flipping upside down. Although it could have affected several more cars and trucks, there was one vehicle I clipped while turning over. That car crashed head on into the median. My mangled car came to a complete stop. I tasted blood in my mouth; my eyes were sealed shut. I passed out. The next thing I remembered was waking in a hospital room, tubes and wires covering my body. All I could hear was the incessant beep of the monitors that were keeping me alive. I couldn't move, couldn't speak. I woke periodically, only to lose consciousness quickly afterwards. After a week, I completely opened my eyes and was able to see my mother and father standing over the bed. They each held my hand, telling me I was alive and that everything would be fine. I tried to talk, but nothing came out from my mouth because a tube ran down my throat and was taped securely in place. For ten days, I existed in a state of semi-conscious fog, and I couldn't recall a thing. All I remember to this day about that first week after the accident was that my parents never left my side and held my hand the entire time, whispering words I never heard. At the two-week mark, the doctors removed the tube from my throat and disconnected several others. I went through two surgeries, and I could barely move any part of my body. The doctor told me I was lucky to be alive, although I didn't feel the least bit fortunate. My memory slowly returned, but I started to have nightmares and woke screaming many times. My mother and father took turns lying in the cramped hospital bed to hold me until I calmed. I must have caused them to age ten years in the process. I began calling them Mommy and Daddy again, rather than the very grown-up mom and dad of a twenty-year-old college student. My siblings and best friends came to visit, but I didn't want to see anyone except my parents. The worst was when I fully recovered my memory and began to question the events of the accident. I knew there was another car involved, but I didn't know what happened to it. When I asked my father, he looked over at my mom and she nodded her head."

"Sweetheart, your car hit a van that had no time to react," my father said.

"Daddy, what happened? Is the driver okay?" I asked.

He stared at my mother again.

"Daddy! Is that person okay?" I shouted. My head hurt again.

My mother came to my side. She hesitated before she spoke. "Melinda, there was a family in the van. A mother, father, and their two small children."

"Oh, God," I moaned. "Tell me."

"The mother was not wearing her seat belt. The police report said she had unfastened it to reach back to grab something when the impact occurred. She was thrown from the vehicle. Melinda, she died."

I was shaking and sobbing. "I killed her, I killed someone's mother! I deserved to die, not that innocent mother. Oh my God, I want to die."

"My parents tried to calm their hysterical child. My mother pushed the button on the bed to summon the nurse. She entered soon after and gave me a sedative. I welcomed being unconscious. I never wanted to wake up again."

The entire time I was relaying this story to Jack, I kept my head down. Mustering the courage to look up to gauge his reaction, I was surprised to find his face had not changed since I started to relay my story. He nodded.

"Keep going."

"A month later, I was ready to be released from the hospital. Most of my body was on the mend, but my mental state was extremely fragile. My injuries from the accident were extensive, but the worst was the fact that the steering wheel rammed into my pelvis and crushed it. When I returned home, I endured months of physical rehab and counseling with a psychiatrist three days a week. The family of the woman I killed agreed to a financial settlement, and my parents' insurance covered it. With the help of my therapist, I wrote a letter to the victim's husband and children, apologizing for what I had done. I never heard back, and every single day I think about them and what their life has been like without her. I can't even fathom my life without my mother. I told my therapist that God punished me with my injuries. The doctors said most likely I could never have children because I had sustained so much abdominal damage. It was what I deserved, and that is the reason I never had children. I probably can't, and I had no right to be a mother after taking those innocent children's mom away from them."

Jack leaned forward, resting his arms on his knees. "Melinda—it was an accident. You never meant for it to happen."

"Still, it was my fault. I caused the accident to happen. I won't ever be able to escape the guilt and regret. Never. It diminished over time but it's always there."

"So that's why you never went back to college?"

"No. I couldn't. Too many painful memories and I needed to be with my parents at all times. I was crippled by guilt. I didn't deserve anything good to happen to me. I kept punishing myself by denying the attainment of the college degree that was at the root of my culpability. When I first came home, my mother had to sleep with me because of the night terrors. After a year, my parents arranged an intervention with my therapist. They all told me I couldn't go on like I was, and I needed to begin moving forward. It was my father who suggested I move to France, a place I always wanted to go to. My doctor had a friend there who worked in the fashion industry who agreed to rent me a room in her house and give me a job. I reluctantly agreed to go, because I knew my life was slipping away from me and I had to stop punishing myself for what I had done. As I boarded the plane, we all were afraid. My parents were concerned about whether or not I could handle being so far from them. I was about to enter a life where I knew no one and couldn't speak the language."

"And?" Jack asked.

"And it ended up saving me. Being on my own in a country where no one knew me or even cared about me forced me to start my life over. Ines, my doctor's friend, took me in, and I'm sure she was briefed on my situation. I loved her because she never asked me about the accident, never mentioned it. She just fed me, had coffee with me every day, and helped me. When I made my first million, I bought her a small house by the sea that she could retire in. I never forget the kindness of others."

"That aptly describes you. You are the most generous person I have ever met."

"It forced me to grow up fast. I learned the hard way what's important in life. After a month working in Ines's dress shop, she told me that Pierre Roussel, the famous footwear designer, was looking for an intern and she thought I would be perfect for the job. I was becoming more and more interested in fashion, particularly shoes because of my family history in the business. I assembled a portfolio of sketches that Ines thought were good. Long story short, Pierre and I fit like a pair of perfect pumps, and he taught me every aspect of the shoe business. I spent three years with him in France, and at the end of that time, I became fluent in the language and in designing beautiful shoes. When I shared with Pierre my idea for MD Shoes, he thought it was brilliant and agreed to financially back my business. He recommended I move to New York and helped me secure everything I needed."

"And how did the great Melinda Drake repay her mentor?"

"I made him a great deal of money our first year and took care of any relative of his who wanted to come to New York. I even set up his daughter with a business partner of mine, and they married and have four kids. Pierre became a happy grandfather. He is also my guardian angel. Sadly, he passed away last year."

"I'm sorry."

"One of the things I promised myself on the plane ride over to France was that if I ever became successful—which by the way I was determined to do—I would give back, especially to those who struggled. When I returned to New York, I hired a lawyer to establish an anonymous fund for the family of the victim of my accident. The insurance settlement helped, but I wanted to make their life easier after I had destroyed it. It didn't bring her back, but at least I could do something. Call it penance, call it atonement."

"I call it wonderful."

"Guilt played a large part in my decision not to return to Pennwood. I didn't deserve to have my dreams fulfilled when I had taken away those of another. It wasn't right."

I walked toward Jack. He stood, wrapping his arms around me. I buried my face in his neck. "I've never told anyone my story. Only my family and close friends knew the details about the accident. I discussed my issues with a psychiatrist, but it was all very clinical. It feels good to share it. Thank you for listening." I hugged him closer.

"What you just described took courage. I'm certain you've been told a million times it was an accident, but I also imagine wanting to go back in time and change things. Unfortunately, none of us can. All we can do is learn from it, move on, and try to live as good a life as we can."

"Are you sure you want to give it a go with me? I'm not the easiest woman in the world, and I am extremely set in my ways. I hog the bed, I need to eat at least three times a day, and I adore parties," I announced.

"Well, let's see. I'm thin, so I don't require much room in a bed. I also need to eat, and you will be shocked to learn that I am actually the life of any party I attend."

I squinted my eyes to see if he was being facetious.

He burst out laughing. "Just kidding. But I do enjoy being with people, and I love good food and conversation. So I promise: I can keep up with you."

"One other thing, Professor. I've been told I'm a lot to handle." I looked directly in his blue eyes—eyes that peered back no differently than before I had revealed my darkest secret to him.

"Don't you get it?" He pulled me to his side as we walked to his car. "You don't need to be handled. You need to be *loved.*"

CHAPTER TWENTY-NINE

Preparations were in full swing for my fast-approaching graduation. Final projects demanded I spend hours in the design lab piecing together prototypes and models that would be scrutinized by my professors. A ten-page paper in my political science course loomed over me like the grim reaper. I was trying to juggle all this and keep on top of things related to MD Shoes. Thank God for Teresa. She was doing her own job, Alyce's job, and much of mine. I knew I would find a proper way to acknowledge and compensate her after I was done with school and returned as leader of my company. Teresa demonstrated how competent she was every day, but the last few months revealed so much more in regard to her capabilities. I made a mental note. Today, I needed to prioritize my thoughts, directing them toward finishing the damned classes.

Through all the chaos of finishing the semester, I was savoring the glow of a brand new relationship. Jack and I managed to spend every afternoon together since our day at Gettysburg. We would grab a bite somewhere on campus, or I would make something for us at my apartment, and then we would retreat to my bedroom or sofa. Love in the afternoon was a novel concept for me, because I rarely, if ever, was home midday at my place in Manhattan. There is something tawdry and liberating about having sex during the daytime while the world is bustling outside the window. We were like a couple of teenagers, entering my apartment, pulling off each other's clothes. Most evenings he had to go home to be with Spencer, and it was a treat when she would stay at a friend's house overnight and we could wake in each other's arms.

Jack Sweeney surprised me in so many ways. First of all, the man could cook. He put me to shame in the kitchen demonstrating an impressive repertoire of recipes and techniques I had yet to master. Secondly, he was handy. He could fix almost anything. He changed Aiden's flat tire one night when he came banging on my door, hoping I had a repair service he could use. Jack and Aiden ended up liking each other, mostly because I think they both realized it would mean a lot to me if they did.

The third thing about Jack Sweeney that came as a shock was that the professor had skills. Granted, at first he may have been a little rusty from lack of use, but he made up for lost time and I had never been more suited to someone than I was with him. One afternoon, as we were dressing, getting ready to eat lunch before our scheduled classes, Jack addressed an issue that had been nagging him for weeks.

"How are we going to make this work once you graduate and go back to New York? Have you thought about it? Because it's all I can think about. I can't believe how lucky I am to have found you, and soon you're going to be gone. I need to know that we have a future, that we will somehow stay together."

Strolling over to him as I buttoned my blouse, I sat on his lap, taking his face in my hands, kissing him. With my forehead against his, I whispered, "Do you actually think I would be willing to give you up? I've never been happier. I have no doubt we can face the challenges ahead."

"Spencer still has two years of high school. I have tenure here at Pennwood. You run a multi-million dollar business two hours away. We are here; you are there."

"Exactly. We are a measly two hours from each other. That is so doable. Please don't worry. We have weekends, holidays, and my schedule can be as flexible as I make it. Hell—I managed to work out finishing my degree and still run my company, didn't I? We will definitely make it work."

Something else was bothering him apart from the distance. I climbed off of him as he straightened, shoving his hands into his pant pockets.

"What is it?" I asked.

He bit the inside of his lip. "I'm forty-one. I feel like I'm in high school hoping that the prom queen will still like me tomorrow. I love it when I'm with you, but I fear being without you. I hate that I feel so much for you and that I haven't a clue about where our relationship is going. I don't like feeling vulnerable, yet I've never felt more for someone in my entire life."

"Good to know we are on the same page, Professor. I feel the same."

He put his arm around me as we walked to the kitchen where our food had been warming in the oven. It was my turn to ask him a question. I figured now was the time to put it out there.

"I need to ask you something."

"What is it, honey."

He calls me honey. No one ever called me that. I like it.

"Does it ever bother you that I am a very rich woman? Doesn't that normally threaten a man's masculinity and ego? Say we last forever as a couple. Do you think in ten or twenty years you would resent the fact I came in to the relationship with so much more money than you?" We sat at my kitchen island, sharing a meatball sub.

Jack swallowed a large mouthful of sandwich. He lifted his glass of diet root beer for a sip to wash it down. Wiping his mouth with a paper napkin, he looked at me.

"No. If nothing else, I live in the real world and have no problem that, financially speaking, you are so successful. I want my daughter to understand that she can achieve anything in her life, and you are a great role model and mentor to her. I have always embraced the idea of equality, and acknowledge we all have things we excel in. For example, I can write circles around you and have published several books and been hired as a consultant on projects you would have no clue about. I have a doctorate and can speak three languages. I possess an Emmy award for a documentary I…"

"Okay I get it, Sweeney. You made your point abundantly clear. Money is not the only yardstick by which to measure success. I wanted to make sure. Showoff. And just as I suspected: the male ego is alive and well, eating a sub in my kitchen."

"Hoagie," he corrected.

"Sub."

"Hoagie. Actually, it is a grinder because it's hot. Hoagies are cold," he proclaimed.

"Grind her?" I asked as I straddled him.

"That, too." He began kissing my neck when my cell phone rang. "Ignore it. I'm busy."

"Let me look. It may be my parents. You are the same way with yours," I said, smiling as I reluctantly pulled away from his embrace.

Glancing at the screen, I saw it was Teresa. "It's work—do you mind?"

Jack shook his head in surrender as he resumed his decimation of the meatball sub.

Grabbing my phone, I meandered into the living room and settled on my couch, tucking my legs under me. "Hello, Teresa. What's up?"

Huffing, she rambled in a high-pitched voice. "Do you realize you are graduating in three weeks and, unless you didn't tell me, there is no party planned in your honor, right? Is your mother doing anything?"

Leave it to Teresa Jenks. Running her family and my company wasn't enough stress. She was also concerned that her boss/friend wasn't going to get a proper graduation celebration. God, I loved that woman. Even more, I did love a good party.

Jack stood in the doorway, holding his glass. He mouthed, "What?"

Rolling my eyes, I switched my phone to speaker mode and focused my attention on Teresa. "Not that I'm aware of, or at least she hasn't mentioned anything. She has been babysitting her grandchild since my sister went back to work. I think we all have been crazy busy. Anyway, I don't need a party."

"What!" she shouted.

"What!" Jack shouted.

"I told you Jack was good people. He agrees you have to have a party. This is a huge accomplishment. Besides, you have put me through hell for the past year with this getting-a-degree nonsense, so this party would be as much for me as it would for you—maybe more so. Dammit, Mel I want—and deserve—a great big, blow-the-roof-off party."

Jack practically spit out his soda. He ran over and grabbed the phone from my hand.

"Do it, Teresa. Plan the biggest party you can for this woman and spare no expense."

"Go away, Jack. Okay—I give up. Let's have a party. Teresa, call some places here in Philly. See what's available on that date. And as

Jack instructed, spare no expense. You're right. This is a time for us to celebrate."

"Don't worry, I'm on the case. Please, take me off speaker, will you?" she asked.

I clicked the icon to return to its regular setting. "Anything else?"

"No—I wanted to tell you that I like Jack. It's good to see you so happy."

Grinning at the man cleaning the remnants of our lunch without missing a beat, I whispered in to the phone. "I couldn't agree more."

Two days later, my capable assistant booked one of the smaller banquet rooms in a four-star hotel, called my mother to select the menu, gotten a list of guests I wanted in attendance, and reserved rooms. I felt a certain melancholy about leaving Pennwood University, and I thanked Teresa for convincing me to end my tenure with a farewell in grand style. I knew Aiden would adore the fact that he would be treated to wonderful food and top-shelf liquor, and my Baes would die to attend a lit party in my honor. I had Teresa arrange for a spa day prior to graduation for any and all females interested. Heidi was beyond excited to have a night out in the city in an elegant hotel with her hubby. Due to the short time frame, Teresa sent an e-vite, including *formal attire required* in the details. I would pay for all formal wear, and the Baes shouted with excitement. Jack and Aiden made faces at this, but I told them that chicks love a guy in a tuxedo. Aiden hoped he would get lucky; Jack knew he would.

A week before graduation, I was finally done. All my work had been submitted. I picked up my cap and gown and put the final touches on my speech. Did I forget to mention that I would be delivering a speech at the commencement ceremony?

Shortly after Jack and I journeyed to Gettysburg, I received an email from Rose, asking me to meet with President Samuels. We had lunch in a cozy new restaurant near the campus. I was so pleased he wanted to see me; there was much to thank him for.

When I arrived shortly after noon, he was seated in a booth, carefully studying the menu. The hostess led me over, and he stood as I approached.

"Melinda, so good to see you. Please have a seat," he gestured to the chair across from him.

"Hello, Walt."

We laughed.

"I recall you telling me that one day we'd be friends."

"And here we are. How have you been? You look well. Authority agrees with you," I said.

"I must admit I'm thoroughly enjoying the job. I never expected at my age that learning something new would be so enjoyable and fulfilling. At first I was a bit intimidated."

Nodding my head in agreement, I rested my chin in my right hand. "Funny thing, but in retrospect, I had the exact emotion returning to Pennwood as a non-traditional student. So many conflicting feelings compete inside you: excitement, intimidation, fear of failure, fear of judgment. Any new situation is stressful and, yet, challenging. It's truly a wonderful combination."

"Take a look at the menu so we can order. There is something I need to discuss with you."

Narrowing my eyes, I said, "Sounds ominous. You aren't going to rescind my diploma, are you? Or did the registrar discover some missing credits in reviewing my degree audit?"

"Not at all."

The waitress brought tall glasses of ice water, and we ordered wraps with fries. He leaned forward on the table, crossing his arms.

"Please describe what this year has meant to you—the struggles, the highs and lows, the fact that you will soon be an alumna of Pennwood University. I want to hear your impressions."

Taking a sip of the cool water, I traced the ring it left on the wooden tabletop.

"What does it mean to me? Wow. I've been so busy I haven't digested the fact that it's almost over. I set out to do this on the virtual dare of a magazine reporter, and soon I will have the college degree that has eluded me since I was twenty-years-old."

I repeated the circumstances that brought me back to Pennwood, withholding the personal details regarding the car accident. Jack was the only one I trusted with that information.

"I've had the unique perspective of sitting on both sides of the aisle at Pennwood. I arrived as a naïve eighteen-year-old, experiencing the life of a carefree undergrad whose biggest obstacles were the classes I could get so I could have Fridays free and what outfit to wear to a frat party to impress the boys. But real life derailed my trajectory, forcing me to implement a new path for my life. Never thinking I needed to complete my college degree, I placed that dream in a box and hid it away until it was opened by a random reporter asking an innocent question. In turn, that box materialized into many gifts—gifts of knowledge, friendship and yes, even love. This has been my year of discovery, of awakening and of realizing that no matter how old we are or what the circumstances of our life may be, we can always go back to start something new or to accomplish an unfinished goal. Going back to college to complete my degree has been one of the most empowering things I have ever done."

Walter sat and leaned against the back of the booth. "That's quite a testimonial coming from my favorite non-traditional student."

Our food arrived.

"I meant every word." I reached over for the bottle of ketchup.

"Good. Because I would like you to repeat what you just said at the commencement ceremony."

"Excuse me?"

"Each year at graduation, we have two students, one traditional and one non-traditional, each give a five minute speech. Who better to tell their story and relate their experiences at Pennwood than you?"

"Are you serious? Me? You want me to do it?" It was hard to shock me, and this came as a complete surprise.

"Not just me. The faculty in your school and a group of students who I assume are your classmates wrote a letter pleading for you to be selected."

President Samuels pulled an envelope from his breast pocket and slid it across the table. I slowly opened it like it was a delicate treasure. All of my friends—Aiden, the girls, Heidi, the folks in my major, faculty members in the department, Rose, the women who worked in the student union dining hall, and Jack—my Jack—had signed a letter of support for me to speak at commencement. I looked at him after reading it, tears clouding my vision.

"Your biggest cheerleaders have lobbied for you, but it was unnecessary. I knew ten minutes into our first encounter you would stand on that dais at your graduation ceremony and deliver a speech that would resonate with all students, no matter what their age."

"I'm so touched by this gesture. These people mean so much to me. My heart is so full."

"So is that a yes, Ms. Drake?"

"That's a resounding YES! It would be my supreme honor. Yes."

"Excellent. I'm thrilled it's settled. Now, let's eat," he said, taking one of his fries, dipping it in the ketchup on his plate.

"One more thing. I want to thank you for not throwing me out of your office when I attempted to bribe you to bend the rules for me."

"Ah, Melinda? You did bribe me, remember?"

"Desperate people do desperate things," I smirked.

"You did present an intriguing challenge that day. If I remember, there was mention of a sizable donation in the form of a new campus building—am I correct?"

"Why, President Samuels. You have an impeccable memory." I laughed.

"And here I assumed Melinda Drake was a woman of her word," he said, biting into his wrap.

"Oh, I always keep my word and put my heart and soul into everything I do. So don't worry. Your new building on campus is a shoe-in."

Shoe puns are endless.

CHAPTER THIRTY

With one week until graduation, I completed the final draft of my speech. I ironed my gown and, of course, Aiden's. The two robes hung like symbols of victory in my spare bedroom closet. My chest swelled with satisfaction. Both of us were graduating summa cum laude. I stood back, arms folded, gazing at the regal black robe, mentally patting myself on the back for a job well done. Jack snuck up behind me, wrapping his arms around my shoulders. I leaned back into his warm body.

"You worked hard and sacrificed quite a bit to make this happen. I'm so proud of you."

I turned around, hugging him. "It was a struggle to get here. I keep thinking about the ramifications of the accident. I believed not getting my degree was a justified, self-imposed punishment for what I did and that karma interceded."

"Stop beating yourself up. You have more than atoned for past mistakes. Melinda Drake is a good person."

"Thank you. Let's change the subject: have you been fitted for your tux?"

He groaned. "Yes—I would only do this for you. I hope you appreciate it."

I had wanted to take Jack to my tailor to buy him a custom-made tuxedo, but he flat out refused.

"I have to draw the line somewhere. Absolutely not."

"I can't wait to see you all fancy, dancing the night away with me. I'm taking Spencer for a dress tomorrow. Did she tell you?"

"Yes. My little girl dragged me to the store to buy makeup—can you imagine? What have you done to her?"

"We all come into our own at some point. I love seeing her so happy," I said.

"She's thrilled about us being together. She told me last night."

"Good. That kid is amazing. Listen, I'm taking Aiden out tonight, but I won't be late."

"Have fun. Call me later when you get back." He grabbed his bag and kissed me, leaving me lost in my thoughts.

When I broke the news to my parents that I was asked by the president of the university to address the students, faculty, administration, and guests at the ceremony, they could not contain their pride and excitement. The following day, Marion dragged Fred out of the house to go buy new outfits for the party.

My brother called to congratulate me. "Dad is parading around town, chest puffed out like a peacock, telling anyone who will listen that his daughter was personally selected to speak at her graduation. But seriously, Dolly—we are so proud of you, every single day. You've accomplished great things in your life, and should be proud. Stacy, the boys, and I can't wait to watch you be handed that diploma and give your speech. We'll be cheering you on."

"You always have, Bug. I love you. You have been an awesome big brother. I'm so lucky we ended up in the same family," I said, my voice cracking with emotion.

"Back at you, Mel. See you on the big day."

That night, I treated Aiden to a farewell to Pennwood dinner, just the two of us. He arrived at my door in the suit I had bought him, with a new haircut and freshly shaved.

"I only shave for you, Mel. Enjoy it."

"You clean up nice."

I ordered a bottle of champagne. This was, after all, a celebration to honor our graduation and friendship.

After the waiter left, I reached out for Aiden's hand. We looked at each other with wide, satisfied grins.

"If it hadn't been for you, I don't know how I could have survived. You were my first friend in Philly, and I don't ever forget my friends." I reached into my purse and slid a gift-wrapped box across the table.

His face froze in embarrassment. "I don't have anything for you."

"You have given me more than you will ever know. Plus I have

227

money to burn and you don't—not yet, that is."

Aiden was offered a terrific job at Lexor Animation Studios at a great salary and was moving out to California two weeks after graduation.

"Go ahead, open it. For your graduation, and everything else."

"Okay, but we could still hook-up before I leave. I promise I won't breathe a word to the professor," he joked as he tore away the silver wrapping paper.

"Nice try. I hope you like it."

When he opened the rectangular box, his eyes widened in surprise and shock.

"Are you effing kidding me? You got me the latest smartphone? I can't even believe this! I never, ever thought I could upgrade to one of these bad boys. The camera on this thing is sick! Oh my God!"

The best part of wealth is showering others in it.

"Enjoy it, dearest friend. It's a token of my affection for you and a remembrance of a special time in our lives. Thank you for always making me laugh and for hanging out and helping me. I can't wait to see what you accomplish because I'm convinced it will be something special. You are a bright light, Aiden Flanagan. Go set the world on fire."

He stood and pulled me out of my chair into a bear hug. "I adore you, woman," he whispered into my ear.

The champagne arrived. Aiden sat back down as the waiter poured us each a glass. He was mesmerized by all the features on his new phone, and continued to stare at it in disbelief. Turns out I was not only an expert in shoes but also an expert in selecting a Generation Z graduation gift. It was a perfect fit.

When we finished dinner, we waited for my driver in front of the crowded restaurant. In typical Aiden fashion, he spoke in a resounding tone so all could see and hear him.

"How long have we been waiting, babe? Wait, let me check."

And in a dramatic flourish, he pulled out his shiny new phone and examined the screen for all to see. And then, he did something I knew he had been dying to do since the day we met. He took me in his arms and danced with me for a few seconds. As everyone gaped, he dipped me back and planted a big kiss on my lips.

"I love you, Melinda. You will always be my first love."

CHAPTER THIRTY-ONE

Graduation day dawned bright and beautiful, just as I always imagined. Approximately eight hundred students were scheduled to receive their diplomas. We lined up according to our departments inside the large field house. I awoke that morning at six and took a walk around Rittenhouse Square. I would miss this second home, but I was eager to return to my real life back in New York City. I made arrangements with the landlord in my building to keep the apartment for when I visited Jack and Spencer. I gave Jack a key weeks ago, hoping he would still use it during the week.

As we filed out in pairs, heading to the football stadium where the ceremony was to be held, my heart skipped a beat listening to the iconic music drifting from the overhead speakers. I had waited almost twenty years to hear the strains of the march, composed by Edward Elgar: *Pomp and Circumstance*. He originally wrote it in 1901 for a king's coronation. The rousing anthem was guaranteed to elicit tears from both graduates and their proud family members. Standing confidently, head held high in my cap and gown in this majestic moment, I felt like a queen.

The faculty led the procession out of the field house. The president flashed me a thumbs-up, his eyes sparkling with excitement for us and for himself in this new role. Jack looked resplendent in the robe, hood and velvet tam of his alma mater. Handsome and tall, he winked as he passed. I realized in that moment that I loved him. I was in love for the first time in my life. I wanted my old life, but I wanted a life with him and Spencer. Trembling as the tenderness of loving them flowed over me, I vowed on this special day to make it work with Jack, no matter what.

I adjusted my tassel and prepared to embark on the walk I had waited a lifetime for. Gazing down at my feet, I grinned from ear to ear. On this, my commencement day, when I held my diploma, I would be wearing a pair of pumps I created and designed in my own factory.

I had finally come full circle.

After the welcoming remarks were delivered, the president stood behind the podium, emblazoned with the seal of Pennwood University. He was beaming.

"As is customary here at Pennwood, two students are invited to address this audience of parents, friends, and faculty to highlight their experiences as students. A commencement ceremony symbolizes the start of a student's life out in the real world, to begin their professional life. Our first speaker came to us, already a success in the business world. And yet, the attainment of her college degree was so important that she put her life on hold to reach her goal. She has been an inspiration to everyone here on campus, demonstrating the idea that students can have it all, provided they are willing to work hard enough to achieve it. It is with great pride that I introduce to you, Melinda Drake.

After generous applause, I inched my way through the aisle, ascending the stairs to stand before the crowd. I lifted my chin, inhaled deeply and addressed the rapt audience.

"My fellow graduates, President Samuels, Provost McCabe, Board of Trustees, distinguished faculty, family, and friends. I am honored to be here today to speak on behalf of the many non-traditional students who are a vital and necessary component to the landscape of every college campus across our great nation.

Although my story is unique to me, it is similar to the thousands of non-traditional students who enroll in classes every year, hoping to finish or begin their degrees on the road to a better life for themselves and their families. We come to the classroom with unique perspectives and a vast array of life experiences. Our apprehensions are different from our eighteen to twenty-two year old counterparts, but our goals are the same.

I first began my journey to this day twenty years ago. Like many of the graduates sitting here, I was forced by circumstances beyond my control to change my path and become detoured in another direction. Whether it was fate, luck, or sheer coincidence, I was steered back to

Pennwood this past year to finish the dream I started so long ago, earning my Bachelor of Science in Design and Merchandising. I am fortunate to be successful in my career, and yet the void of unfinished business loomed over me. I stand here today along with my peers, poised to receive my degree, one of the greatest accomplishments of my life.

In closing, my advice to the traditional student population is this: work hard while you are here, stay on task, have fun, but take the academic portion of your life seriously. Don't take a minute of your experience here at Pennwood for granted. Thank your parents for their unwavering support, both financially and emotionally. They know so much more than you right now—trust me.

For my fellow non-traditional counterparts, you have sacrificed so much to get here. Hang that diploma where you can see it each and every day and say, "I did it!" As the CEO of MD Shoes, I must say that our quest may have taken us down a much longer, winding road, but we finally arrived, in style. We are ready to put our best foot forward, landing feet first, ready for the next step. Thank you."

Thunderous applause erupted from around the stadium. I had given countless presentations before large groups of people, but nothing compared to this. It was validation; I felt complete. From the sea of black gowns, swinging gold tassels, and multi-colored hoods and honor cords, I couldn't miss seeing Aiden, Blake, and Courtney jump to their feet in a standing ovation. As I exited the stage, Jack flashed a broad smile while mouthing the words, "Well done," while Walter Samuels nodded in satisfaction.

I returned to my seat (after several low and high-fives along the way) where I listened to the remaining speeches. Finally, we were presented to the now-getting-bored-with-this-and-I'm-starving crowd as the newest graduating class of Pennwood University, and it was time to receive my diploma. In reality, the official diploma would arrive several weeks from now by certified mail, but I didn't care. And I knew the exact spot in my office that I would hang it for all, especially me, to see.

"MELINDA DRAKE."

President Samuels announced my name with perfect diction and enthusiasm. Walking toward him, I was overcome with the enormity of it all. We ignored the standard handshake and went all in for a hug.

"Congratulations, Melinda. I'm so proud of you," he whispered.

"Thank you, Walter—for everything." I took the symbolic scroll from his hand and glanced over at Jack, who rose from his seat to snap a picture with his phone. He winked as I walked past, and I breathed a huge sigh. But my sigh was so much more than relief. It was pure, unadulterated contentment.

It was done. I had officially secured all my wildest dreams. I had finally healed myself and found my sole mate. I giggled in glee.

Shoe puns are endless.

CHAPTER THIRTY-TWO

There were flashing strobe lights and, at the insistence of the Bae Watch girls, several songs they personally requested. It was one of the best parties I ever hosted or attended. Teresa outdid herself. The guest list encompassed around eighty-five family, friends, and faculty I wanted to celebrate with, employees from the university and a small circle of close associates from MD Shoes. I had invited Steven, but he was out of the country on business. He sent another enormous flower arrangement to my home, along with a lovely note of congratulations. My wonderful assistant hired a local DJ at the recommendation of Aiden and his cousin Ellie, who also attended with her husband.

The Baes informed me that the party was lit and warned me that they were going to get crae-crae since we YOLO (translated: the party was fun and they were going to have a wild time because you only live once). They cheered when I informed them about the event two weeks prior and that I had arranged two rooms for them at the hotel to crash in afterward with free room service the following morning. They arrived dressed to impress in bright, short dresses, dark-lined eyes, and ruby-red lips, sporting heels they navigated like pros. I loved them all and would miss their snappy comebacks and colorful language that I had finally gotten the hang of. Four of them brought dates, and two came solo after I assured them that I had a couple of single, handsome, eligible younger relatives who were coming to the party.

Aiden and Lucy danced all night together, disappearing for a long stretch of time. Gina and Chelsea, always there for me, came solo and we shared a few dances together on the floor.

Gavin Beck waltzed in with a gorgeous woman on his arm, and he and I shared a couple of dances together.

"Thanks for being here. And thanks for keeping me warm on those lovely nights. I enjoyed our brief time together," I said, placing a chaste, friendly kiss on his cheek that smelled of expensive aftershave.

"If you ever decide to dump Mr. Excitement over there, give me a call," he joked, gesturing toward Jack who danced nearby with Spencer.

Smiling, I replied, "I think I'll keep my professor for a while. I never expected to fit so well with someone. It came as a complete surprise to me, too."

Gavin pulled me close, his lips brushing my ear. "He's a lucky guy. I'm happy for you. I'll be in Manhattan in late July. Let's get together for dinner. You can bring Skippy over there."

I playfully slapped his arm as Jack asked to cut in. Gavin gallantly stepped aside and joined his date who was having a great time at the bar with the suddenly resurrected Aiden.

"Thank God, I finally have you all to myself. Having fun?" Jack asked, holding me close.

"I'm having a great time. I'm so happy," I said, embracing him as we swayed to the slow music filling the ballroom.

Jack nodded to my parents who were watching us as they sat, enjoying after dinner coffee and plates of assorted desserts. "I think they like me. They invited me for dinner on Sunday."

"Did they? My mother makes a mean chicken piccata on Sundays—you're in luck," I said, running my left hand over his lean, strong chest. His dashing transformation in a tuxedo was intoxicating, and all I wanted was to be alone with him back in our room. Now that the graduation was over and the party was winding down, I shifted my focus to the next thing—getting back to work and figuring out a life with Jack and Spencer.

"I am lucky, because I found you. I don't ever want to lose you."

"We're good, Jack. No worries. We'll figure it out," I assured him.

"I already have."

I stopped dancing and searched his face. "What?"

"I'm taking a sabbatical starting July first. I received a grant to write a book about the modern-day legacy of Abraham Lincoln. I won't be tied down by a teaching schedule. After Spencer graduates from high school in two years, I'll re-evaluate my position at Pennwood. I rather enjoy the idea of pursuing opportunities at Columbia or NYU. What do you think?"

"Are you serious? You'd give up your tenured position to follow me to New York?"

Taking my face in his hand, he kissed me. "At this point, I'd follow you anywhere. You are the person who makes everything right. I want to share my life with you. I want to marry you, if you'll have me, and my daughter, of course. She adores you, too. Look at her."

Spencer was watching us. They both planned this, and she walked over to join us.

"Are you in on this scheme to get me to marry your father?" I laughed.

She hugged me. "Thing is, you get both of us in this deal. I love you, but my dad is crae-crae for you. He has this goofy look on his face and stares at pics of you on his phone, and it's kind of nauseating and cute at the same time. But you know what? He's happy. And I like seeing my dad happy. He's a good guy, and he loves you, a whole lot."

Jack slid his arm around Spencer's shoulder. "Okay, sweetheart. This has been a big day for Melinda. I've given her quite a bit to digest. Let's give her some time to think about it."

I experienced a calm that was foreign to my often, frenetic life. I pulled away from the two of them.

"No," I said, firmly.

Jack's face fell. Spencer's turned red.

"No, guys. I don't need time to think about it. What I need is the two of you, because the three of us belong together. So my answer is YES!"

Spencer shrieked, running off to share the good news with her friends I had encouraged her to invite to the party.

Jack searched my face. "Are you sure? I'm certain the last thing you expected to leave Philadelphia with was a ready-made family. I don't need your answer tonight."

"Listen, Jack. This is a huge thing for both of us—for all of us. Sure, it's going to take some time to iron out all the details and logistics of a Drake/Sweeney merger," I smiled.

"God, I'm in love with a tycoon!" He threw his head back and laughed. "But you're right. Nothing will happen immediately."

"All I know is that I love you, Jack, and your daughter. Everything will fall into place because we will make it happen."

My heart was full. Today had been the best day of my life.

The following Monday, I was back at my desk, at home in Manhattan. I wasn't giving up my Philly apartment, so I enjoyed a relaxing weekend with Jack and Spencer and arrived back Sunday evening. Everything felt different. I left here alone, but I arrived back in my old life with shiny new additions—a college degree, lifelong new friends, a soon-to-be stepdaughter, and the best part: a wonderful, sexy, nerdy, fiancé.

I powered my computer as I heard Teresa arrive for the day. She must be exhausted from my graduation party. There she was—the pint-size ball of energy, dirty dancing with her husband, the waiters at the venue, Aiden, and the Bae crew on the glossy, wooden dance floor. Her gold, sparkly tea-length gown shimmered like her personality—she was the hit of the evening. The woman never let me down since the day I told her she was hired.

I was preparing for a second, major announcement. The first had come the other night, at my graduation celebration.

While the wait staff circulated among the well-dressed guests, offering bacon wrapped scallops, succulent, marinated meats on skewers, mini quiches and crab cakes, I snaked my way through the kisses and congratulations of my peeps to ascend to the stage where the DJ played a mix of tunes from the seventies to the present. The music stopped as I approached the microphone, tapping my index finger against it to test for sound.

"Ladies and gentlemen, friends, family, and colleagues. I want to welcome you tonight to a grand celebration. It warms my heart I have so many wonderful people in my life who have helped me realize all my dreams. Thanks to all of you for being here this evening, to share in the many riches of my life. Now I would like to ask for the President of Pennwood University to join me on stage for an announcement."

Walter Samuels looked surprised as he walked up and stood next to me on the stage. With a quizzical expression, he asked, "Melinda?"

Sporting an ear-to-ear grin, I held up my hands. "Don't worry, it's good news."

His shoulders relaxed, but he remained perplexed.

"The first day we met, I promised you a gift that I'm ready to deliver on. Pennwood University will always hold a special place in my heart, for many reasons. But if it weren't for the love and support of my parents, Marion and Fred Drake, I wouldn't have become the woman I am today. So tonight, President Samuels, I would like to present you with a check to be used to build the new dormitory you need to house the increased student enrollment, and I want it to be named Drake Hall, in honor of my dear mother and father."

For the second time that day, the crowd exploded in applause at my remarks. My overwhelmed, yet proud, parents joined me on stage as Teresa appeared with a giant check made out to Pennwood University. I had invited campus media to cover the announcement and take pictures.

Later, in bed, Jack turned to me, propping his head on his hand. We discussed my donation to the university. This is why I love this guy: with a straight face, he said, "Hey Mel, can I borrow a dollar?"

After I tried to smother him with a pillow when he wouldn't stop laughing, he surrendered, and we made love. That night, Jack Sweeney realized just how rich his new fiancé was. And it didn't seem to scare him one bit.

Teresa burst into my office, yammering on about the party while scuttling about, thrilled to have me back on a daily basis. One of the things I loved best about this woman was the vast range of her personality. One minute she was ultra-professional, dignified, and composed, and then faster than you could turn on your heel she was getting down and dirty in language and attitude. Teresa was delightfully charismatic, capable, and cunning. I knew I had made an incredible business decision for MD Shoes.

I settled back in my custom-made leather desk chair. "Teresa—sit. I need to discuss something with you. Close the door, please."

We had been together long enough for her to know that this meant I had confidential information to share or we had incredible office or personal gossip. She was the one person in my circle that I trusted with both.

"Before you start, I need my say."

"Shoot."

"First of all, it's so good to finally have you back. I realized I poo-pooed your whole going-back-to-college thing, but I want you to know that I think it took a lot of guts and sacrifice, and I'm damned proud of you. Melinda Drake talks the talk and walks the walk. You say you're going to do something and you get it done. You continue to be a role model for all of us. Not that I would ever bother going back to school, but I'm impressed that you can add "college graduate" to your résumé."

"Why, thank you, Mrs. Jenks. I hope that crow you just had to eat was dee-licious."

Teresa was on a roll. "Let me tell you, this place was like a ship without a captain while you were gone. I did the best I could, and all your managers did a great job of picking up the slack in your absence. Thank God—it's over. Finally, we can get back to business as usual," she responded, folding her arms across her chest.

"I agree—back to business. So what's on the agenda?"

"To begin with, you need to fill Alyce's position. It's been vacant too long, and we need a president to direct the day-to-day operations of this company and oversee our strategic plan. Now that you are back full-time, you can't possibly cover your responsibilities as CEO and president, too. Unless you split yourself in half or get yourself cloned. I've been trying…"

"And you've been doing the job of three people. You're proud of me? I left my business completely in your hands. I am proud of *you*. You have been my rock, a godsend, and not many people could have juggled this place like you have. I knew the day I hired you to be my assistant that it was a brilliant move, but you have superseded all my expectations. I have decided to reward you for your outstanding work and loyalty."

Teresa smirked, assuming I was going to send her on a cruise or give her a sizable cash bonus.

"I am offering you, Teresa Jenks, the position of president of MD Shoes. No one deserves it more than you. It comes with a huge increase in salary, stock options, annual bonus, and additional responsibilities. I'm convinced you are ready. I'm praying you are willing," I said, standing to walk around my desk and hug her.

I rendered her speechless, a previously impossible task. She covered her face in her hands, overwhelmed. I could feel my own heart pounding in my chest, because I was thrilled with the moment. I had my right arm attached to me all along. I simply needed to feel it.

"Are you sure, Mel? Are you sure you want me? I mean, I have an associate degree, with no executive experience. You don't have to repay me with Alyce's job. Are you thinking clearly? You are newly in love and that can cloud a person's judgment..."

"I am one hundred percent certain that my new president should be you. You've been doing the job for almost a year. I want you to have the recognition you deserve. Aside from myself, no one loves MD Shoes more than you. You are the heart and sole of this place."

We looked at one another and roared.

Shoe puns—like friendships—are endless.

CHAPTER THIRTY-THREE

After two months of being back at work full-time, I longed to return to the life of a college student. When I was a kid, complaining about how much I hated school and couldn't wait to leave it behind and venture in to the real world, my father would sit me down and lecture me.

"Don't rush your life," he would scold, wagging that parental finger in my anxious face. "It goes by too fast. Enjoy the moment. All in good time, Dolly. All in good time."

I was relishing my life as a newly minted college grad while basking in the warmth of being in love for the first time in my life. We had just arrived back in New York after a glorious few days of meeting Jack's parents, siblings and extended family at their annual reunion. They welcomed me with open arms, and I felt as comfortable with them as I did with my amazing fiancé and soon-to-be stepdaughter. With Spencer in Wisconsin visiting her grandparents and cousins for the summer, Jack and I were enjoying our privacy, commuting between Manhattan and the Hamptons, languishing on the beach where I owned a lovely, restored cottage. He had moved several of his things into my apartment, and while I was at work he would shuffle between the library at NYU and our home, where I would often discover him, hunched over the computer, tapping at a frenetic pace to meet his word count goal for the day on his book. We ambled about our living quarters, eating something as basic as hot dogs or sumptuous such as oysters or local scallops dipped in melted butter. Jack brushed and blow-dried my hair after we showered, and I scratched his back as we watched a movie or the news. I proofread the first drafts of his book; he massaged my neck and shoulders after a stressful day at the office. We slipped into a rhythm, cozy as a pair of worn slippers and, yet, thrilling in learning the things that ignited our passion for each other. I had either forgotten or, more likely, never learned what it meant to be part of a couple—to be the half of another person who held your heart. Jack Sweeney was still an infuriating, know-it-all at times, but he was gentle and kind and kissed me slow and sweet, even first thing in the morning.

We had tentatively planned a destination wedding in the South of France after Spencer finised her senior year, including just immediate family and our closest friends. Jack was approved for a twelve-month sabbatical to write his book and complete his research, but he was required to be back at Pennwood shortly after we would return from our two-week honeymoon. He planned to teach at Pennwood for a year and then he would retire from the university. Columbia had reached out to him, indicating they would be interested in having him join their faculty or consider an endowed chair in their history department. I was happy he had options and I was convinced our life together would fall into place at its own pace.

On a sunny Thursday in August, Felix appeared in the doorway to my office, dangling our newest prototype from his talented fingers.

"Melinda—look what I have for you."

My eyes widened with excitement. "Oh my God, Felix—they are beyond gorgeous! Bring them over here—immediately."

Practically jumping over my desk, I toed off my gold and silver sling-backs, gently taking the new shoes from my lead designer.

"One of our best. Feel that vegan leather. It's pristine," he said.

Sitting on the sofa, I slipped the models on my feet. We had come up with the design together, right before I left for the Pennwood campus last January. Normally, we would have produced the sample much sooner, but with me being away it took far longer to approve and construct.

"Oh, Felix," I purred.

"Good, eh?"

"Supple and sweet. I'm going to take them out for a stroll on the streets," I said.

Whenever we created a new design, I was the one who literally road tested it. If I couldn't walk on pavement and wear the shoe comfortably all day, then it failed the MD Shoes test. I assured my customers that it would always have to meet my own rigorous standards before I would let the women of America and those around the world spend their hard-earned money for a pair of my shoes.

"Okay. I'll be back in the showroom. Let me know how they do."

Felix gave a crisp wave as he exited my office. I strutted around the room in the newest addition, already sensing that they would become one of our best sellers. The prototype was a black pump, but we would manufacture it in a variety of colors. The shoe was adorned with a large soft-as-butter bow in pastel pink, with patent leather lining the heel. They were feminine and could be worn high end with a business suit or cocktail sheath, or dressed down, paired with jeans, capris, or a casual skirt. Sporting a three-inch heel, they gave the illusion of a longer, slimmer leg. Women were going to love them.

"Lauren? I'm hitting the road," I said, logging off my computer and grabbing my purse and sunglasses. "I should be back in about an hour. I need to stop and buy a birthday card. Do you want anything while I'm out?" My new assistant was a thirty-year-old, single mom with a dry sense of humor, almost as efficient as the previous occupant of this job. She realized she had big shoes to fill after Teresa.

"No, thanks. Enjoy."

I peeked my head in to Teresa's office across the hall. "Going out for a road test—back in an hour." She was absorbed in her lunch while reading a report. Without looking up, she flashed a peace sign.

Even though she was now a top executive at MD Shoes, the woman still brought lunch from home, often some homemade pasta or stew dish she would invite me to taste.

I pushed through the revolving glass doors of my building, braving the steamy Manhattan sidewalk. Forgive me for having to utter a string of clichés, but the damn shoes made me feel as though I was dancing along Ninth Avenue. There was that cushiony spring in my step, a necessary prerequisite for an MD pump, boot, or shoe. I practically pranced, my face turned toward the sun, basking in the glow of not only another successful product, but also being in love with a sexy, smart man. I was so oblivious, I slammed head on into a fellow New Yorker, who caught me before I landed flat on my tush in the middle of 34th Street.

"Whoa, there. Are you all right?" A deep familiar voice asked as he steadied us. Was I suddenly developing a habit of slamming into random men?

I nearly dropped my purse, and my sunglasses had gone askew on my face. When I regained my composure, I gaped into the familiar face of none other than Philip Gunderson! The man I once secretly cursed for upending my life was the same one I had been meaning to call and thank for my newfound happiness.

"Well, if it isn't Melinda Drake. How are you? You must be more careful. In those heels, you could have injured me and yourself."

He flaunted an amused expression. With his jacket slung over his arm, dressed in a seersucker suit and white buckskin shoes, he could have easily been a model for a fashion house. His hair was cut shorter, probably due to the August heat, and he sported what I assumed was a summer-long Hampton or Stone Harbor tan. The man was still deliciously fine.

Smoothing my skirt and blouse, correcting the angle of my sunglasses, I reached out and hugged him there in the middle of our metropolis. "Phillip! I've been meaning to contact you. I have so much to tell you. Are you free for lunch? You don't realize it, but I owe you quite a bit."

"Is that so? I'm intrigued. As a matter of fact, I just finished an interview and was going to grab a sandwich on my way back to the office. But an offer of lunch with you is far more appealing. I'd be delighted."

Phillip held out his arm for me. I felt a warm blush of kinship as I tucked my hand in the nook of his elbow, as we slowly sauntered to a nearby restaurant.

We sat in a cozy pub, opting for indoors and the much-desired air-conditioned dining room. The owner led us to a table adjacent to a lovely garden hosting a fiery red, Japanese maple, potted plants, and a dainty waterfall. We ordered iced tea and chef salads, agreeing that dessert would be allowed with such a sensible lunch choice.

He settled back in his seat, crossing his legs. "So, Ms. Drake. What has been happening in your life since we last spoke?"

Wait. Was he hiding a secret with that sly fox grin? I guessed he must have been well aware of where I had been and what I was doing.

"You know. Don't you?"

"And what would that be, Ms. Drake?"

"Melinda." I corrected. "You know that I went back to college. I finally finished my degree."

"No! Do tell."

"Cut the crap, Gunderson. You are a reporter—you guys know everything, isn't that right?"

He leaned forward, stirring a packet of sugar in to his tea. After taking a long swallow, he sat back again and folded his arms over his chest.

"Not all reporters, only investigative journalists, like myself."

I peered across the table, squinting my eyes. "What did you do Philip? Why do I suddenly have the impression I've been had?" I realized there was more to this story than my informing him I was officially a college graduate.

"It's a great story. Interested?"

"I'm listening." I folded my hands in my lap, noticing their slight clamminess.

"My editor at *Wealth and Success* had approached me, asking to brainstorm ideas for an upcoming feature article on the most successful female entrepreneurs in Manhattan. As I began my research, I formulated an original list of about twelve women. Most were Ivy-league educated from well-to-do backgrounds, inheriting family dynasties and established businesses. But a few, including you, were self-made millionaires. When I began looking at your résumé and list of accomplishments, I was surprised to not only see that you had no degree, but that you dropped out of college in your senior year under rather mysterious circumstances. After a bit of digging into old court documents, I discovered why."

I lowered my head and closed my eyes. "It was the darkest period of my life, being responsible for the death of another human being."

"Actually, Melinda, you weren't."

Looking up, I asked, "What are you talking about?"

"Your car may have caused the chain of events in the accident, but it was a recalled seat belt that malfunctioned, causing the passenger to be thrown from the vehicle and killed."

"But the police told us she wasn't wearing a seat belt." My throat felt like it was closing shut.

"The victim's husband told the officer she was buckled in, but because he barely spoke English, the officer incorrectly wrote down that she was not wearing it—he misunderstood. The van the family was driving in had been recalled six months prior to correct the faulty seat belt, but they never took it back to the dealer to be repaired. They thought they would have to pay for it and couldn't afford the expense. They had no idea it was covered under the recall."

I could barely breathe. "What are you telling me?"

"If the seat belt had been repaired, the mother would have survived like the other occupants of the vehicle. Melinda—you were not responsible for her death. The car company was."

"Oh my God." Tears streamed down my face. Phillip handed me his handkerchief. "But how did you uncover this information?"

"I told you—I'm good at what I do. I started my career as a reporter working with detectives in the homicide division in the Bronx. I saw it all when I started in this business, and those guys taught me everything—stuff you can't imagine. I learned how to sift through the evidence and piece a story together. When I discovered a discrepancy between the police officer and the husband's account of what happened, I decided to run a search on the make and model number of the car. I had a hunch. It proved to be accurate. The officer who recorded the details of the crash was a rookie. He had only been on the job a few weeks. The report on the accident was hastily filed, and a proper investigation was never conducted due to cutbacks in the department. It simply fell through the cracks of an overcrowded, bureaucratic system. No one ever questioned the final outcome."

I was speechless.

"I'm sure you have lived with guilt all these years. Your parents had no idea about the recall of the van and that it wasn't your fault she was thrown from the car and died due to a malfunction with her seatbelt. They quietly took care of the victim's medical bills and focused on trying to heal their distraught daughter."

I nodded my head. My parents were too overwhelmed in trying to help me move on. The last thing they would have expected was that something else was to blame because I was so consumed with blaming myself.

"So, to continue the story. When I uncovered this information, I understood the reason why you had left Pennwood University. You also paid a price for the accident."

"You can't even compare the two. I lived. She did not and paid the price with her life."

"Yes, but you punished yourself by not ever finishing your dream of going to college. You offered that up as a sacrifice to her, didn't you?"

"I guess you're a psychologist, too? That's a bit over analytical, don't you think?"

"Perhaps. But I'd venture a guess it's true. When I decided to include you in the list of *Wealth and Success* honorees, I decided to also give you a gift. My research revealed Melinda Drake never walked away from a challenge. I knew if I asked the question about your lack of a degree in the exact, right way, I would press a button, planting a seed in your mind that you might want to return to college and actually capture that elusive dream—your undergraduate diploma."

Philip Gunderson extended the olive branch of redemption. I caused the accident those many years ago. There was no denying this fact. And yet, that woman's death may not have been my fault. I would forever carry the responsibility, but perhaps now, I could carry less of the guilt. I prayed she and her family had forgiven me. It was time to forgive myself.

Philip motioned for the waitress.

"Yes, sir?"

"Two glasses of champagne, please. We are here to celebrate."

I reached for his hand. He squeezed mine.

"One other thing. I know about your anonymous foundation—the one providing full college scholarships for underprivileged young women and men."

"Why does that not surprise me? So much for remaining incognito," I said.

"It's our secret. You've done a whole lot of good things in your life, Ms. Drake."

Our champagne arrived. My eyes filled as I held my glass aloft to this man who delivered tidings of great joy on a blistering, summer day.

"To you, Melinda."

"And to you, as well, Philip. Thank you—for healing me."

"Heal or heel?"

"Is that a shoe pun?" I giggled, champagne bubbles tickling my nose.

"No, just a reporter's instinct. I had a hunch the instant I met you that your greatest feat was yet to come."

We clinked glasses. I would never forget Philip Gunderson and what he had set in motion the day we first met in my conference room. How could I have learned that a single circumstance in my life would have brought so much pain and joy?

I was ready to take the next step, putting one foot in front of the other—with Jack Sweeney.

Because I finally discovered that people, like shoes, should stand in pairs.

And love, like a good shoe pun, is endless.

ACKNOWLEDGMENTS

This book was a long time in the making. After I finished my first novel, *Out Of My Dreams*, I promptly began *Pumps and Circumstances* but put it aside to write *The Magic Of Us* at the request of readers who asked for a sequel. So Melinda Drake sat patiently, waiting on the pages of my computer. I hope you enjoyed her journey!

I want to thank Laura Ginsberg and Marco Santomenna for their feedback and support.

To Katie and Matt, thanks for being such enthusiastic cheerleaders.

Many thanks to family and friends who support my writing career by promoting and buying my novels. Word of mouth gets books read and sold, and you have been amazing in helping me reach my goals.

I owe a great debt of gratitude to my daughter Maria. Thanks for making the hundreds of changes to this manuscript with minimum eye rolling and for designing the exact cover I envisioned. You are amazing.

Thanks to my husband Rick. Always my first reader, I know if you like it I have told a good story. Your love and encouragement mean the world to me.

And finally, thanks to my readers for all the lovely messages, texts, posts, and reviews. Your words inspire my words. I am lucky to have you in my corner.

ABOUT THE AUTHOR

Mary Lou Irace is the author of *Out Of My Dreams* and *The Magic Of Us*. She earned a Bachelor of Science in Sociology from Rosemont College and a Master of Science in Education/Student Personnel Services from Monmouth University. A former college academic advisor, she lives in New Jersey with her husband and two daughters. You can follow her on Facebook at Facebook.com/MaryLouIraceAuthor and Twitter at @MaryLouIrace.

Made in the USA
Middletown, DE
08 July 2020